Plague Doctor

by

Laura Strickland

A Buffalo Steampunk Adventure

Plague Doctor

Cover Art by *Diana Carlile*

The Wild Rose Press, Inc.
PO Box 708
Adams Basin, NY 14410-0708
Visit us at www.thewildrosepress.com

Publishing History
First Edition, 2022
Trade Paperback ISBN 978-1-5092-4537-6
Digital ISBN 978-1-5092-4538-3

A Buffalo Steampunk Adventure
Published in the United States of America

He rounded the corner at a half jog, his bundle clutched to his chest, and faltered. A single figure walked toward him out of the gloom between the street lamps.

Tall it appeared—at least it cast a tall shadow. Dressed all in dun brown, it wore robes that whispered when it moved. Real, then—it was real and not an illusion, for he could hear that rustle, and hear its footsteps just like his own, clattering against the pavement.

Its face—

But it did not have a face, not a human one. Instead it possessed a beak and two dark slits for eyes, with which it fixed Kasper in a stare that nearly froze his blood.

A mask—some dim part of Kasper's mind recognized it for a mask. The balance of his mind stuttered and flooded with panic. He recoiled in an almost visceral horror.

On the same side of the street as him, the plague doctor carried a censer, trailing steam, and walked steadily toward him, as if it might walk through him. As if it weren't flesh and blood after all. But Kasper believed to the root of his soul it was.

He heard a strangled sound and only belatedly realized it came from his own throat—a stifled moan. Everything within him wanted to avoid contact with that figure. But he had no time to run.

Praise for Laura Strickland

Two of Laura Strickland's Buffalo Steampunk Adventures—*Cross Checking* and *Steam Tinker*—have won the N. N. Light Book Award for Science Fiction, in 2020 and 2021 respectively.

Her Scottish Historical Romance *The Reiver's Cub*, won the RONE Award in 2021.

And her novella *Forged by Love* won first place in the short historical category of the International Digital Awards.

~*~

"The world building is phenomenal."
~*Daysie W. at My Book Addiction and More*
~*~

"Laura Strickland creates a world that…draws you in…the kind of book that keeps you awake well into the wee hours, and sighing with satisfaction when you've finished the very last page." ~*Nicole McCaffrey, author*
~*~

"As I read I became so involved with the story, I found it difficult to put down the book. …Definitely …an author to watch." ~*Dandelion at Long & Short Reviews*
***

Previous Buffalo Steampunk Adventures
Dead Handsome
Off Kilter
Sheer Madness
Steel Kisses
Last Orders
Tough Prospect
Cross Checking
Steam Tinker

Chapter One

Buffalo, The Niagara Frontier, Summer, 1885

"They say he's been sighted again," Daisy told Mrs. Marner in a lurid whisper. "Two nights ago it was, outside the Catholic orphanage on North Street. And sure enough, one of the children there fell ill the very next day."

"Who says this?" Mrs. Marner demanded repressively.

"Eh?" Daisy squawked.

"You told me '*they* say.' Who are 'they'?" Mrs. Marner, who managed the Lost Waifs orphanage, did not suffer fools gladly.

"Oh. I heard it down the tavern, this afternoon."

A short, sharp silence fell, and Tori Anderson, who stood with an armload of dirty sheets, eavesdropping shamelessly on the two women, wondered if her boss— for such was Mrs. Marner—would berate Daisy for what she did during her time off, or put an end to the conversation.

All three of them worked at Lost Waifs Home for Children on Buffalo's west side. With the exception of a newly-hired caretaker, they were the only humans employed at the establishment. Three ancient and decrepit steam units helped them look after twenty-five children.

Lost Waifs was just one of many small, independent orphanages in the city, all barely staying afloat. Though reforms were underway and changes driven by wealthy patrons did come about, those certainly hadn't reached Lost Waifs as yet.

As a consequence, the employees, who were supposed to work in shifts, spent far more time there than the hours for which they were paid. Since Tori, currently past quitting time, considered her present duty voluntary, she felt very little actual shame in standing out of sight now and listening.

Mrs. Marner said, "You should not be down at the taverns, Daisy, or drinking on the afternoons you have off."

"Then," Daisy, a young Irishwoman, answered defiantly, "I'd never get a drink. Besides, Mrs. Marner, and it's the truth, if I didn't take a fortifying nip or two from time to time, I don't think I could face working in this place."

True enough, Tori acknowledged. It was an awful purgatory of a place to work. Take her present situation, for instance. She should have gone home hours ago when Daisy came in for the night shift. Instead, she stood here with her back and feet aching, clutching an armful of sheets that reeked of urine. There weren't enough hands to go around, that was what. And if she went home when she was supposed to, some of the children would go wanting.

Mrs. Marner had told her, over and over again, there was nothing wrong with letting the children go wanting. They were orphans, not cherished little princes and princesses. So long as their basic needs got met, they—the employees of Lost Waifs—did their duty.

Such a philosophy made Tori's heart hurt. There was duty, and then there was *duty*.

Take little Benny Woods, for instance. He had bad dreams—a lot of bad dreams—and when he did, he wet his bed. Mrs. Marner ordered them to let him lie in the wet sheets, in order to teach him a lesson. They couldn't be pampering him, she claimed, and anyway, the steam automaton unit that worked in the laundry couldn't keep up with the dirty linens.

Which explained why Tori stood at the end of a dim corridor overhearing other people's conversations. She'd intended to run Benny's soiled sheets out back to the laundry and try to put them through the mangle herself.

The idea of leaving a frightened child in a wet bed would haunt her, if she went home. And in truth, *home* wasn't much better than being here.

She would like to find another position elsewhere, but jobs weren't easy to obtain, not for a young woman with a withered arm. Anyway, one thing she could say was she felt needed here at Lost Waifs.

Mrs. Marner was what you might call hard-nosed. She usually shut down any hint of gossip. Would she deem talk of the mysterious plague doctor, who'd been sighted all around the city, as such?

For to that person did Daisy refer when she said *he'd* been sighted again. A plague stalked the streets of Buffalo, these warm summer days and nights. It seemed to be heralded by a terrible figure, glimpsed by witnesses both credible and otherwise.

Terrifying of aspect he was said to be, dressed from head to toe in a long cloak like that of a monk or a magician. He always appeared from nowhere—and disappeared into the same. Moreover, he wore a mask, no ordinary mask this, but a bird-visaged horror like those of the medieval plague doctors long ago.

Those doctors had treated the Black Death in Europe. No one knew if this masked individual was truly a doctor, but he'd first appeared at the same time as the mysterious illness now scourging Buffalo.

Did he bring it, or come to cure it? That question was on everyone's lips.

"Are any of our children sick?" Mrs. Marner asked in a whisper so harsh it sent a shiver up Tori's spine.

Daisy replied, "Not so's I can tell. Tori keeps checking on them, as do I. There's the usual—runny noses and tummy aches." Caused by their limited diet, Tori reflected. "But none of *them* symptoms."

The mysterious illness was marked by a high fever. Its victims reportedly wanted to shed their skin and sometimes tried to claw it off. Headache and an intensely sore throat emerged a day or so later, and eventually dark purple spots on the skin. Those in a weakened state, such as the elderly or young children poorly nourished, succumbed once the spots turned black. So far, nearly half the victims hadn't survived.

The black spots made everyone think of the plague of old, as did the appearance of the plague doctor on the streets of the city. Buffalo's physicians, however, assured everyone this was not in fact the Bubonic Plague but some other heretofore unseen illness. It spread quickly, though, and—so it seemed—most readily in the city's orphanages.

"Keep a close eye," Mrs. Marner bade Daisy, "and bring me word immediately if any of our residents fall ill."

"Sure and I will, Mrs. Marner. And I'll keep a close

eye out for the plague doctor."

The two women went their separate ways, and Tori crept off with her soiled linens, unheard and unseen. She passed a room where, between rows of cots that contained sleeping children, an ancient steam unit mopped the floor. The unit creaked as it plied the mop, but none of the children stirred, far too used to the sound.

The three steamies worked here round the clock. There had been four until the laundry maid broke down and was declared past repair. Tori and Daisy were supposed to do twelve-hour shifts, but they rarely got away on time.

Tori had to admit Mrs. Marner, who had quarters behind her office on the ground floor, was on duty most all the hours of the day and night also.

The Lost Waifs orphanage was owned and mostly funded by an ancient woman called Miss Radmacher, daughter of a wealthy man. Tori had never seen her but knew she lived in a fine house up on Bidwell Parkway. Mrs. Marner made a point of never speaking ill of Miss Radmacher, though she did remark it was difficult to run the orphanage on the funds they were allowed.

Mrs. Marner had applied for extra help after the last steam unit broke down and had been given permission to hire the new caretaker. Tori had only seen him in passing when he'd started that morning—a tall young fellow who probably had no idea what he'd gotten into.

She shoved open the door to the laundry room, a dank chamber tacked onto the back of the orphanage behind the kitchen. Only one dim light burned there. They rarely had coal enough to keep the steam plant in the cellar running at full capacity to light the house well. Tori's footsteps echoed off the walls, and Becky, the broken laundry unit, stood slumped in the corner, looking ghostly and vacant.

"I hate this place," Tori said aloud, and that echoed also. She wished once again she could find work elsewhere. But she had her mother to worry about. Ma suffered from rheumatism, yet still went out to work when she could, cleaning other people's houses. Anyway, potential employers took one look at Tori and shook their heads. No one wanted to hire a worker with only one good arm and a slightly gimpy leg.

People Tori met often asked her how she'd got this way, whether she'd suffered some accident. The fact was she'd been born with a withered left arm and one leg turned inward. She'd learned to cope with the leg. Her long skirts covered most everything, and she could move without a stick. The arm was a problem, though—no hiding it, and it hampered her activities.

It made people stare.

She drew the wringer washer out from the wall on its rollers, and dumped the sheets into the tub. She'd have to fill it with water and run the sheets through the mechanism or there wouldn't be enough clean linen for tomorrow. Upon such dismal necessities did her life run.

As she turned to snatch up the bucket, she thought she caught a movement from the corner of her eye, and her heart leaped. Had Becky moved? But no, Becky couldn't move; she'd been shut down, and her joints were probably rusted fast from the damp.

It was a shadow she'd seen move. She turned toward the door. Maybe Daisy had followed her down.

No one there.

"I have the heebie-jeebies," she told herself out loud and didn't like the way her voice sounded. Too much talk about the plague doctor—it had put her on edge. Why, there had even been a drawing of him in the newspaper, based on eyewitness descriptions. He'd looked terrifying, with his rusty cloak and the mask fashioned into the likeness of a bird's head, complete with beak.

She splashed water into the tub, only to have a chill chase its way up her spine. A sudden conviction seized her. If she turned, the plague doctor would be standing right behind her. Tall, evilly sinister, with a stillness akin to that of death.

Quiet your overactive imagination, girl, she heard Ma say in her head.

Yet the conviction wouldn't let go of her. If she spun quickly enough she would catch him, grim and solemn, watching her.

She spun and gasped. A tall figure did in fact stand behind her, perfectly motionless in the dim doorway. She jumped, and her twisted foot threatened to go out from under her. A ragged gasp tore from her throat even as she dropped the bucket from suddenly nerveless fingers. Water sloshed everywhere.

The figure raised its hands and came for her.

Chapter Two

"Get away from me!" Tori warned the looming figure in alarm.

Somewhat to her surprise, he stopped in his tracks. By then, though, he'd come into the light, and she got a proper look at him.

Not the plague doctor after all. In fact he wore quite ordinary clothing, a pair of workman's pants and a neat woolen shirt, along with a pair of well-worn boots. No mask and no beak, though he did have a rather prominent nose, a little like that of a hawk.

"I wanted only to help," he said, waving his hands at Tori in what she now saw to be a soothing gesture. As soon as he spoke, she knew him—the new caretaker Mrs. Marner had hired. He had a heavy accent and seemed to choose his words carefully, as she'd noticed this morning when she'd been introduced to him.

Residual fear made her ask, "What are you doing back here? Why did you sneak up on me?"

"Not sneaking." He reiterated, "I wanted to help. You—with your arm."

Tori flushed. People did tend to point out her shortcomings with amazing candor and lack of tact. That didn't mean she had to enjoy it, especially when it came from a virtual stranger. Why, at the moment she couldn't even remember his name.

Her chin jerked up. "I'm perfectly capable of

performing my duties, thank you."

"My duties also, yes?"

He took another step closer, and the light behind Tori flooded him. The new janitor, yes. She'd had no more than a glimpse of him earlier, being engaged with little Fern White when Mrs. Marner brought him round. But goodness, now that she took a good look at him—

He was a startlingly handsome man.

Tall and well-built, with rangy shoulders and no spare weight on him, he moved with careful grace. Dark hair—it looked black in the laundry room light—spilled over his forehead and kissed cheekbones sharp enough to have been carved with a blade. A pair of fine lips tightened as she studied him, emphasizing a perfectly formed chin. Dark brows hovered above a pair of eyes so blue they might put sapphires to shame.

Tori gaped at him, no doubt appearing like the pitiful specimen she was with her mousy brown hair, apron covered in stains, and yes, her withered arm. For the life of her, she couldn't think of anything to say.

He filled the silence by speaking softly into the echoing room. "I did not mean to startle you."

"No, it's all right. Forgive me, I recognize you now. The new man."

"Kasper Czak," he acknowledged and held out his hand. "We were introduced earlier." A certain gentlemanly courtliness accompanied his words. Tori tried not to be utterly charmed, and failed.

She shook his hand. "Tori Anderson."

"It is a pleasure to know you, Tori Anderson."

What kind of accent was that, coloring his words? She couldn't tell, and it felt rude to ask. She'd already been sufficiently rude.

"I heard someone moving around back here," he explained, "and thought it might be an intruder. Do you always work so late, Miss Anderson?"

"Yes." She turned back to the washer in an effort to duck his intense blue gaze. "I'm not supposed to work past six or so, but one of the boys wet his bed, and there aren't enough sheets, with the laundry unit broken down."

He glanced at the automaton in the corner. "What is wrong with her?"

"I don't know. Something seized up, no doubt. There's no money to get her mended, and we go through a terrible amount of laundry here."

"I see. Please allow me to help." He took the bucket from her and filled it at the leaky tap. When he bent to the task, his glossy hair fell over his forehead. Tori went dizzy.

Oh, my. Oh, my!

He filled the steel tub with water and stood with his hands on his hips while she added the soap flakes.

"Why are you here so late?" she asked.

"Getting to know the place. Trying to. There is a lot to be done."

"Oh, yes. Never enough hands."

His gaze flew to her withered arm before jerking away, and Tori flushed again. What must he think of her, grubby after a full day of work, her hair tumbling down her neck, and her clothing wet from the water she'd splashed everywhere? Difficult to tell. He bent his gaze on the washer and asked, "How does this work?"

"I turn the crank and it agitates. See? To wring the sheets out, I turn this other crank and feed them through the mangle."

"Allow me."

With the utmost courtesy he edged her aside and applied himself to the handle. Tori was about to express her indignation once more when she realized she'd much rather watch the play of his muscles beneath the plain woolen shirt than complain.

Hmm. She didn't like him pitying her or thinking she couldn't perform her job because of her arm. No, she did not. But—goodness!

As he worked the crank, he said, "I may be able to look at the laundress steam unit."

"Fix her, you mean? Are you a mechanic?"

"No. But sometimes I am good at looking how things are meant to go together and putting them back that way."

"It would be most helpful, if you could repair her. I don't know what Mrs. Marner told you, when she hired you. There's never enough help or enough money."

He shrugged. "Mrs. Marner told me pay is small. Said I would have to turn my hand to many things." He indicated the washer and quirked an ironic brow. "I am willing."

He might feel that way now. Tori wondered how long it would last. She herself had started here with considerable enthusiasm and compassion in her heart for the poor children. She still had compassion, but the enthusiasm had all drained away.

She was tired. Used up at barely twenty years of age.

"Jobs are not easy to find," he said. "Especially when one has broken English."

"I think your English is very good."

"Thank you. I work hard at it. They do not like incomers, here. People from other countries."

"Some folks don't. Which is funny when you come to think on it, because nearly everybody in Buffalo's an immigrant of one kind or another. Some came from down south, with their roots all the way in Africa. A lot came from Ireland. Some from Germany or—well, you name it."

He shot her a burning blue glance. "I have been told to my face, 'We will not hire you because you are stupid.' People from my country are considered so. If we cannot speak properly, we are of course deemed stupid." He shrugged. "Mrs. Marner did not say that."

She wouldn't. She'd probably been too happy to find a fit, able-bodied man for what she intended to pay. A very fit man.

"What is it like working here, Tori Anderson?"

She sighed. "You want the truth?"

"I would appreciate that."

She didn't want to tell him the truth. For then surely he would find another position—even one where they considered him stupid—and leave. And she discovered she didn't want that, not at all.

"It's difficult work. Like I say, there's never enough time or resources to give the children what they need. Your heart aches for them till it can't ache any more."

She stopped abruptly. She hadn't meant to say so much. He stared at her.

"And now with the sickness in the city—you've heard about that?"

"Yes. My mother is very worried."

"Your mother?"

He paused in his cranking. "I brought her with me, from our village in Poland."

Poland? He was from Poland.

"We had lost everything there. We had no reason to stay. Now she is afraid to leave the room we rent."

"You live with her? I live with my mother too." Something they had in common. "Have you heard about this figure that's been seen around the city, the plague doctor?"

Kasper shook his head.

"He dresses like one of those medieval doctors with the long robes and a mask like a bird's head, and wherever he goes the sickness seems to follow." She admitted sheepishly, "When first I saw you standing behind me there, I thought it was him."

He gave her an odd look. "I had not heard of this. Is he truly a doctor?"

"No one seems to know what he is, whether he spreads the sickness or comes to cure it. But I don't want to see him here." She shivered.

"No. We must hope he will not appear." Kasper indicated the machine. "These are washed enough?"

"Yes. Now we must put them through the mangle."

But when they tried to feed the sheets through the rollers, the upper crank froze. They had to wring out the heavy linens by hand before Tori took them to the warm kitchen, to hang.

All in all, she didn't know how she would have managed without Kasper.

"Thank you for your help," she told him fervently as she turned to leave the laundry.

"You are welcome, Tori Anderson." He tapped the roller on the mangle and gave her a smile that fair curled her toes. "I will look at this in the morning and see can I make it work again."

"That would be wonderful. And if I didn't say it

earlier, welcome to Lost Waifs."

Chapter Three

"Well, how was it, your first day?" Mama asked as soon as Kasper ducked through the door. She stood with her hands clasped, looking worried—a tiny woman who now encompassed the better part of his world. "You are so very late."

She spoke, of course, in Polish—the only language she knew—and sounded as fretful as she looked.

In an effort to calm her, Kasper said soothingly, "There is much to be done at this orphanage."

"Did they feed you all day?"

"No, Mama. My meals are not included in my wage." From what Tori Anderson had said, Lost Waifs was barely able to feed the children.

"Fine, then. I saved your supper."

Her supper, more likely. He eyed the plate on the table suspiciously. Their cupboards were nearly bare.

"Come," she said, correctly interpreting his reluctance. "You cannot work and earn for us if you do not eat. Sit and tell me all about your day."

He did, though in an effort to put as good a light on it as possible, he didn't relate everything. He failed to mention the poverty of the orphanage, as it might make her fear he'd get struck off. He didn't say how sad and pitiful the inmates appeared, focusing instead on the tasks he'd accomplished. And he didn't mention the frightening figure about which Tori Anderson had told him—the plague doctor.

Mama was worried enough and didn't need that specter haunting her mind.

But Kasper could picture it—oh, yes, he could. Back when he'd been small, in Poland—during better days— he'd had a number of books. Picture books, they were, and one had depicted a figure such as Tori had described, going about a medieval village while children followed him, and sang. He'd carried a censer in his hands full of burning herbs.

Kasper had always hated that picture. He wasn't too pleased by the idea of a mysterious illness haunting the streets of Buffalo, either. They'd come here at great trouble and expense to get away from that kind of ugliness.

No, he could not tell Mama. He hoped she would not find out some other way.

"Son, do you think you will like working there at the orphanage?"

He shrugged. He had his doubts, but he wouldn't tell Mama that, either. It seemed a sad, heavy place, far too short-staffed.

Carefully he pushed his plate away, having left a portion of his food on it. "I cannot finish, *Matka*. Why do you not eat?"

He went on speaking so she wouldn't guess he was still hungry. "You know, I have never seen so many steam units as here in this city. They are everywhere— not like back home. The ones at the orphanage, there are only three, operate very poorly. They are called Hank and Molly and Tom. I think Molly works mostly in the kitchen, though I also saw it in the children's rooms. Tom also helps to look after the children, though you should see the way he leaks steam. I suppose I should have the most to do with Hank, as he seems focused on maintenance."

"Goodness!" Mama picked at the leftovers on the plate idly, while she listened. "Are there no people like us?"

"Just three. Mrs. Marner, the woman who hired me, and two maids only, Daisy and Tori."

Tori. An image of her flashed across his mind. Brown hair straggling down from a bun that seemed too heavy for her fragile neck, clothing wetted and stained from her day's labor, and that arm…how did she ever manage? He would have to be careful if he wished to help her. She didn't like pity and would become all prickly with him if he forced his assistance.

Did he wish to help her? He was meant to help all of them, wasn't he?

But Tori, she had the most enchanting green eyes.

He wanted to tell Mama, *This Tori Anderson, her eyes are green as new leaves in the spring.*

But he couldn't. Mama would get the wrong idea.

When she'd hired him, Mrs. Marner had warned there was to be no fraternizing with the girls. It had been the same back home. Fraternizing, which he expected meant getting too friendly, would get him discharged.

He needed this job. Mama needed him to keep it. But he could provide Tori with his assistance, couldn't he?

"I hope," Mama said as she finished his supper, "you will be happy working there."

Happiness? That seemed too much to ask for. He only hoped he could hold onto the position, at least till he got paid.

17

****

The next morning he arrived at the orphanage at his appointed time, to find chaos. When she hired him, Mrs. Marner had told him he would work from seven in the morning till seven at night. He expected everyone else also worked twelve-hour shifts, except the steam units, of course. They were always on duty.

Yesterday, his first on the job, he'd found the building was mostly quiet. Oh, there was crying, of course, and a certain amount of operational noise from the steamies. And Mrs. Marner's tapping footsteps as she moved around.

This morning, the air felt charged. He met Tom on the front steps. When he bade the steam unit good morning and asked him why he was standing outside, the unit told him in a mournful rumble, "I am keeping watch."

Kasper went in. Mrs. Marner and Daisy stood at the entrance to one of the ground-floor classrooms, huddled close together. The normally immaculately groomed Mrs. Marner appeared disheveled, and Daisy's eyes were wild.

Of Tori there was no immediate sign. Kasper wondered if she'd arrived yet for her day shift.

"Good morning, Mrs. Marner. Is something amiss?" He could hear children not only crying but running around, which had not happened yesterday.

Mrs. Marner turned to him in apparent relief. "Oh, Kasper, I'm afraid much is amiss." She waved her hands in a distracted fashion.

Kasper joined her and Daisy. "Has there been an accident? Is someone hurt?" He hoped Tori hadn't tried to empty the washer on her own after he left, and overturned it on herself.

Daisy answered, sounding both horrified and oddly excited. "There's been a sighting. Here, in our street."

He stared from one to the other of them in confusion.

"A sighting of this—this plague doctor." Mrs. Marner whispered the words as if ashamed.

Ah, the medieval figure Tori had described. Well, and he did not like the sound of that.

"It has been seen? By whom?" He stared at Mrs. Marner. She seemed such a practical and unfanciful woman. If she said she believed in this thing, he must take it seriously.

"By the maid in that big house on the corner. One of the neighbors came round to tell us first thing this morning. She went out early to retrieve the milk and saw it." Mrs. Marner went pale. "Heading for our house, or so she said."

Kasper couldn't help but give a shiver, remembering that old picture in his book. He glanced over his shoulder to where Tom kept guard. "The house is locked at night, no? Nobody could get in."

"So one would think," Mrs. Marner said unhappily.

Daisy suggested avidly, "What if he's magic and can't be stopped by ordinary things like locks?"

Kasper eyed the girl in alarm. "That is not possible—magic."

Mrs. Marner told him, "Of course it isn't. But there's all sorts of wild speculation going 'round, and superstition seems to accompany this figure. The children have got wind of it and the house is in an uproar."

"Do you want me to search the building," he asked calmly, "and put everyone's mind at ease?"

Mrs. Marner looked relieved. "A very good idea, Kasper. The maid who supposedly saw the plague doctor ran and told her employer. She said she saw it walk down the street away from her and—and pause by our gate. By the time he arrived on the scene, the figure had disappeared. There is a great deal of uncertainty, as no one seems to know where it went after she took her eyes off it. The entire neighborhood is on edge."

The situation seemed silly to Kasper, though he wouldn't say so. The women obviously took it seriously. He nodded.

"I will start at the cellar and work upward."

"Thank you, Kasper. I'll just leave Tom on guard out front for now. Daisy, please come and help me calm the children."

Instead of obeying, Daisy said, "It'll be a feather in your cap if you can catch him, Kasper. The whole city's searching, and the mayor's ordered him caught, since seeing him is such a bad omen."

"A bad omen?" Kasper repeated, thinking of what Tori had told him last night.

Mrs. Marner looked even more uncomfortable. "It's said that wherever he goes, this new sickness follows. We certainly don't want it here."

"No," Kasper agreed. "We do not."

Daisy said, her Irish accent thickening, "Now the coppers are goin' door to door—"

"The coppers?"

"Police," Mrs. Marner pronounced carefully. "In an effort to home in on this—this miscreant."

"Let me take a look around the house," Kasper told her, in the same soothing tone he used with Mama. "I'm sure I will discover that all is well here at Lost Waifs."

Chapter Four

Tori arrived several minutes late for her shift that morning. Ma's rheumatism had been acting up, and Tori had spent precious time trying to persuade her to stay home from her taxing job as a scrubwoman. To no avail. Ma had a stubborn streak—possibly a good thing since it kept her going in the face of her aches and pains.

As a consequence, Tori had to run all the way from the trolley stop up on Elmwood and arrived breathless. It struck her there was a lot of activity on their street for seven in the morning, but not till she saw Tom standing out in front of the orphanage did she pause to think about it.

"Good morning, Tom. What's up? What are you doing out here?"

Tom swiveled toward her. His face, sculpted from metal, had no eyes as such, just two dished areas beneath ridged brows. He had a crude mouth set with a patch of screen for his voice box and funny little ears tucked on the sides of his head. His finish had worn significantly and rust crept over his surface like a rash. Tori couldn't even begin to guess how old he was.

"Specter, Miss Tori," he ground out.

"I beg your pardon?" She paused and stared.

"The way I understand it, a specter has been sighted here in the street."

All the blood drained from Tori's face. "Not—not

that plague doctor?"

"I believe that is the one. I am keeping watch."

"Oh, Lord! Is everyone all right, inside?"

"Yes, but I will need to refill my hopper with coal soon."

"Very well." She glanced up and down the street. People stood outside nearly all the houses talking to each other, and a group of men moved up and down. "Come inside with me for just a moment."

A mood of sharp discomfort prevailed inside the orphanage. Tori could hear children crying as she led Tom from the front to the back of the house. No one in the kitchen—they must all be upstairs, but it seemed odd for Molly to be absent from the kitchen where she should be preparing breakfast.

On the little back porch she filled Tom's hopper with coal—their supply was once more perilously low—and topped up his water before sending him back out to his post. Her nerves jangled, and she'd just decided to begin a search for her fellow employees when a clatter of footsteps sounded from the cellar stairs.

She spun with her heart in her mouth, only to see Kasper emerge from the doorway. He had dust in his dark hair and cobwebs clinging to his shirt and trousers.

"Kasper? What on earth is going on?"

He grimaced and made a gesture with his hands. "Someone down the street—a young girl—has seen this plague doctor. The one you spoke about last night."

"That's what I thought Tom said. Not good. Where is everyone?"

"Upstairs trying to calm the children. I'm searching the house. The cellar is filthy and needs to be swept." He brushed himself off. "The steam plant down there is so old, I cannot believe it works."

"Sometimes it doesn't. Mrs. Marner has been asking Miss Radmacher—she owns this place—for a new one, to no avail."

Daisy entered the kitchen, her eyes wild and her manner distracted. "Oh, Tori, did you hear? It's been sighted—right here in our street."

"Kasper just told me."

Daisy pressed a hand to her chest. "I declare, I'll not survive the terror of it. The children are all in an uproar. Try as we may, they do get wind of things."

Tori nodded. "You're past time for going home. You get off, Daisy, and I'll take over here."

"Goodness! I can't be leaving till things settle down a mite."

"Where's Molly? Why hasn't she started breakfast?"

"Molly's helping Mrs. Marner."

"I'll start breakfast, then." Tori set her things down on the table and turned to the giant porridge pot on the back of the stove.

With a nod, Daisy hurried off. But Kasper stood watching Tori, and when she reached for the huge pot he sprang into action.

"Allow me to lift that."

"I am capable, you know." She cast him an indignant look.

"I did not say otherwise."

She tipped up her chin. "I was born with my arm like this, so I've learned to cope."

"I am sure you have." Still he didn't move and stood watching as she shifted the pot, and began measuring water.

"I can manage most things with just the one hand."

He raised both his palms, placating her. "I am sorry I offended you by offering to help."

He went past her out of the kitchen, and she bit her lip. What was the matter with her, snapping at Kasper that way? But faced with such an attractive man she just felt—well, that much more awkward.

Never mind, my girl. You have real problems to deal with here today.

Molly came rumbling into the kitchen, her faulty wheels wobbling over the uneven flagstones of the floor. Like Tom, Molly was an aged automaton that had seen better days. She'd been here at Lost Waifs when Tori started two years ago and had seen very little maintenance since then. Her finish was worn and stained, and she had a tendency to overheat at times, which made her spontaneously shut down.

Tori had become accustomed to her, however, and spoke to her as she might any other co-worker.

"Morning, Molly. I'm getting the porridge started. What's going on upstairs?"

Molly waved her arms, which were covered in chipped rubber. "The children are upset and crying."

"I can hear that. Where's Hank?"

"Mopping. There have been many accidents."

"I see. Well maybe if we can get them to breakfast, the routine will help calm them down. Do you think you can set the tables?"

The room next door had two long tables crowded by many chairs. Service was not fancy, but everyone got three meals a day.

Since coming to work here, Tori had heard of other orphanages where only two meals were provided, or even just one. Children died of starvation and disease. Lost Waifs wasn't that bad, but it was certainly not the lap of luxury, either.

People said Mitch Carter—the wealthy city real estate titan—was buying up the orphanages one by one and improving them. He'd been raised at the infamous Carter's Home for Boys—children there took the last name of their benefactor—and sought to effect reform. But it would likely take him a long while to work his way down to a small operation like Lost Waifs.

Molly rumbled off to do as requested, and Tori stirred the thick pot of gruel. Despite the price of oats, she refused to serve their children a watery slop.

Her efforts were interrupted by a furious pounding at the front door. She arrived there right behind Daisy, who hauled the panel open and stared in awe at the tall, strapping police officer who stood on the stoop.

"Good morning, miss," he greeted each of them, with a smile and a tip of his cap.

The smile was engaging, and both the face and brogue screamed Ireland. Daisy relaxed visibly. "Officer?"

"Patrick Kelly, miss, at your service."

"Daisy Kilkarney." She gave a bob of a curtsey. "Won't you step in?"

The officer did, taking in Tori and her surroundings in one comprehensive glance. Behind him, before Daisy shut the door, Tori caught a glimpse of other policemen going door to door.

Excitedly, Daisy asked, "Are ye lookin' for this plague doctor, then?"

Officer Kelly looked her over with bright green eyes. "We are that, miss, canvassing the neighborhood, so to speak. Sightings of the figure have been heaviest at and around orphanages, so I wanted in particular to inquire here. Is all well?"

"To be sure, we're all at sixes and sevens, and our caretaker, he's going over the house from top to bottom, making sure there's nobody lurking, so to speak. I don't think he's found anything yet."

Mrs. Marner came down the stairs. "Officer?"

"Ma'am, the neighborhood's all clear so far. Might I have a short word with your caretaker?"

"Certainly. Tori, go find Kasper." She turned back to the officer. "His name is Kasper Czak. He's from Poland."

Not sure where to look, Tori took the back stairs and did a floor-by-floor search, finding Kasper at last in a corridor speaking with Hank.

"The police are here," she said, breathless.

"Are they?" He looked taken aback.

"About the plague doctor. Asking to talk to you. Will you come?"

He didn't look happy about it, but he followed her silently.

When they got downstairs, Tori discovered Daisy remained planted beside the handsome police officer. He spoke in reassuring tones to both her and Mrs. Marner.

"You may rest assured we'll do all we can to resolve this mystery."

Mrs. Marner appeared annoyed. "But surely it's a prank of some kind."

"Ma'am, we just don't know at the present time. The young lady who made the sighting this morning seems very certain of what she saw."

"Then it has to be someone dressing up," Mrs.

Marner asserted.

"To what purpose, ma'am?" Officer Kelly inquired.

"I don't know, do I? To frighten people. It's absurd."

"Ah." The police officer's expression remained bland. "Just so. Why would a medieval figure be roaming the streets of Buffalo? There must be something behind it."

"It's very disruptive. All our residents are upset." Indignantly, Mrs. Marner charged him, "I hope you will find out quickly."

"Yes, ma'am."

She stalked away in the direction of her office, ignoring the crying that still came from upstairs. The officer turned to Tori and Kasper, who stood listening.

"Mr. Czak, how long have you worked here?"

"This is only my second day, Officer."

Kelly eyed Kasper up and down. "And have you seen anything suspicious since you've been working here?"

Kasper raised his hands and shrugged. "It is difficult to know what is out of the ordinary, as yet. Nothing has caught my notice."

"You have searched the premises?"

"Yes, sir."

"You will not mind if we sweep the building again?"

Daisy spoke up. "Mrs. Marner will be livid if a load of policemen come through frightening the children worse than they already are." She eyed Kelly again. "Why don't ye let me show ye about?"

"Miss, that would be most kind."

After asking both Kasper and Tori what time they'd arrived that morning, Officer Kelly moved off with

Daisy. Tori and Kasper stared at one another.

"Strange," she commented.

"Yes, it is."

"Do you think that—that thing was headed for Lost Waifs?" Tori gazed up the stairs where Daisy and the police officer had gone. "I hope none of the children get sick. In other places where it's been sighted, people soon sicken. And die."

Kasper looked grave. "I would not wish to take any sickness home to my mother. She is already so frail."

Tori nodded. "We will need to keep close watch, I suppose."

Not knowing whether the policeman would want to speak with them again, they stood where they were until he and Daisy came back down the front stairs, Daisy chattering a mile a minute.

"We found nothin'," Daisy told Tori and Kasper, with a relieved smile. "If that thing's stalking our street, it hasn't come inside here."

Officer Kelly replaced his uniform cap on his head. "Please inform us immediately if anyone here sees anything."

"We will. Oh, and officer"—Daisy gave him her most winsome smile—"if you'd ever like to share a wee drink with me in the tavern, I most assuredly would not say no."

"Ah, miss. I'm very much afraid I cannot."

"Against regulations, is it?" asked the redoubtable Daisy.

"Not if I am off duty, miss. But I am, in fact, married."

"Oh." Daisy's face fell almost comically.

Kelly leaned toward her confidingly. "In addition,

miss, I am a hybrid automaton."

All three of them stared in astonishment as he tipped his cap again, and went out.

"Well, I'll be damned!" Daisy exclaimed then. "You can't blame a girl for trying. But that's a lot of man, for a machine."

Neither Tori nor Kasper laughed, though as Tori turned away she caught a smile in Kasper's eyes that matched her own.

It felt good having someone to share her ironic enjoyment. And someone to whom she might, perhaps, turn for reassurance? Time alone would tell.

Chapter Five

The children remained fractious and troubled all the rest of that day. Usually biddable for the most part, they now refused to settle. Lily Ramsey got in a hair-pulling match with Candace Byers, who was always up for a quarrel. Tori had to sit them both down and give them a stern talking-to.

Even after the police cleared the area, residents from the other houses on Breckenridge Street stood outside gossiping with one another. And the little maid from the house on the corner—her name was Kerry Butler—had become a celebrity with whom everyone wanted to speak. It was even rumored someone from the *Courier Express* intended to come and interview her.

Kasper observed all this when he took out the dust bins. He stood for a moment absorbing the scene, and wondering.

Had the sighting of this plague doctor been genuine or a fancy on Miss Butler's part? As Kasper well knew, early in the morning things tended to look—well, different. Back home while abroad early on some errand, he'd been sure he saw mounted Cossacks riding down the road toward him, emerging from the early mist and shadows. On one occasion he'd even hidden from them till the rising sun burned the mist away.

He glanced up at the orphanage—a world away from the rural life he remembered back home.

Sometimes it seemed as if nothing was real, including his memories. How had he come to be here? To take it a step farther, was he truly here? What if everything—life itself—was the mere product of imagining?

Life back home had been hard and treacherous. Life here, though, almost defied understanding. He'd but rarely seen a steam unit before they'd sailed from home. There, only the very wealthy owned such.

Here, automatons were everywhere, in all states of repair. And they seemed to own themselves.

That policeman this morning, Officer Kelly. He'd looked and acted like a man. In truth he was one of these hybrid automatons of which Kasper had heard. Part steel and part flesh and organs harvested from cadavers, of all things. And he held down a job like anyone else.

Kasper shook himself. Mother always told him all things were the will of God and must be borne accordingly. He wasn't sure he agreed.

He took himself back inside where he stood listening for a moment. Mrs. Marner, Tori Anderson, and the automaton called Molly seemed to have restored a measure of peace. Kasper wasn't sure how they endured this day after day. Daisy had at last been persuaded to go home—he smiled just thinking of her—and would be back for her night shift in just a few hours.

This place had the capacity to overtake one's existence—he could quite clearly see how it could happen to him. But never mind that now. He'd promised Tori he'd take a look at that broken automaton in the laundry, and so he intended to do.

He'd just reached the laundry, a damp and highly unpleasant room, when knocking broke out at the back door. Not wishing for it to raise the whole house again, he hurried back and flung the door open.

A familiar figure stood outside, which was remarkable since Kasper knew few enough people in the city. Yes, he knew this fellow.

Tall and bean-pole thin, the young man had a shock of very blond hair and slightly crazed blue eyes. Kasper's heart sank at the sight of him.

"Josef? What are you doing here?" How had Josef—whom he and Mother had met aboard the steamer on which they'd crossed the Atlantic along with a plethora of others fleeing the unrest at home—found him? And why?

Josef was what Mama would call an unsavory character. She'd spent some time aboard ship pitying his young wife, toward whom he did not behave very kindly.

"I came looking for a friendly face. So," Josef said, peering past Kasper into the kitchen, "this is where you fetched up." He spoke in Polish, and sounded put out.

"*Tak*," Kasper agreed, wondering how to get rid of Josef as quickly as possible. "How did you know to look for me here?"

"Mattus Kaslewski saw you walking in here the last two mornings. There are eyes everywhere in this city, *tak*? Just like home."

"Not like home." Kasper's hands contracted on the edge of the door. He wanted very badly to shut it in Josef's face.

"What is this place?" Josef asked, sounding a bit more friendly.

"Orphanage."

Josef made a face but asked, "Any other jobs here?"

"No, and I'll lose mine if I'm seen being idle, talking to you."

"I am having the devil's own time finding work. My wife and I, we have been thrown on the mercy of the church."

Surely that was only to be expected. The church had helped guide them here to this city among all the others in North America, and was supposed to continue to lend support. But in truth, there were so many to be helped, the church had insufficient resources to go around.

Still, not like home.

Josef said, "I am on a list for work at the docks. Like my father did at home, eh? But the bosses there, they don't want to hire us. They call us thick and slow. They would rather take on mechanicals who work long hours for less. It seems even here we are at the bottom of the pile, considered nothing but shit."

"Look," Kasper said, his feelings coalescing into a discernable wall of dislike, "I have no time for this. You will have to go."

"All right, all right. But it is good to speak our language, *tak*?"

Kasper nodded.

"I came to say we need to stick together, here in Buffalo. There are so few of us. There is power in numbers, and we do not wish to be powerless—again."

"All right." At the moment, Kasper just wanted Josef to leave.

"Strange bedfellows and all that." Josef grinned. "Come to the Red Eagle tavern. It's on Sobieski Street. That is where all of us gather when the day is done."

"Gather? For what?"

"For talk." Josef's lips twisted. "Support. To hear our language, to stick together." He grinned suddenly. "For vodka."

And, Kasper wondered, where did Josef get money to buy vodka when he could not support his wife?

Politely he lied, "I will come if I can. And if I hear of any other jobs around here, I will let you know."

Josef, apparently satisfied, gave him a salute and moved off.

Strange bedfellows or not, Kasper would rather share his sheets with a roach than the likes of Josef Zymanski.

****

Tori, on her way to the laundry with yet another armful of soiled bedding, heard voices coming from the back door. Two men spoke together, their words quick and unintelligible.

One voice she recognized as Kasper Czak's. He did not speak English. She paused and peered around the corner that separated the hallway from the kitchen.

Yes, there he stood clutching the edge of the door as if he wanted to slam it shut. The second man lounged in the doorway facing him. Tall and fair-haired, he had a careless yet edgy air.

None of her business. Quickly, she moved on into the laundry and dumped the linens in a pile on the floor. A moment later, Kasper came in.

"Who was that?" she asked before she realized if it was none of her business, she shouldn't inquire.

For an instant, Kasper looked trapped. But he answered without taking any apparent offense, "Someone Mother and I met during the voyage."

"Ah. A friend?"

Kasper shook his dark head. "Acquaintance is, I believe, the word."

"It is. He seems—" But Tori had no description for

the way the tall young man made her feel. She shook her head.

Kasper said, "He makes Mama feel uncomfortable too."

"It's none of my business. I didn't mean to butt in." It was just that she got feelings about people sometimes, strong and instinctive. Like she had about Kasper as soon as she spoke with him, only that had been a good feeling.

"More laundry?" he remarked with a smile. "I was just about to make an attempt to repair your laundress." He nodded at the rusty unit in the corner.

"Like I said, there's always plenty of laundry."

"If you are going to use the crank washer, I will help you with that first."

Tori brushed aside the tendrils of hair that wisped free from her bun and gathered around her face. "That's not your job."

"As I told you last night, my job is to help."

"Then I would appreciate that very much. And if you can get Becky fixed, that would be even better."

To her delight, Kasper took over the hard job of filling the wash tub with water from the tap. No matter how she'd learned to adapt to life with a maimed arm, the task of lifting a filled bucket taxed her. Besides, she appreciated another opportunity to watch the way the muscles of his arms and back flexed when he moved, and how the black hair shimmered when it tumbled over his forehead.

A handsome man, was Kasper Czak, one she wouldn't mind observing all day long. But no, "handsome" didn't cover the perfectly molded planes of his face or the angle of his brows, which looked so pleasing. She'd call him beautiful, if the term didn't denote far too much femininity to fit him.

Nothing feminine about him.

As if he could hear her thoughts—mercy, she hoped not—he shot her a look and smiled. "All filled."

"I can take it from here, thank you. You go ahead and work on Becky."

They subsided into mutual silence, except for the sloshing of water and the complaint of rusted bolts as Kasper set to work. It felt nice, companionable. Tori could get used to having this man around.

"You let me know when you are ready to wring out those sheets," Kasper told her. "I will help."

"Thank you. I need to get these out on the line. There's another load upstairs."

"Why so much?"

"The children tend to have accidents. It does no good to scold them. Daisy, who's worked here far longer than I have, says the woman who was in charge before Mrs. Marner came used to beat the children for having accidents." She chased a wisp of hair that teased her cheek, once more. "It only made things worse. The children here are—well, not well-equipped to face life's vicissitudes, so to speak."

"Vicissitudes?"

"Troubles."

"Ah, yes. The woman before Mrs. Marner sounds very cruel."

"She does, doesn't she? I mean, the poor tykes can't help it, though it does make an awful lot of work. I hope you can fix Becky."

"Me also."

Tori rattled on, wondering why she chattered so much—a thing she rarely did. He seemed easy to talk to.

"Mrs. Marner is strict. She has to be. But she's not so bad. Never cruel."

"This I am glad to hear. It would be good to have more help." He gestured with the wrench in his hand. "More automatons."

"Old Miss Radmacher holds the purse strings far too fiercely. She's said to be tighter than a size-four shoe."

"So meanwhile, we do the best we can."

"Yes, that's it."

"And," he looked her in the eye, "we are cruel to no one."

"You have that right, Master Czak. There's already enough cruelty in this world."

Chapter Six

The front page of the next morning's *Courier Express* featured a depiction of the plague doctor. Kasper saw it on his way up Breckenridge Street from the tram and paused to peer at the sheet in the newsboy's hand.

"Want to buy a copy, mister?"

The picture had a caption printed in large letters, most of which Kasper couldn't read. He was much better at speaking English, still, than reading it.

"Where was this figure seen?" he asked the boy, who gave him an affronted stare.

"Near the hospital down Niagara Street. Want to buy a copy? I can't let you read for free."

Kasper shook his head and walked on. He hoped nobody—none of their neighbors or anyone at the church where Mama frequently went—told her about this. She was already fretting too much over things in general.

"Son, will we have enough money at the end of the month to pay the rent? To eat?"

"Calm yourself, Mother. Have I not a good job?"

Not a good job, so to speak, but he felt pretty sure he'd be able to get Becky up and running today. A little hum of satisfaction started through him when he thought how happy that would make Tori Anderson.

Tori, with her soft brown hair and expressive green eyes. Did she realize how much she conveyed with them? He'd known a lot of brave people back in Poland-that-was-no-longer-Poland. Folks who struggled against impossible difficulties. Was any braver than Tori with her withered arm and her limp, who nevertheless strove to work as hard as anyone else?

When he finished fixing Becky, he promised himself he'd attempt repairs on the wringer washer. Anything to make life here easier.

But when he let himself in the back door of the orphanage, he could tell right off things at Lost Waifs were anything but easy this morning. Voices and cries echoed from upstairs. Tom came clattering down the back stairs on his rusty wheels, and a neglected kettle in the kitchen spewed steam wildly.

Something appeared very much amiss.

"Tom?" He intercepted the battered unit. "What is wrong?"

The unit looked at him, or seemed to do. It possessed only a suggestion of eyes in its sculpted face. "Good morning, sir."

"What's going on?"

"One of the children has taken ill. Miss Daisy found him when she went in to check the boys at the end of her shift."

"Ill? Surely that happens a lot?"

"It does. Apparently this particular illness is cause for unusual alarm."

"Not—the plague sickness!"

"I do not know, sir. Perhaps Miss Daisy can tell you."

Daisy came hurrying down the stairs, her face flushed, and paused beside the unit. "Tom, you get Tori them sheets like she asked. I'll fetch the basin."

"What has happened?" Kasper asked Daisy.

She shook her head, looking upset. "We don't know. Good thing Tori came in early."

"Is it—"

"We don't know," Daisy repeated. "But I'm afraid. I'll tell you that flat out. It's just Matty's gone sick for now. Tori's going to move him to a storeroom, but we need to clean up. You want to help? Take up a basin of hot water. The kettle's boiling."

Did Kasper want to enter the room where the suffering child lay? What if he took the illness home to Mama?

He faltered. "I'm not sure—"

"We don't even know if it is that plague, as yet."

Hell! What was he to do?

Daisy snatched a basin from beside the sink, plopped it on the table, and filled it with hot water from the steaming kettle. Then she poured the rest of the hot water into a bucket and added some soap flakes.

"Matty's been sick all over his bed and the floor. We have to get it cleaned up, in case—"

In case it was the plague. So no one else would be exposed.

"*Tak*," Kasper agreed, and picked up the basin.

Half way up the back stairs he realized he'd forgotten to ask in which room the poorly child had been domiciled. It didn't matter. When he reached the second floor he encountered Mrs. Marner standing in the hallway as if marooned there, twisting her hands together.

"Mrs. Marner?"

She stared through him, obviously distracted.

He looked into the room beyond, where he could see Tori bent over one of the small cots. The sound of weeping poured from not only that room but also the others.

Ignoring the distracted manageress, he moved past her into the room.

Twenty-five orphaned children lived at Lost Waifs. Of those perhaps nine—all of them boys—occupied this room, their beds marching down both sides of the chamber.

Another large room housed the girls, and still another the infants, under three or so.

Such close quarters did not afford much room between the cots—just enough, as it happened, for an adult to stand.

Tori hovered at the third bed down, on the far wall, wherein lay a child. She appeared to be preparing to pick him up.

Should she, if he was ill?

"Wait," Kasper called.

He didn't want to enter that room. He'd learned enough about sickness, about death in general, in his youth and while living in poverty since. Wisdom—if not a strong streak of self-preservation—bade him keep out of it. Yet how could he let Tori lift the child with but her one good arm?

Tori turned and looked at him, her eyes wide and brimming with emotions. He set the basin on a nearby table and went to the foot of the child's cot.

A grim and terrible sight. So far, Kasper had interacted very little with the residents, but even a stranger might tell this child was unwell. He lay with his eyes closed, a sheen of perspiration marking his skin. The room stank of vomit. Matty had indeed been sick all over his bed and the floor. Tori had thrown the offending bed coverings aside before preparing to lift the boy.

This was bad, very bad.

"Mrs. Marner cleared the storeroom at the end of the hall and put up a cot there. I have to carry him—"

"Allow me."

"I can't do that." Tori gave him a wide-eyed stare. "He may be contagious."

"But—your arm—"

"I can manage." She bit her lip. "I think."

The children occupying the cots on either side of Matthew's stared, both crying, as did the others in the room. Quite plainly, Kasper had to do something.

Very gently he nudged Tori aside. "Allow me," he said again.

Silently, she backed off.

Matty's eyelids fluttered when Kasper picked him up. His skin looked pale and blotched with red, and he gave off a tremendous heat. Tenderly, Kasper lifted him in his arms.

"Where do we go?"

"The end of the hall."

Mrs. Marner jerked to life when they entered the corridor, and she led the way. The storeroom, built over the front stairs, contained no window and had space for perhaps only two or three cots. Not a good place for a sick child, but who was Kasper to judge?

He laid the suffering boy on the cot, which contained but a single sheet. Daisy came clattering up the stairs with the mop and bucket. The four of them stood outside the storeroom in a huddle while the sound of wailing filled the air.

Mrs. Marner said, "Someone must go for the doctor."

"Will the doctor come?" Tori asked. "If they think it's the—the—" She didn't speak the word.

"Dr. Rasmussen may be the only one. Daisy, you run and fetch him, please, before you go home."

Daisy thrust the mop into Kasper's hands. "That I will."

Mrs. Marner stopped her for a moment. "Perhaps best not to mention our fears about what sort of illness this is. Or the sighting yesterday morning."

Daisy nodded before pelting off for the stairs, her apron strings flying.

Kasper and Tori exchanged one horrified look. Clearly, Mrs. Marner feared the worst—that the illness already within their doors had been brought by the plague doctor.

Chapter Seven

Tori never saw Dr. Rasmussen arrive. She kept busy settling poor Matty into his cramped quarters, changing his nightshirt, and then returning, along with Hank, to clean the room from which he'd been taken.

She didn't have time to speak with Kasper even though he looked the way she felt—queasy with fear and dread. A worst nightmare was this—something Tori had prayed might not happen ever since the first stories of this disease started circulating around the city.

Of course, they didn't know for sure exactly what had befallen Matty. A hundred other ailments beset children. It could be anything.

Then why did her heart pound so hard as she went about her tasks? Why did she feel weak with misgiving?

The other boys in the room, upset and frightened, made more of a fuss than usual when she and Hank got them up. Billy was quarrelsome, and Jim Carlson—no dummy, he—kept asking questions Tori couldn't answer. She had opened the windows of the room to try and air it out and concentrated on getting everyone dressed and downstairs for breakfast.

"Make sure and ask them if they feel sick," Mrs. Marner hissed at her before going off to tend Matty. So she did; she gazed into the eyes of each boy as he passed by, headed for the dining room, and asked if he felt sick like Matty. They all replied in the negative.

She struggled to remember what she'd heard about the plague. Precious little, except that it started with a high fever followed by a sore throat, and made its victims very, very sick with a purple rash that eventually turned black. No one seemed to know from whence it had stemmed or if it had a name. Doctors had never seen it before.

Once she got the boys up and moving, she tended to the girls in their dormitory. They, too, had more questions than she could answer, though she did her best. Meanwhile the babies cried to be fed. Molly tended them on her own, as Tori found when she popped her head into the crib-filled room.

So she missed Dr. Rasmussen's arrival and only realized he'd come when Daisy appeared.

"I thought you were going home," she greeted Daisy, who made a face.

"How can I, with all this goin' on? I'm needed, aren't I?"

"Did you bring Dr. Rasmussen?"

Daisy, still out of breath, nodded. "He's with Matty now."

"Does he think—"

Quickly, Daisy shook her head. "Didn't say. You know how Dr. Rasmussen is."

Tori definitely did. A Swedish immigrant who spoke heavily-accented English, Dr. Rasmussen attended those to whom other doctors might refuse to offer care—other immigrants like himself, prostitutes, those mired in poverty who could not pay or could pay very little.

Lost Waifs fell into that last category. As Mrs. Marner always said, their budget provided for only the most rudimentary care.

"At least he came," Daisy said darkly, as she began helping Tori clean the girls' room. "I've heard there are plenty of doctors who won't, if they suspect—you know."

"Yes."

"He's a good man."

Rasmussen was a curious sort of man, in Tori's opinion. He said very little. He noticed things but rarely expressed an opinion on them. Yet he always seemed to pay extra attention to Tori and had once questioned her about her arm.

"Excuse me, miss. You have had that from birth?"

"Yes," she'd admitted, blushing. "Came out of my mother's womb this way, I did."

He'd run searching blue eyes over her. "No other defects?"

Defect. He hadn't meant to be unkind. In fact Tori felt sure he was quite kind under his rather grave exterior. But she hated that word, hated feeling defective. She'd poked her foot out of the hem of her skirt reluctantly, and watched his eyes when she said, "I've a turned foot as well. I cope."

His expression hadn't changed but she fancied she saw the truth—that she was in fact defective—reflected in his face, just as in the eyes of those she met every day.

And now she had to see herself reflected in Kasper's deep blue eyes.

Speaking of Kasper, where had he gone? Slipped away from the second floor and probably returned to his duties downstairs.

She told Daisy as they worked together, "I hope Dr. Rasmussen decides this is just an ordinary fever and that no one else falls ill."

Daisy bit her lip. "I might have mentioned our fears and that the plague doctor was seen here on the street. You know how I am for holding me tongue, especially when the other person is not speaking. It runs away with me, so it does."

"What did he say?"

"Nothin'. That's just the point, ain't it?"

By mutual consent, they stayed on the floor till Dr. Rasmussen and Mrs. Marner emerged from the storeroom. Both Tori and Daisy held babies by then. Tori had discovered if she cradled an infant in her right arm, she could hold a bottle in her withered left hand and manage the task of feeding.

Dr. Rasmussen approached them, followed by Mrs. Marner, but stopped short of getting too close. The doctor's expression looked grave.

"I hope," he greeted them, "you have both washed your hands before touching those infants."

Daisy gasped. "Is it—"

"I am not certain," Dr. Rasmussen admitted, "but I fear the worst. I have been called to other orphanages in the city, as well as—brothels." His lips tightened. "You will need to exercise the most stringent cautions until we can determine exactly what this illness is."

"How—how can we determine that?" Tori asked anxiously.

Dr. Rasmussen's gaze softened a bit when he looked at her. "The child's fever, it will spike. It is already very high. He will break out in dark purple spots that will eventually turn black. His throat will swell so he cannot swallow and will have difficulty breathing. Death may follow."

"Jaysus, Mary, and Joseph!" Daisy breathed and crossed herself.

Dr. Rasmussen turned back to Mrs. Marner. "Do you have someone you can dedicate to nursing the boy?"

"N-no."

"Find someone. If this is what we fear, it is highly contagious. An automaton attendant would be best."

"An automaton?" Tori repeated, and his gaze touched her again.

"They cannot get sick."

"Ah." Looking desperate, Mrs. Marner said, "Perhaps we can assign Molly to the task for now."

Tori thought of the dozens of jobs Molly performed daily—and nightly—without complaint. Who was to manage all that if she stayed in the storeroom?

"I will return this evening to see how the boy does. Meanwhile, I want the most strenuous cleanliness. Disinfect with care. Do you understand?"

All three of his listeners nodded.

"Monitor the other children. Get as much liquid into the boy as you can."

"Doctor—" Tori wanted to reach for his arm but didn't, "you are not sure this is—well, what we fear, right?"

"I am not. But it is smart to take the precautions, *ja*?"

"Doctor," Daisy spoke in turn, "does the disease have a name?"

"They are calling it the Black Fever."

****

Kasper reassembled Becky for the third time, filled her thorax with water, and got it up to a fine simmer before he flipped her switch. The switch itself, so he'd determined, had been part of her problem, so corroded by salts and soap residue it made but a poor connection. Others of her internal parts had also been gummed up. He'd spent more time scraping off goo and polishing with solvent than actually repairing.

Yet this made his third attempt, and he held his breath until the unit actually jerked to life, moving her arms.

"Becky?" he breathed.

She turned her face toward him. Her neck joint squealed in protest, and he realized he should have polished that too.

"Master?" she croaked through the screen that served her as a mouth.

"I am not your master," he corrected. "Call me Kasper."

"Kasper."

"How do you feel?"

She tipped her head and appeared to consider the question. The indents that served her for eyes reflected only glints of light from the lamp that hung overhead.

"I feel strange."

"Strange how?"

She flexed her limbs. "My arms and legs move more easily."

"That is good."

"Did you repair me, Kasper?"

"I did my best."

"No one has ever bothered to repair me." She leaned closer to him.

For some reason, though he'd seen all her inner workings, the scrutiny made Kasper uncomfortable. "It seems no one has performed regular maintenance on you. We can remedy that, though."

"You will maintain me in future?"

"I will."

She shivered, a whole body movement.

"Becky, are you operating correctly?"

"Very much so, Kasper. What can I do for you?"

"For me? Nothing. But if you feel equal to performing some work, you can take up your former duties. As you see, there are piles and piles of laundry."

"Oh, dear. How long was I inoperative?"

"I'm not sure. I only started working here a few days ago."

"A fortunate addition to the household."

"It is nice of you to say so. Do you feel capable of tackling this laundry?" Kasper figured the best thing he could do to help Tori was remove that monstrous chore.

"Yes."

"Only I'm afraid the mangle is also broken. I mean to look at that next."

"Not a problem." She held out her hands, with their rubberized, whitened fingers. "My hands are very strong."

"That is good."

"Will you remain here and repair the mangle, Kasper, while I work?"

"Unless I am needed elsewhere."

Apparently contented, Becky set to work with a will.

Chapter Eight

As promised, Dr. Rasmussen returned early that evening to check on the ailing child. Tori let him in, and he treated her to his grave smile.

"Miss Anderson, how is the patient?"

"Not doing very well I'm afraid, Doctor."

"He has got worse? How is the fever?"

"Higher, we think. And that flush on his cheeks? It's—it's turning into a rash."

"Tsk, tsk." He actually spoke the words, looking unhappy.

As she led him up the stairs, she asked, "Do you think it's this Black Fever?"

"I will need to look at him again."

"Only—Daisy never went home today, and I don't know if I should go home, either. I have an aging mother, and—"

He laid a kindly hand on her good arm. "Let me look at him, eh?"

"Yes, yes, of course. It's just I'm—"

"Ah, Dr. Rasmussen!" Mrs. Marner descended upon him. "I'm so glad you're here. He's worse, I'm afraid."

She led him off to Matty's cubbyhole. Daisy came out from the girls' room and joined Tori in the hallway.

"What's he say?"

"He won't know till he sees Matty again."

"Jaysus. Tori, I don't know how to conduct meself.

I've prayed till I can pray no more."

"You're exhausted. Maybe you should go home."

"I just want to wait and see what we're dealing with here, before I decide to. If I take something home to my younger brothers and sisters—"

"I know, I feel the same. But Mother will worry."

"We'll have to send a message. Maybe Tom can go." They exchanged a look. "He's a mechanical—like the doctor said, he can't get sick."

****

They still stood together, Daisy with her hands wrapped in her apron, when the doctor emerged from the sickroom followed by Mrs. Marner, who had a handkerchief pressed to her face.

"Oh, no," Daisy mourned.

Grave as a specter, Dr. Rasmussen approached them.

"What is it?" Tori quavered.

Disregarding her piteous question he asked, "Are any other children sick?"

"N-no," Tori faltered. "Not yet."

"The boys all slept in one room together before Matthew fell ill?"

"Yes—all the boys above a certain age."

He glanced at Mrs. Marner. "They will have to be watched most carefully. Ideally, they should be kept away from the girls and infants, though it's likely already too late."

Tori gasped. "It is this Black Fever, then?"

"I fear so. We will know by morning. If he starts vomiting blood—"

Daisy stepped up. "Shouldn't Matty be taken to the hospital?"

"I will have to notify them. They will in turn notify the police. Just so you know, officers may turn up here."

Mrs. Marner grew indignant. "I've done nothing wrong in caring for these children."

Dr. Rasmussen glanced around the hallway. "Indeed, you have done the best you can." He grimaced. "As do we all. Keep him warm and as clean as possible. I will be back in the morning."

He started down the stairs. Tori followed him.

"Doctor—"

He turned at the door, his gaze once more softening. "You should not be here. You are vulnerable."

"Because of my arm, you mean? I'm just as strong as anyone else."

"Ja, and we are all vulnerable."

"Is it safe for me to go home to my mother?"

"I would not, if there is a cot you can occupy here."

"You do think it's the Black Fever, then."

He said nothing, though his eyes answered her.

"Oh, God, what are we going to do?"

"Try to have faith all will come right."

"How? How am I supposed to do that?"

"Miss Anderson, I see much in my practice. If I can hope, so can you."

"Yes. Yes, of course." Yet Tori's heart faltered beneath the weight of dread.

"Try to get some rest. Oh, and let your mechanicals do as much as possible for the children."

He went out into the gathering night.

Mechanicals. They had only Hank—on his last wheel—Molly already tending Matty, Tom…and Becky, now that Kasper had miraculously repaired her, a feat she'd not had time to see for herself. Supposing Kasper should be informed of Dr. Rasmussen's diagnosis, she continued on down to the kitchen and the laundry beyond.

Not only had Kasper repaired Becky, who was up and running, but apparently the mangle on the washer also, for Becky manned the crank, turning it with enthusiasm. The piles of laundry had been reduced to but a few, and clean, folded sheets were stacked on the work table.

"Oh, Becky, you've got nearly all the sheets and clothing done. I can't tell you what a help that is."

"Master Kasper suggested it."

Master Kasper? "Where is he?"

"He went out." Becky turned her face toward the door. "I only wish he would return."

"Oh?" Tori fought down a quite inappropriate surge of—was that jealousy? Ridiculous. "You like him, do you?"

"He brought me back to life."

Tori agreed, that made a powerful attraction. Even if Kasper weren't so handsome.

"I hope he didn't go home. Matty's very sick. The doctor suggested we all stay here."

"I always stay here."

So she did. Tori grimaced. Again, life reminded her there were worse things than a withered arm.

Giving Becky an uncertain smile, Tori continued her search for Kasper. She at last found him out in the darkening yard, struggling to tie up an extra clothesline.

"All these others are full," he explained, "and Becky has more laundry to hang." He shot Tori a close look. "What is wrong?"

"Dr. Rasmussen thinks—he's pretty sure that Matty

has the Black Fever. He's coming back in the morning to make sure. Meanwhile he suggests we should keep the children apart as much as possible and that we should probably sleep here till—till we know what's to be done."

His eyebrows soared. "But I have my mother at home."

"As do I. And Daisy has her whole family. We're planning to send Tom around to inform our households." Though she could just imagine how Ma would worry.

"I will go speak to Mrs. Marner."

He ran into the house. Tori followed more slowly, wondering what she was going to do for clean clothing tomorrow morning, for a nightgown tonight. She desperately wanted a cup of tea but felt too tired to make one.

Daisy came in, her eyes wide. "Kasper is upstairs arguing with Mrs. Marner. You told him?"

Tori nodded.

"You don't think he'll get dismissed, do you?"

"I hope not." The very idea made Tori feel sick.

"We're short-handed already. Tori, lass, how are we ever going to manage?"

"Dr. Rasmussen says to have faith. Maybe he's right. We don't even know for sure Matty's got this Black Fever."

But Dr. Rasmussen had been certain; Tori had seen that in his eyes.

"Well," Daisy said, "I need to get up to the nursery. Those poor lambs will be squalling." Tears filled her eyes. "If one o' them falls ill, I don't think I can endure it."

Daisy always had a soft spot for the smallest of their

charges and paid them as much attention as possible, though there was never enough time.

"I'll go put the girls to bed and then the boys," Tori volunteered.

Daisy paused and looked at her. "Is that safe, goin' back and forth?"

"Who knows, Daisy? We're walking on uncertain ground."

****

"You must be sensible," Mrs. Marner told Kasper. "You can send your mother a message via Tom. He's going to tell Tori's mother and Daisy's family they can't come home just yet."

"You do not understand. My mother—she does not speak any English. She cannot communicate with any of our neighbors and will not understand what Tom tells her." To say nothing of the fact that she'd likely be terrified at finding an automaton at her door.

"That is indeed unfortunate, Mr. Czak." Mrs. Marner put a hand to her brow. "I am afraid I have my own problems and do not have time to argue it with you."

"I see that, and I do not mean to argue. Are we strictly forbidden from going home? Has Dr. Rasmussen said so?"

"Well, no. But—"

"Then I will hurry home, tell my mother what has happened, make sure she is all right, and come back here to help you. Otherwise—"

Mrs. Marner met his gaze. "Otherwise you'll quit? I can't have that. I'm already dreadfully short-staffed." She sighed. "Try to get back as soon as you can. And do not make any other stops along the way, please."

"Yes, Mrs. Marner. I promise."

"Ah, Mr. Czak, that is a promise I do hope you'll keep."

Chapter Nine

An hour later, Kasper realized he should have made no promise at all. His mother, hearing his story, became distraught. She wept and clung to him even though he told her over and over he'd just come from a house of illness.

"Son, you cannot leave me. What am I to do here alone?"

"I know it is bad, Mama. But until we know for sure what illness it is that the young boy has—"

"I am sorry for him, indeed I am, and I will pray for him just as I pray for you. But you cannot abandon me here." Her eyes were wild. "I know no one."

Kasper's thoughts flew. Was there anyone to whom he might turn for help on Mama's behalf? They'd met people—like Josef and his wife—during the crossing. But he had no contact with Josef's family now.

He snapped his fingers. The church! Many of those from the boat attended the same church, St. Stanislaus. In fact, it was only a few blocks away.

"I tell you what, Mama. On my way back to the orphanage, I will stop at St. Stanislaus and ask them to check in on you. Maybe someone could escort you to the market. There is a little bit of money in the tin box on the mantel. But it's safest for you to stay here as much as you can, just in case—in case—"

He stumbled to a halt. Should she contract this dread

illness and die, well, he could not conceive of it. Already he'd lost so many. Papa and his grandparents, his brothers Janusz and Pavel. Mama was his last remaining link with his past, the only one to share memories of what had been. Yet she looked so frail, gazing up at him with her blue eyes swimming with tears.

"Oh, son!" She embraced him. "Must you leave me?"

He supposed not. He reckoned that rather than abandon Mama he could abandon those back at Lost Waifs instead. He'd known them only a few days.

Yet the orphanage was in such a bad way, and already so short of help. He thought of all the children sleeping in their neat rows. Of Daisy run off her feet and of the expression in Tori's green eyes when she looked at him.

Tori was special. He just couldn't say why.

"Mama, *tak*, I have to go back. I made a promise."

Her gaze fell in defeat. "We do not break promises."

"No, we do not. Listen—I hope this will all blow over and I will be able to return home very soon."

He gathered up some spare clothing—he didn't have much—and bundled it together before kissing Mama on the cheek. "Mama, please stay well. I will check in at the church and ask them to help you."

Full dark had fallen before he returned to the street. The crowded neighborhood had quieted down and lights burned behind many windows.

He hurried to the church, fearing no one would be there at this hour, but the doors stood open, and people from the neighborhood, mostly women, prayed inside.

He found the priest, Father Wisniewski, standing to one side of the altar.

"Father, if I might have a word?"

The comforting thing about Father Wisniewski was that he spoke their language and had lived many of their woes—the loss of family and country. The expression on his rather cherubic face grew grim as he listened to Kasper's account, and he crossed himself.

"I understand. This is a dread illness, so I hear, worse than anything that touched us even back home."

"Father, I feel it is my duty to return to my job at the orphanage. But I worry for my mother."

"You have a good and stout heart. Go follow your duty. We will look in on your mother."

Relief flooded Kasper. "Thank you, Father."

"And may God protect you from any hint of this contagion."

Despite Father Wisniewski's assurances, Kasper still doubted. Even as he made his way back to Breckenridge Street, he wondered whether he did the right thing placing any loyalty at all before that he owed his mother.

The streets seemed very dark and empty. Were folks all shutting themselves away inside, afraid of contact with one another? His footsteps echoed on the pavement and off the shuttered buildings he passed, and a cold feeling of dread crept up his spine. When he saw the corner of Breckenridge and Elmwood up ahead, he quickened his pace, knowing Lost Waifs lay only halfway down the next block.

He rounded the corner at a half jog, his bundle clutched to his chest, and faltered. A single figure walked toward him out of the gloom between the street lamps.

Tall it appeared—at least it cast a tall shadow. Dressed all in dun brown, it wore robes that whispered when it moved. Real, then—it was real and not an illusion, for he could hear that rustle, and hear its footsteps just like his own, clattering against the pavement.

Its face—

But it did not have a face, not a human one. Instead it possessed a beak and two dark slits for eyes, with which it fixed Kasper in a stare that nearly froze his blood.

A mask—some dim part of Kasper's mind recognized it for a mask. The balance of his mind stuttered and flooded with panic. He recoiled in an almost visceral horror.

On the same side of the street as him, the plague doctor carried a censer, trailing steam, and walked steadily toward him, as if it might walk through him. As if it weren't flesh and blood after all. But Kasper believed to the root of his soul it was.

He heard a strangled sound and only belatedly realized it came from his own throat—a stifled moan. Everything within him wanted to avoid contact with that figure. But he had no time to run.

He leaped sideways into the yard of the house in front of which he stood. Vaguely he noted there was a fence—scant protection, but he crouched behind it like a guilty child.

The plague doctor passed. It passed so closely he might have reached through the fence and touched its robes, though nothing on earth would have persuaded him to. It kept its gaze fixed on him as it passed, turning its head as far as possible. He fancied he caught a glimpse of eyes between the slits in the mask. And he caught a hint of a vile odor emanating from the censer.

He prayed.

He prayed and the figure went by, continuing its way down Breckenridge Street before dematerializing into the gloom.

Kasper remained where he was and tried to remember how to breathe. Not normally a coward, this terror had moved him beyond the ordinary.

What if it had touched him? Would he then have fallen ill with the Black Fever? Had he been close enough to it, now, to contract the contagion? Had it been carried in the foul odor he'd inhaled?

Eventually he got to his feet and brushed himself down, both physically and mentally. He had to get hold of his emotions. He had to get back to the orphanage.

He needed to raise the alarm. Death walked the very streets of Buffalo.

Chapter Ten

"Get yourself around the outside o' that, son,"
Patrick Kelly said, his Irish accent rolling over Kasper
like a warm and comforting blanket. He nodded at the
glass of whiskey Mrs. Marner had rather surprisingly
placed in Kasper's hand, right after summoning the
police. "I understand it has a wonderfully steadying
effect."

They all stood around him—Mrs. Marner, Daisy,
Tori, and the police officer—in Mrs. Marner's office
where Kasper had collapsed. She kept the bottle in the
bottom drawer of her desk, a thing Kasper might never
have suspected.

She looked so staid and sober. Except now that he'd
blurted out his story, she looked as spooked as Kasper
felt. They all did.

He waved a hand at his audience. The hand trembled
visibly. "You should all keep back, away from me. What
if I caught something from it?"

Everyone but Kelly backed off several steps. He
said, "Lord love you, *sor*, I'm an automaton. I can't get
sick. It's why they're sending us on these calls, ye
know."

"Ah. Yes. That is—handy."

"I am very handy, *sor*, yes. Now drink your whiskey
and give me an exact account of what ye saw."

Kasper drank. The warm burn of the liquid spread

through him. It helped, though not as much as he might wish.

He made his account as clearly as he could. His audience listened, Daisy's face blanching in horror. Mrs. Marner's grew tight. Tori's green eyes became impossibly round.

The tall hybrid police officer heard him out patiently, even when he stumbled over his English, unable to find the words in this moment of extremity.

"So you got a close look at it, *sor*."

"Very close. Too close."

"That is an excellent description and matches others from around the city."

"But Officer," Daisy faltered, "why would it be seen twice here on Breckenridge Street?"

"Miss, its appearance seems to be connected with threat of the sickness, which occurs most frequently in institutions like this one—orphanages, elders' homes—many of which are congregated in this area."

"Do you think the plague doctor brings the sickness, Officer Kelly?"

"It is too soon to tell. A curious thing, though—there have been simultaneous sightings."

"Eh?" Kasper balked.

"At the same time you saw this figure here, *sor*, we also received a report he was seen on Porter Avenue, where there is a church home for the aged."

Mrs. Marner put her hand to her throat. "You're saying there's more than one of them?"

"So it would appear, Mrs. Marner."

"But—what does that mean?"

"Either there is magic involved—"

"Magic?" they all exclaimed.

Mrs. Marner added, "Officer Kelly, surely you don't believe in that sort of thing."

"Magic?" He looked at her with his uncannily perceptive green eyes. "Why not? Because I am, in fact, made of metal as well as flesh?"

"Well—" Mrs. Marner looked mildly embarrassed.

"But there is considerable evidence for the existence of magic. I do a great deal of reading." Modestly, he explained, "It is how I've learned about the world. Magic, so it seems, is present in every aspect of what we call life. It keeps the gasses of the air in balance, the seas within their shores. It keeps gravity operational and the sun in the sky."

"I thought that was God," Kasper whispered involuntarily.

"Or—or science," Mrs. Marner added.

Patrick Kelly shrugged. "God or science. Whatever one wishes to call it. Is there a difference?"

Kasper exchanged an incredulous look with Tori.

"Do you and your—er—kind believe in God? In prayer?" Mrs. Marner asked.

"Many of us do, madam. Though we pray to different things."

"The question o' magic, now," Daisy took it up. "Me, I believe in magic, bein' Irish like yourself, Officer Kelly. But even I fail to see how magic could account for that terrible specter bein' seen in two places at the same time—oh." She considered it.

"I am not saying, miss, that is what has occurred. But," he tapped the side of his head, "I consider all possibilities. Someone—or more than one person—may be playing at being this plague doctor in order to send a message. Or there may be a Deeper Meaning." Emphasis capitalized the last two words.

"Officer Kelly," Mrs. Marner lamented, "what are we to do?"

"Keep close and keep watch. Hope no others of your charges fall ill. We members of the Irish Squad will patrol the street. Call upon any of us if there is another sighting."

"Yes, Officer, we will."

About to depart through the front door, Pat Kelly turned and looked at them again. "This is a very special city. I believe there's something beneath the very streets—"

"Magic?" Daisy breathed again.

He nodded. "Some sort of force, running deep. Where else might automatons build churches and where else might folks from all over the world"—he waved a hand at them—"find a way to share their dreams? Try to have faith that all will be well."

Mrs. Marner nodded. "Thank you, Officer Kelly."

He went out, admitting just a little darkness. Mrs. Marner sighed. "Someone needs to go up and check on the children."

"I'll go," Daisy volunteered. "In fact, I was thinkin' of sleeping in the nursery tonight."

They all stared at her. "My dear, are you certain about that?" Mrs. Marner asked. "You'll get little rest."

"I don't expect to get much rest anyway. And if that plague doctor finds his way in here—by magic or other means—I'll be there to protect those bairns."

Tori, looking terrified, murmured, "Have there been any reports of it coming inside?"

"I don't think so. Not yet."

Daisy hurried off, and Mrs. Marner looked at

Kasper. "Take your time recovering. And I meant to say, thank you for getting Becky up and running. It is a great help."

She too hurried off, leaving Tori and Kasper alone together in her office.

Tori shivered. "What was it like, seeing that thing?"

"I am not ashamed to say it frightened me on a—a deep level. It felt as if, well, I have no words, at least not in English. As it passed me by, it looked at me, and—"

"Your blood turned cold?"

Kasper nodded.

"I am so scared," she admitted in a whisper. "What if they all get sick?" She nodded toward the second floor. "What if we do?"

Wordless, he rose and held out his arms. She availed herself of the shelter he offered, huddling in tight against him, one human seeking comfort from another. Kasper, hungry for the same comfort and sustenance, wrapped his arms around her tight.

She felt very small—fragile, for one who had to bear so much. Her head just reached his shoulder, and she tucked it in close to his neck as if they'd done this a thousand times.

Warmth stole through him in company with a rush of emotions that included, to his rueful surprise, a good measure of lust. He wanted to kiss her, but that would be a terrible violation of her trust.

This—this one moment, must be enough.

After several minutes he murmured, "I'm sure the automaton policemen will be keeping watch. And I am here." Now why had he said that? He was the same person who'd leaped over a fence to get away from that—thing.

Must be the whiskey talking. But with Tori in his arms he felt braver and stronger.

"Thank you." She raised her face from his shoulder and looked at him, green eyes gazing so intently into his it made him shiver in reaction. She brushed her lips very lightly over his—so lightly it could barely be called a kiss—and it felt solemn and profound.

Tori Anderson, whether she knew it or not, was very special.

And maybe getting marooned here at Lost Waifs wouldn't be all bad.

Chapter Eleven

Mrs. Marner wept the next morning when they saw that little Matty's spots had turned black. Tori found it deeply distressing to witness the usually restrained woman breaking down that way. There had been times since she'd started working at Lost Waifs when Tori wondered if Mrs. Marner truly cared about her charges.

She did.

"Oh, oh!" Mrs. Marner huffed into her handkerchief after Daisy brought her the news. "What are we to do?"

"Care for him, I suppose," Daisy replied, tears also sparkling in her eyes. "Or perhaps Dr. Rasmussen will send him to the hospital when he comes."

Tori tiptoed into the tiny storeroom to peer at Matty, who appeared feverish and still very sweaty. He lay as if asleep, yet not peaceful, turning his head on the pillow.

She stood there torn between her reluctance to touch him and her desire to see the evidence of the fever. At last, very cautiously she peeked through the front of his nightshirt. And gasped.

The rash had thickened so it appeared one color—a blot. Dark red no longer, it definitely appeared black.

"Oh, Matty. Oh, Matty!" Forgetting her reluctance in a rush of compassion, she smoothed the hair back from his brow. Poor waif, indeed. Only seven years old, left fatherless and motherless, and now having this terrible illness visited upon him.

And what about the rest of them? Could they hope to keep from catching this?

She went out to find Mrs. Marner still in the hallway. "How awful," Tori said.

"It is deeply distressing. I do not think I can allow Daisy to tend him any longer, if she is going back and forth to the nursery. Should one of those tiny babes fall ill, I will never forgive myself."

"Will you leave it with Molly, then? Is there any way I can help?"

"No, I dare not let you fall ill either. I am afraid we will have to dedicate Molly to the task full time, just as Dr. Rasmussen suggested. Becky will have to pick up some of Molly's duties in addition to the laundry."

Poor Matty. Molly was sometimes clumsy and not as gentle as she might be.

When Tori expressed this concern, Mrs. Marner said, "She is very old, and her limbs no longer operate smoothly."

"We need more help."

"We cannot afford another steam unit, and bringing in an employee now would be irresponsible, even if we could find someone willing to work for what we can offer."

"Could you ask Miss Radmacher for more funds? In the circumstances, I would think she'd feel charitable."

"Miss Radmacher? Charitable?" Mrs. Marner sighed again. "I will think about it. Meanwhile, I believe I hear Dr. Rasmussen arriving. Will you please go bring him up?"

Tori hurried off to obey. Dr. Rasmussen stood at the door, looking weary and grim. It had begun to rain, and his demeanor matched the weather.

"Oh, Doctor, please come in. Mrs. Marner is upstairs with Matty."

"How are you, Miss Anderson?" He peered at her through his rimless spectacles.

"I'm sure I don't know. Matty—we think it is the Black Fever, Doctor. His chest is covered in spots all run together and nearly black."

Dr. Rasmussen took the stairs two at a time to the second floor, where Mrs. Marner greeted him.

Daisy stepped out from the nursery with little Letty in her arms. "Tori, can you help me with these babies? They're all crying."

"They aren't sick, are they?"

"Just wet and hungry, I think."

"Daisy, should we be tending them when we were just in there by Matty?"

"There's no one else."

She was right. Tom was in with the girls—Tori could hear him trying to get them out of bed—and Hank tended the boys.

She scrubbed her hands at the basin in the hallway and followed Daisy into the nursery, which smelled of wet nappies. Before they had all the infants changed, they heard Mrs. Marner calling them.

"Everyone, gather round!"

"But the babies—"

"You will have to leave them for the moment. Dr. Rasmussen has something to tell us. Mr. Czak?" she called down the stairs, and a startled-looking Kasper appeared from the back of the house. "Come up here, please."

He ran up the stairs, looking wary.

Dr. Rasmussen began to speak. "Your young boy,

Matthew, has the Black Fever. There can be no doubt. His fever is very high and his rash has turned black. His throat is sore and almost swollen shut."

Daisy gasped.

Rasmussen went on, "I am going to take him to the hospital. I will leave here directly and summon an ambulance."

"Ambulance!" Mrs. Marner looked horrified. "I cannot afford that."

"I do not have a carriage and cannot take him on public transport. I think the charity hospital on Grant Street may admit him for free."

"That place?" Daisy sniffed. "More people die in there than come out alive."

"I feel it is important to remove him from here," Dr. Rasmussen said, "before others of your children fall ill."

"Very well," Mrs. Marner agreed.

"What about the rest of us?" Kasper asked. "How likely are we to fall ill? It is just that I have an aged mother."

"Of course." Dr. Rasmussen rubbed at his forehead. "I cannot say. We have never before seen this fever and do not know exactly how it behaves."

"If you've never seen it before, where did it come from?"

"Miss Kilkarney, we do not know that either."

"The plague doctor," Daisy whispered. "It was seen in this street—twice."

"Nonsense," Dr. Rasmussen declared.

"I saw it myself, this terrible figure," Kasper said quietly. "Here in Breckenridge Street."

Rasmussen glared at him. "Even so, such a figure, how could it bring contagion? Make sure, all of you, to wash your hands scrupulously. Employ your steam units as much as you can. Is there a chance you can obtain more?"

Mrs. Marner shook her head.

"I will see what I can do," Dr. Rasmussen said.

But what could he do about their staff shortage? Tori could only wonder.

"Yes, Doctor. Thank you."

The ambulance arrived an hour and a half later. Tom carried Matty downstairs most carefully, and the attendants placed the child inside the vehicle. He hadn't yet regained his senses.

After they left, Tori stood outside for a few moments. Rain still fell, and windows across the way were early lit.

From behind curtains, the neighbors peered out, Tori saw.

"Miss Anderson, come back in," Kasper called from behind her. "You're getting all wet."

She turned and faced him where he stood just inside the doorway, frowning.

"You mean I could catch my death?" she called back. "But we're all in danger of catching that now, right?"

He ran out and shrugged out of his coat, which he placed around her shoulders. "Are you all right?"

"I don't know. I honestly don't. What if others fall ill and we've sent that poor child away to strangers for nothing?"

"We must hope they won't."

But, late that evening, nine-year-old Janie started with a sore throat, and overnight her fever soared.

"I don't understand it," Daisy nearly wept. "She

isn't even in the same dorm as Matty was."

"But we all go back and forth," Tori pointed out, "and have been this whole time. Daisy, with all this going on, it surely isn't safe to go home, is it?"

"I'm afraid not, love."

"Ma will be frantic."

"They all will."

Early next morning, however, they discovered the city had trouble far beyond the walls of Lost Waifs. A newsboy went down Breckenridge Street hawking his papers with a cry shrill enough to reach Tori's ears.

"Sickness spreads! Mayor to shut borders of Buffalo!"

"What?" Tori gasped to herself and ran out front. The rain had stopped and sunlight strained through the clouds, turning the wet pavement to gold.

She shouldn't be out here. And she shouldn't spend what little money she had on a copy of the *Courier Express*. Most definitely the newsboy—who looked about thirteen—shouldn't be out and about on his rounds.

She grabbed a copy of the paper and paid him a nickel anyway.

Inside, they all pored over the paper, which Tori spread across the kitchen table. No one had snatched much sleep. Molly had sat with the ailing Janie, who'd been moved to the storage closet, but both Tori and Daisy had been on call. Accordingly, the newsprint danced in front of Tori's blurry eyes.

The lead story informed them that the Black Fever had now been diagnosed in all wards of the city. Mayor Piffen had indeed advised no travel in or out of city limits, except for emergencies. Movement within the city was discouraged and residents were advised to stay at home as much as possible.

"What does it say?" Kasper asked, hanging over Tori's shoulder, so she read it out loud to him.

"How did that happen so fast?" Daisy wondered. "And all over the city."

"It's not just us," Mrs. Marner murmured in response. "I don't know if that makes it better or worse."

"Worse," Tori breathed.

"Well," Kasper tapped the paper with one finger, "people have to go out to work, yes? There are jobs that have to be done—like ours. And many, many others. Doctors, police, those who sell food—"

"The list is endless," Mrs. Marner agreed. "I do not see how the mayor can hope to impose such restrictions."

A lively city, so Tori acknowledged, Buffalo thrived on comings and goings. She scanned the rest of the front page and her gaze fell on a supporting story farther down.

Sightings of Mysterious Figure Cover City.

"Oh, my," she breathed. "Look at this."

She read that aloud too while her companions listened. Reports had flooded in all over Buffalo of the figure dressed like a medieval plague doctor. Buffalo police were investigating, and members of the public were urged to cooperate with them. Everywhere a sighting had been made, someone soon fell ill with Black Fever, and the question of cause and effect was under consideration.

A partial list of sightings followed. It did, indeed, include every ward and sector. Their own street was duly listed.

"But," Daisy protested, "how could this—this

specter be in so many places?"

"It is as if it wants people to see it," Kasper agreed.

They all stared at each other, and Tori came to the only conclusion she could. "Someone is doing this—spreading this—deliberately. But who?"

Chapter Twelve

Tori wasn't the only Buffalo resident to jump to that conclusion. As they learned when Dr. Rasmussen stopped in later that day, the city ran riot with speculation.

"It is all nonsense," he declared in a sweeping manner. The good doctor looked grim, even more so than previously, and frankly unwell. Tori figured he probably hadn't slept at all and was run ragged.

If this kept up, there wouldn't be enough doctors to go around.

Mrs. Marner had sent for Dr. Rasmussen when Janie was no better that morning. Tori and Mrs. Marner stood outside the storeroom in a huddle with Molly, while he examined the girl.

As if she didn't have enough to worry her, Tori had concerns about Molly, who wasn't operating correctly. Her limbs had begun jerking sporadically and whining at inopportune moments. Even now she stood as if on shut down, rubberized fingers hanging limp.

Maybe Tori could ask Kasper to take a look at her, for they absolutely couldn't be short-handed.

"The child has Black Fever," Dr. Rasmussen pronounced shortly when he emerged from the storeroom.

"Oh, no," Mrs. Marner moaned, even though they'd all recognized the symptoms. "Will she need to go to the hospital?"

Dr. Rasmussen shook his head. "The hospitals are full and asking that patients be looked after at home, except in the most drastic cases."

Tori glanced around. This did not make much of a home but would have to do.

Mrs. Marner protested, "But won't keeping Janie here pose a danger to the other children?"

"*Ja*, Mrs. Marner. But the illness—it is already within these walls. Do the best you can." He looked at her. "One thing I hope may help—I have sent a letter to Mr. Mitch Carter."

"Mitch Carter?" Mrs. Marner looked astonished. "The real estate magnate?"

"He is much more than that. Perhaps you know he was raised at Carter's Home for Boys and has lately become involved in orphanage reform. He has been buying up city orphanages, seeking to improve them."

"Yes. But that's the bigger operations, right? He'd never touch a place like Lost Waifs."

"I do not know. I have informed him of your predicament. He may be able to provide you with extra manpower."

"How?"

"He has been placing refurbished steam units into these institutions. I am not sure how many are available. But it may help."

Mrs. Marner looked dazed. "Yes. Yes—but, steam units?"

"Be thankful for them," Dr. Rasmussen said shortly. "Especially now. Without them we would have no police. The docks would soon be deserted, and if we remain locked down and goods stop coming in—"

"Yes, of course. I am grateful."

"What can we do for Janie?" Tori asked.

"Make sure she drinks plenty of water. Bathe her as often as possible. If she begins to convulse, call me."

"Convulse!" Both Tori and Mrs. Marner exclaimed.

"We are seeing that happen," Dr. Rasmussen said shortly. "The fever goes so high the patient convulses and dies."

Mrs. Marner looked horrified. "Does no one get better?"

"Yes. Perhaps one patient in ten has the fever break. Pray for that. Now if you will excuse me, I am needed elsewhere."

He ran down the stairs. Tori followed and caught him at the front door.

"Dr. Rasmussen, do you know how Matty is doing?"

He turned and faced her. As always, his gaze softened when it found her face. "Not well. Best to prepare yourselves."

"Oh, no. Are we going to lose him?"

Dr. Rasmussen gave a hard nod. "It is most likely."

"I can't bear to think of him at the charity hospital alone."

He laid a kindly hand on her good arm. "He does not know where he is, or with whom. It is the only mercy."

She nodded in turn. "Thank you, Doctor. You've been—well, just wonderful."

"Take care, Miss Anderson. And if I do not see you again—"

"Why wouldn't you see me again? Oh!" She gasped, tumbling to it.

He gave a tight smile. "Doctors too fall ill."

He went out then, his shoes slapping over the damp

pavement.

Tori shut the door and turned back to find Kasper hovering in the foyer.

"What is it, Tori?"

"The doctor says Matty is very bad and might not make it. He says—" She couldn't go on.

"Here. Come into the kitchen for a moment. Have you had any breakfast?"

"I couldn't eat, honestly."

"Some tea, then." He drew out a chair from the table and gently pushed her into it.

"How did all this happen, Kasper?" She waved her hand distractedly. "One day we were just going about our lives, complaining about—well, about ordinary things. That the milk delivery was late. That one of the children wet the bed. That there was laundry to do. How did it get so terrible, so quickly?"

"I do not know." He set a cup of tea in front of her.

"And why Buffalo? Are other cities suffering like this?"

He shrugged and took the chair across from her. Tori could hear Becky working in the laundry beyond the kitchen, cranking the wringer.

"No one seems to know from whence the fever came or if it's spread beyond the city."

"Dr. Rasmussen says it's fortunate we have so many automatons, here. They will be able to keep things running even if—if we all fall ill. I did hear a lot of steam units had taken the dangerous jobs on the waterfront now that they're legally entitled to be paid. There were protests over it last month. People—humans, that is— don't like them taking the jobs."

Kasper made a face. "There were continual protests

back home in the larger cities like Krakow and Warsaw. It never got people anywhere."

"Is that where you're from, one of those cities?"

He shook his head. "We lived in the country, back when things were—well, normal. A small town called Tadpole."

"Tadpole?" That made her smile.

"So it is, I believe, in your language. We were happy." His eyes took on a faraway expression as if he strove to remember such a state. "My father, mother, two brothers, and myself. Father, he had a small farm. We had a snug house. Mother painted it up."

"I beg your pardon?"

A smile stretched his lips. "Something that was done in our part of the country. She painted flowers all over the exterior of the house. Exterior, is that the right word? The walls and window frames and all. Flowers, leaves, other decorations."

"That must have been beautiful."

"It was. Then the Russians came. Their government had decided our land—our part of the country—belonged to them. They sent their army to enforce it. We fought—Father and one of my brothers were wounded. I was the youngest, you see, and did not fight, not then.

"We had to leave, took refuge in the city. I watched my father begin to shut down. He could not live there, you see, away from his land. He withered as a plant does when it has no rain."

"Oh, Kasper, I'm so sorry."

"My brothers said we should go back and fight for what was ours. There was a resistance centered in the forest. My brother, Pavel, said anything was better than watching Father die by bits."

Tori set her tea cup down. "Go on."

"We joined the resistance and lived that way for five years. I had just come of age—I was eighteen—and had gained the right to fight. A trap was set. My father and both my brothers were taken. I escaped only because they left me behind to care for Mother, who did not feel well that day.

"My father and Pavel were taken to prison in Russia. We learned that Father died there soon after. My other brother, Janusz, died that very day in the fighting."

"That's terrible," Tori whispered. "I'm so very sorry."

He shrugged awkwardly as if uncomfortable with her sympathy—or pity. "I did not know what to do then. I still had Mama to care for, and she was—shattered, as you may imagine."

"Yes," Tori said simply.

"We returned to the city, where we struggled to survive. It is not easy to survive when your roots have been torn up that way."

"I can imagine."

"Neighbors told us to leave Poland, said there were opportunities in the new world. They said there was a community in Buffalo that spoke as we did. We sold nearly everything we owned for our passage. Now—this. Mother is alone and—and things are still out of control."

Tori covered his hand with hers, where it rested on the table. He turned his fingers in hers and gripped hold, tight.

"It sounds unbearable, Kasper. How do you go on? How—how stay so cheerful and patient?"

"Am I cheerful?" He lifted his brows.

"Yes, most of the time."

"The same way you do, I suppose, despite your arm."

She nodded.

"People do not enjoy being near others who display their misery."

"That's the truth. Some damages don't show on the outside." He looked like a beautiful young man with a caring nature and a ready smile. His scars, though, ran deep.

"Kasper," she said, "we will get through this somehow. We'll come out the other side. My ma says these kinds of things make you stronger. I know that's just a platitude, but—"

His gaze softened on her, much as Dr. Rasmussen's had. Suddenly she recalled brushing her lips across his, the contact soft and enchanting.

He was not for the likes of her. Because her maiming showed on the outside. She might hope to be friends with a man like Kasper Czak. Nothing, nothing more.

Chapter Thirteen

Kasper had Molly partially disassembled on the floor of the laundry, which had more or less become his workroom, when he thought he heard something. He raised his head and listened. Becky had gone upstairs to take Molly's place in the girls' room. The laundry lay quiet.

What was that? While Kasper stretched his ears, the sound came again. Someone knocking at the back door.

By now, evening had arrived. In the waning light, when Kasper hauled the door open, stood three men all wearing hoods. For an instant he thought they were three plague doctors and his heart skipped a beat.

The foremost figure slapped a palm against the door before Kasper could shut it. "Kasprczak? You have to let us in."

"Josef?" Kasper peered beneath the gray hood the speaker wore. Sure enough, his earlier visitor had returned, this time with companions.

He gripped the door harder. "Absolutely not."

"You have to let us in. Quick!"

"*Nie*, Josef. We have sickness in this house."

"I don't care." Josef flipped back his hood and stared at Kasper with crazed blue eyes. A graze seeping blood marked his jaw. "We are in trouble. Need to hide out just for a while."

He spoke in Polish, as did Kasper, unthinking.

"You reek of drink."

"We were at the tavern. Got in a fight."

"Fools!"

"Those there started it, called us dumb polacks. What were we to do, refuse to fight them? Roll over like cowed dogs? Of course we stuck up for ourselves. By Jesus, I hate this place. I never should have left home."

"You cannot stay here."

"We must. Let us hide in your cellar."

Josef pushed past Kasper, shoving him hard, and Kasper saw red. He thought he'd disciplined his anger back in the forest, after witnessing the unbearable. A man could lose his temper, but only when it was likely to do him some good.

Fighting for the sake of it was the height of idiocy. "You cannot stay here, I tell you. This is my place of employment."

"I tell you in turn, we will not stay long. Where is the cellar?"

There were bifold doors in the laundry room which had likely been added on to the original structure at some time in its history. Joseph, seeing them, hauled one open. Kasper cast doubtful looks at the other two men as Josef led them down.

What must one do for a countryman? What should he do?

The steam plant, which was woefully old and rust-infested, occupied the cellar along with a small pile of coal. Damp marked the walls. Not a pleasant place to be.

Good, Kasper thought. *They will not stay here long.*

Josef shrugged his hood back farther on his shoulders, displaying rising bruises. The other two men followed suit. Kasper recognized neither of them.

"These are my cousins. They came to this grand new world ahead of us—and we are all still starving." Obviously intoxicated, Josef began to rant. "All the jobs are taken, most by those damned automatons. They should all be destroyed. Then maybe there would be work for honest men!"

"Shh! Keep your voice down."

Josef ignored the warning. "This is Lech, and Stor."

Stor, who had hair so fair it looked white, leaned toward Kasper and said earnestly, still in Polish, "I think we killed a policeman."

"What?"

"Shut up, Stor. It was just a brawl, Kasprczak, like a thousand others."

Lech spoke in a deep voice. "The policemen came pushing in, trying to break it up. The one officer, he fell and hit his head."

"Fell?"

"Was punched." Josef said it jerkily. "We are not sure he is dead."

"You cannot be here! This is an orphanage. There's a child with the fever—"

"Just let us shelter here tonight while the police are looking. In the morning we'll be gone."

"Can you get us any water, bandages?" Lech asked. "I've been stabbed." He displayed his arm, which bore a ragged wound.

Kasper swore bitterly. "No bandages."

"Water, then," Josef insisted. "You cannot tell me there's no water. And bring us food."

"Absolutely not. It is for the children."

Josef leered at him. "Are we not all children in the eyes of God?"

"I do not care." Stor went and curled up in the corner. "I want only to sleep."

"Go upstairs," Josef advised Kasper. "Pretend we are not here. But bring food and water if you can."

****

"Two more children have taken sick." Tory told Kasper later that night. "Little Deborah Bligh and Richie Collins, one each in the boys' and girls' rooms."

"That is terrible." They'd met at the foot of the back stairs when she brought down some trays. It had been decided the children should take their meals in their separate dormitories rather than congregating in the dining hall.

It hadn't helped, though. Kasper had been upstairs a number of times. The children were restless—or ill. He'd finished putting Molly back together fully greased, listening all the while for sounds from the cellar, had restarted the automaton and sent her back up where she was needed.

"Tom has moved them into the storeroom with Janie. Oh, Kasper—she's worse. Much worse."

"Do you want me to go for the doctor?"

"Not yet. Mrs. Marner wants to wait till morning." Tori's eyes filled with tears. "I only hope Janie holds on till then."

Kasper touched her softly on the shoulder. "Have you had any rest?"

She shook her head.

"You and Daisy should at least take turns up in the attic." They'd all snatched rooms there, up under the eaves. Kasper had barely seen his bed.

"I will. The children are all frightened and won't settle. I don't know if they'll sleep much tonight."

"Let Molly or Becky stay with them."

"Yes. Thank goodness for the automatons."

Kasper thought of Josef and his rant against steam units. "Not everyone would agree with you."

"I know. The city's terribly divided over it. There was even a riot last summer. There are those who want them all destroyed, but honestly, Kasper, what would we do without them now?"

****

Daisy woke Tori from a light doze early the next morning. "I hate to disturb ye, lass, but Mrs. Marner says we must send Tom for Dr. Rasmussen. Janie's worse, much worse."

Tori sat up in her cot, dizzy at the sudden alarm, and put her hand to her head. How could the child be worse than yesterday?

"Mrs. Marner is hoping to catch Dr. Rasmussen before he's out and about. Will you tell Tom? Little Marion was just sick in the girls' room. I'll help Becky clean it up."

Tori got to her feet and, not bothering to dress or bundle her hair, donned a shawl over the underdress in which she'd gone to bed, and went. Where would Tom be at this hour, if not on the children's floor? The unit never slept.

After a frantic search she located him at the cellar door, exchanging words with Kasper.

"But sir, I must go into the cellar. I need to stoke the steam plant, plus I must restock the supply of coal on the back porch, for the rest of us."

"I will do that. I'm sure you're needed upstairs." Kasper caught sight of Tori and froze, his lips parted. "Good morning."

"What's going on?"

"Nothing. I'm just telling Tom I will take care of the boiler and bring up coal for the units. It is something I can do to help." Kasper's gaze slid down Tori's body, lingering on her tumbled hair, and a flush colored his cheek.

Tori turned to Tom. "Please go fetch Dr. Rasmussen as quickly as possible. You know where to find his office, don't you?"

"Yes, miss."

"Go now and try to catch him before he leaves on his rounds. Tell him it's very important and that Janie is much worse."

"Yes, miss."

"Do you have enough coal for the trip?"

"Yes, miss."

Tom left, puffing wisps of steam.

"Are we going to lose that poor little girl?" Kasper whispered.

"I don't know. She wanted so much to be adopted. Used to chatter to me about it." Tori blinked away tears. She wished Kasper would hold out his arms to her as he had the other day, inviting her to shelter, but he didn't. He merely stood there looking anxious to go into the cellar.

"I'll leave you to it, then," she said and took herself off back to the kitchen. She felt Kasper's gaze follow her, though he didn't say a word.

Chapter Fourteen

Dr. Rasmussen did not come, not until much later.
Instead he sent a message for Mrs. Marner, via Tom.

Though possibly their best mechanical specimen,
Tom wasn't particularly vocal—not like Molly, who
asked a lot of questions. Tom's conversational style
might be described as brief, concise, and disappointing.

Mrs. Marner and Tori were changing linens in the
girls' room, having sent the children out into the back
yard for some air, when Tom returned and dragged
himself up the stairs.

"Where is Dr. Rasmussen?" Mrs. Marner asked him.

"Not here."

"I can see he is not here." The normally unflappable
Mrs. Marner appeared to be riding her last nerve. "Why
not? Didn't you bring him?"

"No, ma'am."

"He wasn't there?"

"He was, ma'am, but you did not ask me to bring
him." Sadly Tom added, "I failed to understand. Was I
meant to take him by force?"

Mrs. Marner drew an audible breath. "No, Tom. Let
us start over. Did you speak with Dr. Rasmussen?"

"Yes, ma'am."

"Why is he not here with you?"

"He had other more urgent calls to answer."

Mrs. Marner's gaze met Tori's. More urgent than a

dying child?

"Is he not coming, then?" Tori asked the unit.

"Later, miss, when he can. He said the hospitals are full."

Mrs. Marner looked frantic.

"He also said to tell you"—Tom's artificial intelligence clicked as he retrieved the information—"further automatons are coming."

"What's that supposed to mean?" Mrs. Marner asked Tori rather than Tom. Tori shook her head.

"Very well, Tom. Go take up other duties."

"I need coal."

"Go fill your hopper, then."

The unit trundled off, and Mrs. Marner said, "The world has gone mad."

"Yes, Mrs. Marner." And Tori suspected they would all go mad with it.

By two o'clock that afternoon, when Dr. Rasmussen arrived, Janie's condition had further deteriorated. Daisy had elbowed Molly aside and taken her place in the sickroom with a terse, "No child should die alone."

Kasper had brought a load of coal up to the rear porch—for the convenience of the steamies, he said, though he looked as upset as Tori felt when they encountered one another briefly in the kitchen.

"How is Janie?" he whispered.

"Not good."

"Any more gone sick?"

"Not yet."

"Well that's fortunate, anyway."

When Dr. Rasmussen showed up, he looked exhausted. Tori let him in, and Mrs. Marner came running down the stairs to meet him.

"Oh, Dr. Rasmussen! Janie's fever is off the charts, and she is having difficulty breathing."

Dr. Rasmussen merely nodded and followed Mrs. Marner upstairs. Tori trailed them, full of dread.

"You should not be in here," Dr. Rasmussen told Daisy when he stepped into the storeroom cum sickroom where all three ailing children now lay. There was not much space. Even Molly, assigned there, had trundled out and waved her rubberized fingers in distress.

Daisy stepped up to the doctor. "If ye think I'm after leaving a child who's clearly waitin' for the angels to come and take her, ye don't know me very well."

Dr. Rasmussen blinked at her. They made an almost comical pair, or would have, had the situation been less dire, Daisy who barely topped five feet toeing up to the six-foot-something doctor.

"You are risking yourself and all the others here."

"Bugger that! The wee lass needs me."

Dr. Rasmussen did not argue it further, but went on into the room.

Through the open doorway, Tori watched while he checked Janie over and then the other two children in turn.

He came out and eyed the waiting women and automaton.

"I do not need to tell you, her condition deteriorates."

"She's dyin'?" Daisy whispered.

He gave a hard nod.

"Oh, Jaysus!" Fervently, Daisy crossed herself. "Is there nothin' we can do?"

"Keep bathing her. Try to get her to swallow some water."

"She'll take nothin'."

"The throat swells shut—at the end."

"Dr. Rasmussen," Mrs. Marner asked, "where did this awful disease come from? How did it start?"

"We still do not know. No one has seen anything quite like it before. If I did not know better, I would say it originated right here in Buffalo."

"Could it have landed from some foreign country, say, through the docks?" Tori asked.

"Anything is possible. But it is sweeping the city with ferocious speed and spreading beyond, despite the mayor having forbidden any travel." Dr. Rasmussen grimaced. "Wiser minds than mine are busy pondering it."

"Other doctors?" Mrs. Marner asked.

"Yes, undoubtedly, but I was referring to the hybrids. Thank God for them. When they put their collective minds to a problem, they can accomplish astonishing things."

Obviously, the good doctor was an automaton supporter.

He snapped his fingers. "That reminds me. You got my message about additional automatons via your man, earlier?"

"Yes but I have to say, I did not understand it."

"Mr. Carter is sending reinforcements to help you out—four refurbished units. It should allow you to take your duties in shifts and get some rest." His gaze touched Tori. "So you do not grow ill."

"Oh, I see." Mrs. Marner looked shocked.

"I informed Mr. Carter how desperately you need help. He has a crew down at Pike's Automaton Repair, which he patronizes, fitting up units as quickly as they can. I understand other shops are gearing up also."

"More automatons?" Mrs. Marner glanced at Molly and lowered her voice. "That will not be a popular development in some quarters."

"In a situation like this, Mrs. Marner, the automatons may well be the ones to save us."

****

"You must leave." Kasper eyed the men who lounged in the dim recess of the cellar and rage licked up through him. Not a violent man by nature, he'd learned there were times when his anger was justified. He'd felt that glorious rush of rage back in the forest when Janusz was killed, and when his father and Pavel were taken. And later, in Krakow, when he fought to care for Mama alone.

Mama. He spared a thought for her. She must be frantic, and he could only hope the church was keeping its promise and looking out for her.

He glared at Josef, who half sat, half leaned in the shadow of the chugging steam plant. "You said you would leave this morning, first thing. That was hours ago."

"Yes, but it is dangerous out there. Those damned hybrid policemen run the city, 'keeping order' as they say."

"There is going to be a riot," Lech put in.

Stor added, "We do not want to be in the middle of that."

"I do not care what you want. You will keep your word and leave." Kasper balled his hands into fists.

Josef eyed him. "You planning to make me, are you?"

"If I must."

Almost lazily, Josef got to his feet. Kasper had seen enough aboard ship to know the man was a brutal fighter. At the moment, he didn't feel prepared to let that daunt him. His anger made him feel as if he could drag all three of them up the stairs and toss them out by force.

He growled, "What kind of man does not keep his word?"

"In an ideal world, I would agree with you. It is good to keep one's word. But we talk of survival here. And men like us, we know what it takes to survive, eh?"

Kasper did. He hoped it needn't include the surrender of honor.

"Get out or I will summon those hybrid policemen."

"Oh, you would not want to do that. Not if you wish to keep safe all the children and the ladies here."

Tori. Her name flashed through Kasper's mind before he threw the first punch. His fist took Josef right in the middle of his face and rocked him back on his heels. Both Josef's companions exclaimed and leaped to their feet.

Kasper bared his teeth. Josef had not expected him to be so quick. Kasper could see that by the shock in Josef's blue eyes. But that shock swiftly evaporated, burned away in a nasty flare of rage.

Before Josef could recover, Kasper hit him again. This time with a roar, Josef struck back, throwing a mean upper cut that just grazed Kasper's jaw as he ducked aside.

He had time only to be grateful the ancient steam plant chugged so loudly. Maybe nobody upstairs would hear what was going on. And thank heaven Lech and Stor stood back. If the three of them rushed him at once, he was done.

After that, all coherent thought disappeared in a blaze of white, protective anger. When he eventually came to himself, Josef lay sprawled on the floor at his feet and the two others stared at him.

Kasper himself dripped blood, and his hands hurt.

"Get him out of here," he told Stor and Lech. "Don't let anybody see you, and don't come back."

Stor looked from Josef to Kasper and back again. "I fear you have made an enemy there, Kasprczak. And he is not a good man to have for an enemy."

"You're probably right." But what was done was done. He couldn't let anyone threaten to harm Tori.

Lech ran a hand across his chin. "The thing is, Josef likes to be the cock of the walk. You have, as they say, wiped the floor with him. He will want revenge."

"*Tak*," Stor agreed. "Does he know where your mother lives? You had better hope not."

Kasper's stomach turned over in a sickening roll. No, Josef might not know the location of the room where Mama was living. But in their tiny Polish community, he could soon find out.

Chapter Fifteen

A soft gasp turned Kasper from the back door where he'd just seen his unwelcome visitors on their way.

"Oh! What's happened to you?"

He turned from the sight of Stor and Lech limping away through the back yard, supporting Josef between them. Josef had regained his senses but not enough to make a fuss.

Not yet.

Kasper feared for the future.

Tori stood behind him, holding a basin. Thank goodness it was her and not Mrs. Marner.

Her green gaze embraced him, touched all the same places as Josef's fists, and abruptly narrowed.

He might lie to her. He might try and weave some tale about an accident, but he found he didn't want to.

She waited patiently, clutching the basin in the circle of her good arm, the other folded against her chest. The idea of anyone threatening to hurt her—especially because of him—convulsed his heart and made him angry all over again.

Breaking eye contact with her, he looked down at himself ruefully. Blood marked his shirt, and he could feel the bruises rising. "I have been in a fight."

"You have? Goodness! I did not think you the sort of man to brawl."

"That is the thing. I am not." Until pushed.

She glanced at the door. "Whom did you fight?"

"An acquaintance from the boat on which Mother and I booked passage. He came here asking for help I cannot give."

"I see." Clearly, she didn't.

"The man is a bully. He wanted to hurt you. I've seen enough people I care for hurt. I can't allow that."

"He wanted to hurt *me*?"

"Everyone here in this house."

She wrinkled her nose. "I detest bullies."

"So do I." A fundamental truth, bred deep inside him.

"We'd better get you cleaned up before Mrs. Marner sees this."

"Would she dismiss me?"

"I'm not sure, given the circumstances. Every hand is needed. But she won't be best pleased."

She led him into the kitchen where she scrubbed out the basin most carefully and refilled it from the kettle on the stove. "Sit down."

He obeyed. A few painful moments ensued while she bathed his scrapes and cuts. He found he truly didn't mind. Tori was touching him. Her soft, misty green eyes rested on him and him alone. That filled him with a whole new set of emotions.

"Why did those men come here?" she asked softly.

"Hiding from the police."

"Oh? They are bad ones, then."

"The thing is—" How much should he tell her? "Their leader, his name is Josef, didn't like me turning them out, and I fear he's capable of retaliating against my mother."

"That's awful." Tori paled. "Not much of a man, is

he, if he'd do something like that."

"That is what I thought. With me stuck here and unable to reach her with a warning—"

"You should report him to the police. That nice Officer Kelly, for instance. Ask him to look out for your ma, if he can."

"Yes. He seems kind, for—"

"An automaton?" Tori bathed his cheek gently. "I've worked with steamies ever since I came here and find they are kind, on the whole. And they have a very finely tuned sense of right and wrong. Of justice."

"People hate them."

"Some do, yes. It's sharply divided. There are those who'd like to see them all turned into scrap and their jobs given to ordinary folk." Tori made a face. "Not that most people would be willing to perform the kind of jobs steamies do."

"This is true."

"Right." She smoothed the hair back from his brow. "That's you patched up. But what will we tell Mrs. Marner? I do not like to lie."

"Nor do I."

She tipped her head to one side, considering. "At any point when that bugger hit you, did you fall down?"

"I may have stumbled, *tak*."

"Then it wouldn't be a lie to say you had a fall, would it? Everything else is just between us."

"Tori, thank you. I do not mean to bring you into my trouble—"

"Goodness!" She flushed pink, suddenly seeming to realize just how close she stood to him.

Should he tell her how she made him feel? How often he thought about her? How every time he looked at her, a warm hum started up inside him like a steam plant warming up, producing heat?

She'd be shocked. They'd known each other only a few days. Yet these were extraordinary circumstances. And he'd learned the hard way that if a man did not express his feelings he might never get a second chance.

Accordingly, he seized her hand—the withered one since the other still clutched a bloodied cloth—in both of his.

She stiffened and a new look flooded her eyes. "What—"

"Tori, I think you are very special. Like no woman I have ever known."

She paled before flushing an even darker pink. "I should think so. How many women have you known who are deformed?"

"Deformed?"

She flexed her hand, in his. It felt like a bird fluttering. "You shouldn't touch me. You should be far too disgusted to—"

"I am not disgusted." He lifted her hand to his lips. Shock at his action poured through her and into him, via their clasped fingers, but he ignored it. If he could feel what she felt, surely she could feel what he felt too.

Tenderly he drew her nearer, between his knees, and nearer still. Carefully gentle, he pressed his lips to hers, her fingers still caught against his chest.

For an instant only she resisted, before tumbling headlong into the kiss. He experienced her capitulation right along with her, that breathless moment when she began to participate. Lips fused to lips and parted. Tongue met tongue and spirit leaped to spirit. A question that had hung in the back of Kasper's mind for far too long was answered.

There was a place for him, a place to belong in this new world. Only, it was a *person*.

The high impropriety of kissing a fellow employee in the orphanage kitchen—during a plague—never touched him. But it did find Tori and caused her to end the kiss far too soon for his liking.

"What are we doing? We can't—" Her green eyes stared into his, wild and distracted.

"I think I care for you very much, Tori Anderson."

The kiss had seared his senses and apparently loosened his tongue. He had to search for the English. So much easier this would be, in his native language. But she didn't speak his own language and where she was, he wanted to be.

"What are you saying?" she gasped. "That can't be. My hand—"

"You suppose that matters?"

"Yes." She nodded, utterly certain. "It always matters."

He still clutched the hand in question, flat against his chest. "*Nie*, my dear. *Nie*."

"You," she had to pause for breath, "you are such a handsome man—"

"And you. Beautiful. Inside and out."

"No." She tore from his grasp and backed away a couple of steps. "Look at me. Look!"

He looked. In fact, he took great delight in it.

She stood but a few inches above five feet, slender everywhere except in what Kasper considered the right places. Her hair—not tended since early that morning—had come loose from its moorings and straggled down her slender neck, tresses escaping every which way. Her green eyes blazed in a face pale with strain, defiant. She was delicate and beautiful and strong in a way that made his heart clench in his chest.

"You are wonderful. I have a thousand better words in Polish."

She held her withered arm out in front of her like a lurid injury. Like a shield. Doubt and temptation flickered in her eyes. "Can't you see this?" The maimed hand quivered.

"I see it." Again, he took the hand in his, planted a kiss in the palm. "Tori, I see you."

A clatter from the hallway interrupted them. Becky came in, followed by Daisy, who carried a pile of laundry. Daisy's quick eyes took in the scene and narrowed.

"What's this, then?"

Tori leaped farther away from Kasper and gestured to the basin. "Kasper had an accident. A fall. I was just—assisting him."

Daisy tossed her head. "Is that what ye were doin'? And he was after thanking you, I suppose, by kissing your hand."

"Yes, actually." Kasper got to his feet.

"An accident, was it?" Daisy eyed him closely. "The back steps come up and punch you in the face?"

"Yes, that is what happened."

"My, my. As if the state of the city isn't bad enough—"

Becky spoke unexpectedly in her tinny whine. "I like Master Kasper. He brought me back to life."

Daisy grinned. "Looks like he's brought Miss Tori to life too. Maybe that's what he does, eh?"

Tori flushed scarlet. "This wasn't how it must have

looked."

"It looked like the two of you might have shared a tender moment. Maybe even a kiss. If so, I hope it's all innocent enough and you know what you're after doing." She took a breath and continued, "And some good news. Janie seems better. Her breathing's easier. I've come to prepare a hot poultice for her chest."

"Oh, that is good to hear! How are the others?"

"No worse. I think we may be able to best this horrid thing."

"Well…" Tori stole a look at Kasper. "Will miracles never cease?"

He smiled at her. Not if he could help it.

Chapter Sixteen

A loud knocking on the door brought both Tori and Daisy on the run, from opposite ends of the house.

"Coming! Hold your horses," Daisy grumbled as she swung the panel open. "Don't ye know—"

She fell silent, confronted by what stood on the steps. A crowd of automatons. Four of them, to be exact.

The foremost, a rounded specimen with a bulging thorax, still had its hand raised to knock again. Another, taller unit with a head like a train whistle stood just behind it. And down a few steps stood two others, both considerably smaller.

"We were sent by Mr. Mitch Carter," the foremost declared stoutly.

"Were ye, now? Yes, Mrs. Marner did say. You're the extra help, are ye?"

A rattle answered her as they all nodded.

"Well, I suppose ye'd better come in."

Once in the foyer, it became evident that none of the units was new. Well-polished and probably refurbished, they were as varied from one another as they could possibly be.

"I am Henry," said the tubby unit. "This is Omar"— the tall unit. "Nellie and Trina." The two units with female names were the smallest, Trina standing only as high as Henry's shoulder.

Omar leaned forward to ask, "What sort of

household is this? Are steam units given fair treatment?"

"Well," Daisy looked taken aback, "we do our best. There's water. And coal. Considering the present crisis—"

"Ignore him," Henry advised. "He is an activist for automaton rights."

"As we all should be," Omar inserted.

"Yes, quite." Daisy shot an incredulous look at Tori. "I'll just run and tell Mrs. Marner you've arrived, shall I?"

She dashed off, leaving Tori surrounded by the new arrivals.

Trina pushed forward and looked at Tori through blue glass eyes. "Your name?" she inquired in a squeak.

"Oh, I am Tori. And she is Daisy."

"Miss Tori, are you defective?"

"I beg your pardon?"

"Your arm looks incorrect. You should see the Steam Tinker who rebuilt us. You might be able to get a new mechanical one."

****

"They appear to have personalities," Tori reported to Kasper later when they met in the kitchen. "I've never seen the like. Well, all steamies do develop personalities over time, but these arrived fully loaded, so to speak."

Kasper grunted. "I never had much to do with automatons back home. They were toys of the elite." There, he reflected, he and his countrymen had possessed the status of the automatons here, little respected and ill-used. At least here the steamies, as Tori called them, had gained some rights.

"The tall one, Omar—he's quite militant and almost aggressive about his rights. Henry's even-tempered, if a

105

bit heavy-handed about things. Trina—well, she's frank. She asked me right after we met if I wouldn't rather have a mechanical arm than this." She crooked her withered limb.

"I do not suppose they have much sense of propriety."

"Mind you," Tori scrutinized her own arm, "if I could have one of those hybrid limbs that nobody could tell from natural, I might consider it. Not that I have a hope of ever being able to afford such a luxury."

"I find you quite perfect the way you are."

Tori flushed and drew away from him. "You have to stop saying such things."

"Why?"

"I'm not perfect and never have been. Do you know what it's like growing up different in this city? Having other children point at you and laugh? Being called a freak. Never being able to accomplish even simple tasks gracefully, or well."

Kasper reached out and cradled her face between his hands. Should he tell her just how much he thought of her? How she haunted his awareness day and night, so he kept track of just where she was in the house. Should he mention that the delicacy of her neck holding up that cloud of brown hair, and her green eyes that revealed all her emotions, meant far more to him than any misshapen limb?

He thought he was falling in love with her. But he'd better not tell her that either. The half-panicked look in her eyes argued she might run, and that was the last thing he wanted.

Instead, very gently, he said, "Who can say what is perfect to someone else? You are perfect to me."

"You're sweet to say that, Kasper, but—"

Before she got any farther he leaned forward and kissed her. He did it with infinite care, as one would approach a skittish bird, but what started out as comforting assurance quickly heated to something far more. How soft her lips were and how sweet. How trusting she was when, after only an instant, her resistance melted. She eased in against him and curled her good arm up around his neck.

He couldn't declare his feelings then either, because the kiss stole all his words. But maybe she could feel what he couldn't say. With that hope in mind, he kissed her more deeply, putting all his intention into it. She quivered in his arms, and he wondered if her heart pounded the way his did, deafeningly.

When at last he drew his lips from hers, she lay limp against him. Her eyes met his questioningly, wonderingly, before she whispered, "Kasper? Oh, Kasper."

He buried his face in her hair. Soft, soft and warm. It smelled like heaven. Mad thoughts careened through his head, few of which he could express in English—fortunately, for he doubted she'd want to hear how much he longed to have her in his bed.

Stumbling with the words, he said, "When I kiss you, Tori—when I kiss you I forget my English."

That made her giggle.

"I forget everything."

She gazed into his eyes from between deep brown lashes. "I like kissing you too," she confessed shyly.

"How is it you do not know you are beautiful? Has no one ever told you? Are all the men in this city fools?"

"My arm—"

"I am not speaking of that. Your eyes and your hair—both are beautiful. And the shape of your face." He shouldn't mention the shape of her body, generous where it should be and delicate everywhere else. He wanted to see her with all that heavy brown hair hanging down around her naked shoulders. But a man did not say that to a decent woman. Not to any woman, if he were a real man.

So he kissed her again, until a rattle in the hallway heralded the arrival of Becky, carrying a pail and bucket. He and Tori sprang apart just in time, as Mrs. Marner followed the rumbling unit.

The director looked both exhausted and distracted, fortunately for Kasper and Tori, neither of whom had time to recover their composure.

"Ah, there you are," Mrs. Marner said. "I've just sent Daisy up to bed. Why don't the two of you go also?"

Tori shot Kasper a wild look. "Mrs. Marner?"

"With the new units on duty, I figure we can take shifts again and perhaps catch a decent night's sleep."

"Ah." Tori nodded. "I see."

"I'll sit outside the sickroom this evening, with Molly assigned inside. The new units can keep watch over the rest of the children and call one of us if there's a problem."

"Yes, thank you, Mrs. Marner. How is Janie?"

"Better. Her breathing continues to improve."

"That's wonderful."

"Yes, it is. A great relief, but we must remain vigilant."

"Mrs. Marner," Kasper ventured, "since we have extra help, would it be possible for me to go home tomorrow to check my mother's welfare? She will be very worried and frightened."

"Oh, yes," Tori chimed in. "I would very much like to check on my mother also."

Mrs. Marner looked torn. "I will not say but you both deserve the time off. But we have been told to shelter in place."

"I will be very quick," Kasper promised, not without desperation. Even since the possibility of Josef seeking revenge had raised its ugly head, he'd longed to lay eyes on his mother.

"Yes, well," Mrs. Marner decided, "the two of you may go together, tomorrow morning. For just a half hour, mind. Stop nowhere on the way, talk to no one, and stay together. Oh, and Kasper—no more tripping on the stairs. You're a mess. Your poor mother will think you've been in a brawl."

****

It felt as if they'd been confined to Lost Waifs for a month rather than just a few days. When they stepped out the next morning, the world looked brighter, the sky a prettier shade of blue, and Tori's heart rose buoyantly.

Away from the orphanage, bound to see her mother and in Kasper's company, what could spoil her mood?

Well, she supposed it would be better were they not hurrying through streets half empty of people and, apparently, populated mostly by automatons. Of course, Tori reminded herself, it was safe for automatons to be out. They couldn't get sick. But it looked and felt very much as if they'd taken over the city.

Indeed, someone who opposed automaton rights on general principle might say the steam units had been awaiting just such an opportunity as this.

On the corner of Grant and Elmwood, enroute to

Kasper's lodgings, they came upon a scene that had their steps dragging to a halt. A man stood on a wooden platform with a crowd of men and women—the most they'd seen so far—gathered closely around him. And the man on the platform held forth, spewing words like venom.

"Ask yourself!" he raged as Kasper and Tori walked up. "From whence did this dread sickness come? And who stands to benefit from it?"

The members of the crowd, many of whom also seemed quite angry, stirred and muttered.

"A sickness like this doesn't just arise out of nowhere! I say to you, my friends, it was created! Manufactured just like those damned hybrid children the automatons are making. It was unleashed on us! Think about it. The automatons populating our city are clever enough to find a way of eliminating us—or they think they are!"

"Why would they do that?" a man shouted back. "We're givin' 'em their rights, aren't we? We're even being forced by the new laws to pay the damned things."

"So we are!" the man on the platform hollered back. "And how have they repaid us? By buying up houses and most of our downtown properties. By building churches, by getting married—an unholy practice. They won't be satisfied till they get rid of us. And what better way than to create an illness that will kill us all off and leave them untouched?"

The crowd howled in response, sounding like yelping hyenas. Tori reached out and seized Kasper's arm with her good hand.

"That's not true," she whispered. She thought of Becky's long, patient days in the laundry and Hank's endless mopping despite his creaking joints. The faithful years of service in return for no more than water, coal, and a lick of grease on occasion.

"And don't suppose they could not do this dire and terrible thing—this act of murder," the speaker thundered on. "Of murder done over and over again. They are hell-born, these hybrids that now lead our steam units into iniquity. Created by those monsters, Mason and Charles. Any creations with the know-how to build more like themselves can certainly dredge up the spores of a dread disease and unleash it on our city."

"No!" Tori shouted before she had time to think better of it. "That's not true."

"Sympathizers!" the man on the platform roared. "The only thing worse than an accursed automaton is a human who takes up with them!" He pointed a bony finger at Tori and Kasper.

The crowd turned as one. Tori found herself staring into the face of violence multiplied over and over again.

Kasper said something in Polish and added quickly, "Run!"

Chapter Seventeen

They ran faster than Tori ever believed she could. The sounds of roaring voices—those of people clearly out for blood—and thundering footsteps from behind lent her feet wings. When the breath started coming hard in her lungs, Kasper towed her onward, his fingers laced through hers.

Still, the howling mob pursued them up Grant Street and around a corner, down yet another street at full tilt and between two houses where a woman came out her side door and threw a pan at them.

We're going to die. Tori would have said it out loud, but she didn't have the breath. *If they catch us, they'll beat us to death the way a housewife smashes a spider.*

They broke out into the open in yet another street, and Kasper swung left. Heavens, but the man could run. He half carried Tori now, having surrendered her hand and tucked his arm around her waist.

She couldn't stumble, despite her turned foot. She couldn't because if one of them fell—

At that moment the toes of her in-turned foot caught on a curb as Kasper vaulted over it. A whistle blew somewhere close at hand and a river of blue flowed past them, parting like water around a rock, skirting the place Tori had gone down, with Kasper beside her.

"Thank God," Kasper gasped. "Thank God."

"Are ye all right, miss?" A police officer bent over

them, his handsome face one of the most welcome things Tori had ever seen.

"I think I cut my knee. When I tripped."

The police officer straightened. "Let's get you out of here, shall we?" He gave a sharp whistle and waved an arm, and a paddy wagon trundled around the corner.

"I hope ye don't mind ridin' in the wagon, miss. Do ye need to be conveyed to the hospital?"

"Not there, Terry," called the officer driving the wagon. "The hospitals are full."

"Ah, to be sure," the handsome copper agreed. "We'll take ye back to the station where I'm sure we can get ye patched up."

Kasper helped Tori to her feet. They stared after the wall of blue-coated policemen who had intercepted the rioters and set about making arrests.

"What is going on?" Tori asked the police officer.

He looked at her with clear blue eyes. "Fear, miss, and misinformation. There's a lot of it going around. They think our kind is out to hurt them. In truth, we're only here to help."

His kind?

Tori waited till she and Kasper were alone in the back of the wagon to say it aloud. "His kind? Was he a—"

"Hybrid, I think." Kasper gathered her into his arms and held her on his knee. "It's safer for them to be out on the streets now than for human police officers. Are you sure you're all right?"

Tori could feel blood trickling down her knee, and she'd gone limp with relief. All that was lost, however, in the thrill of being in Kasper's arms.

To her own surprise she said, "I would be, if you

kissed me."

Riding in the back of a paddy wagon while maintaining lip contact proved an interesting exercise. The only light came through the bars fitted in the rear door, and the horse trotted briskly, taking the corners at a clip that tossed them around on their bench.

It didn't matter. Nothing did, except the taste of Kasper on her tongue and the way he cradled her. Not even her withered arm, caught between them, could spoil the experience.

"Tori," he murmured, trailing his lips across her cheek to her ear. "I think I—"

The wagon came to an abrupt halt, and the back door was thrown open. Yet another Irish officer stood there.

"Let's get you inside where it's safe, miss, *sor*. These streets are treacherous today."

Kasper stood up with Tori in his arms. "I'll carry you in."

"Goodness no, Kasper. I'm fine to walk."

"You are not."

To her half-embarrassment, half-delight, he carried her out of the wagon and onto the street in front of the police station.

The Irish police officer nodded with what appeared to be approval. "This way, *sor*."

"Is it safe to go in there?" Tori whispered to Kasper.

"I think so. It looks like they're mostly automatons."

The interior of the police station bustled with orderly activity. Many hybrids—Tori was beginning to learn the look of them now: composed expressions and cheerful demeanors—rubbed elbows with a number of regular steam units. A door emblazoned with the name *Captain Brendan Fagan* stood open to reveal an inner office to one side, but the office lay empty.

"We keep a first-aid kit for just such situations as this," Officer Terry told them. "Come right this way."

"Put me down, Kasper. Really—"

"Not till they've seen to your knee."

Terry led the way to a corner and a large wooden chair where Kasper carefully deposited Tori.

"No real privacy, I'm afraid," Officer Terry said cheerfully. "Allow me to fetch the first-aid kit."

Tori's head began to spin. The room smelled of heated metal, coal, and steam, and for an instant she feared she would be sick.

"Are we the only humans here?" she whispered to Kasper.

"No matter, so long as you're safe." He dropped to his knee in front of her, and his gaze met hers, eyes burning blue with intense emotion. He parted his lips to speak to her…something significant?

But he said only, "Let's take a look."

It should have been embarrassing, having her skirts lifted in full view of so many—males, she supposed they should be called. It proved titillating instead because Kasper was the one who had hold of her hem and lifted it slowly—slowly—baring her shins, then her knees. He kept his gaze on hers, failing to check the injury after all, and folded the thick material of her skirt across her thighs.

It felt—well, it felt like the two of them were alone.

"Kasper!" It came in a gasp.

She wanted to kiss him. Yes, she did. And she saw by the look in his eyes he wanted it too, right there in front of two dozen hybrid policemen and automatons.

"There," he said, and dropped his gaze at last to her

injury. Before her disappointment could bloom for the lack of a kiss, he gave her one—though not on the lips. Instead he dropped a kiss onto her knee, just above where the skin was torn.

Tori felt the impact of that kiss in locations she'd never expected to. Despite place and time, heat rushed through her, bringing shocking thoughts in its wake.

"You have beautiful legs," he said.

One, perhaps. It seemed the Almighty or whatever other deity held sway up in the sky had seen fit to give her that, even if the other leg remained turned in at the ankle. When his gaze skimmed over her limbs, did he neglect to remember that?

"You are beautiful altogether," she returned madly. It had been a mad morning. She wanted a mad night to follow. What if he kept kissing his way up her leg? Could she endure the ensuing heat?

She'd just decided to ask him when Officer Terry popped up beside them once more, a white metal case marked with a red cross in his hand.

"Here we go. That does look nasty." He gave Tori a comprehensive glance. "I do believe you could use a few stitches."

"I don't want to go to the hospital."

"Just so. Allow me to take care of it. I have a little experience in tending such injuries. My wife is a doctor, you see."

"Wife?" Tori and Kasper both stared at him.

"Oh, yes. Perhaps you have heard of her—Mrs. Chastity Greely. She is quite famous."

"Oh, yes," Tori responded faintly. She had indeed heard that name. The hybrid automaton had once been a prostitute at a brothel called the Crystal Palace, and since then had risen to heights in the field of hybrid construction. She'd been instrumental in the creation last year of the first hybrid child, a little girl named Kiera. She'd also caused an uproar of ill feeling in the city. Those who believed automatons were just machines declared they should no more have the right to reproduce than wringer washers or steamcabs might.

But automatons, who now married, built churches and owned property, wanted children also.

"Too bad she is not here," Terry went on with obvious pride. "She would mend your injury a treat."

Pride. In an automaton, hybrid or otherwise. It seemed miraculous.

"That's fine," Tori told him. "You're doing a wonderful job."

In fact he'd distracted her with his chatter so she barely noticed he'd closed her wound and secured it with neat rows of tape. How could mechanical hands be so gentle?

"Now…" Officer Greely got to his feet and wiped his hands on a cloth. "We'll get your statements taken and escort you home."

Kasper also stood. "I cannot go home until I've seen my mother. I'm dreadfully worried about her, you see. She speaks no English and will be worried, with me staying at my place of work."

"I see. We may be able to help you with that." Officer Greely turned and surveyed the room. Kasper followed suit.

"Is that Officer Kelly?" he asked, and Tori spied the tall figure halfway across the busy room.

"Yes it is. That's right, you know Pat." Office Greely made an odd sound Tori decided was his version of laughter. "Most everyone knows Pat. I will see if he has time to take your statement."

"He's very kind," Tori said after Officer Greely hurried off. "For a—"

"Machine?" Kasper finished for her.

"He doesn't seem like a machine, does he? And if I had to choose between this crowd and the one we ran into back there, I know which I'd choose."

And, Tori wondered, did that in fact make them sympathizers?

Chapter Eighteen

Pat Kelly escorted them to the house where Kasper's mother was lodging. He wanted to make sure Kasper introduced him to Mrs. Czak, so she would know him the next time he stopped in to check on her.

"I could not possibly take you from your work to do that," Kasper protested.

"You are not taking me from anything, sir. I am offering."

"With the city in its present state—"

"Just why we need to check on our most vulnerable citizens. I can always make time for a welfare check."

Tori asked, "Would you be able to check in on my mother too? She's also alone, and I'm terribly worried about her. Should she fall ill—"

"Certainly, Miss Anderson. In fact, might I venture to suggest we introduce these two ladies to one another? Since the two of you are courting, I mean."

Tori flushed bright red. "We aren't." Her wide green eyes found Kasper's. "Are we?"

Before he could answer, Pat Kelly said, "Forgive me. From your manner with each other, I assumed you were in fact a couple. I am usually quite adept at discerning people's demeanors. Evidently I still have a lot to learn."

"No." Kasper's heart began pounding. "That is, we haven't spoken of it, but I would...would very much like

119

to be courting Miss Anderson."

"You would?" She paled, then flushed still more rosily. And what did that reaction mean? Kasper berated himself for not keeping his mouth shut. What had she thought those kisses meant, though?

Hastily, he added, "With everything that's going on—"

She said nothing.

"It is a mad time for certain." Officer Kelly beamed. "But I am assured there is always time for love."

When they reached her room, Kasper's mother threw herself into his arms, clung to him, and wept. As Tori and Office Kelly stood by, Kasper did his best to reassure her and impress upon her the necessity for staying inside.

"I will try to have whatever you need sent from the shops," he told her in Polish. "Do not go out. Have the people from the church been by?"

"On Sunday someone escorted me to mass, and two women came to drop off a packet of food. But they said they must not come in and visit. Son, is it really so dangerous, this illness?"

He eyed her frail form and worn face. "Very dangerous, Mama, yes. But that is not the worst of it. There are violent people in the streets." He did not want to frighten her further by telling her he and Tori had been pursued.

But her eyes filled with dread. She whimpered, "Just like home."

"No, Mama, not like that." His mind, though, couldn't help but draw parallels. Back home a man could get beaten on the street merely for belonging to the wrong ethnic group. Here, for standing up on behalf of those treated unfairly. Hatred was hatred, and prejudice was prejudice.

Mama wept. "When will you be able to come home?"

"I do not know, Mama."

"Well when will you come and see me again?"

"As soon as I can. Mama," he spoke still in the tongue they shared. "I know you are lonely." He glanced at Tori, who gazed at him sympathetically. "Would you like to meet Tori's mother? She is alone now too."

"Tori." Mama lowered her voice even though neither Tom nor presumably Officer Kelly could understand. "Are you sweet on her? Then *tak*, I think I should make her mother's acquaintance."

Following that emotional visit, Pat took them to the rooms Tori shared with her mother. Mrs. Anderson assured Tori she was no longer going out to work, since the women for whom she'd been scrubbing no longer wanted anyone coming in. She agreed to visit Mrs. Czak so long as she had an escort.

"Mrs. Trimble on the first floor said her son was beaten yesterday morning, right on the street, just because he tried to intervene in a crime. A crowd of thugs was dismantling a steam unit right there on the sidewalk. They blame the automatons for starting this terrible illness." She looked straight at Pat. "Officer, do you think they are to blame?"

Obviously she did not see Pat as anything but human. He spoke calmly. "No, ma'am. I don't think that. No automaton I know would ever create something meant to hurt others."

"Do you know many automatons?"

"Yes, ma'am. I have close acquaintance with a fair

few." Pat Kelly winked at Tori. *Winked.* Or had she been mistaken that the lid over one green eye quirked down?

"Ma'am, I will be happy to escort you to Mrs. Czak's domicile. You choose a time and I will be here."

"My mother," Kasper told Mrs. Anderson, "does not speak English."

"Poor thing, she must feel so isolated. Perhaps I can begin teaching her."

"I would be happy to learn Polish," Kelly said. "I already speak English, French, and a bit o' the Gaelic. A few phrases in German, also."

"Officer Kelly, you must be terribly clever."

When they left the Andersons' flat, they found a steamcab waiting, along with a single police officer.

"Pat, you're needed over on Franklin Street. More rioting."

"Ah, yes. Miss Anderson and Mr. Czak, this cab will take you back to the orphanage."

Embarrassed, Kasper said, "I'm afraid I can't afford the fare."

"Paid for by the department," Kelly assured them. He waited to see them safely into the cab before the two officers pelted away like a matched set of dray horses.

In the cab, Tori said, "That was strange and unsettling. The riot, the police station—all of it. But I do like Officer Kelly."

"Yes."

"It does not seem possible that he or others like him could create this awful sickness just to get rid of us."

"It does not."

"Would the same automatons who help us care for the children want to watch them die? I know there are bad 'uns, as Ma says, among every kind of people, but—

"

"Tori?" Kasper interrupted her.

"Yes?"

He touched her face as gently as he could. "I want very much to kiss you before we arrive back at the orphanage."

"Oh!" Her eyes glittered in the dim light of the cab's interior. "You'd best do it, then."

The kiss proved long, deep, and full of heat. It raised the temperature inside the steamcab by several degrees.

"Oh, God," Kasper said most piously when it ended. "I have been waiting to do that since I pulled your skirts up above your knees."

"I see." Slowly she clamped the fingers of her good hand on her skirts and drew them up. "Like this?"

"Yes, exactly." Slowly, the way a man might lower his hand toward the top of a stove to test the temperature, he placed his palm on her knee—the unbandaged one. She wore knitted hose, one leg of which had torn and was now rolled down to accommodate the bandage. The other went up. And *up*.

He followed it, sliding his palm ever higher, waiting for a reproof, but none came. She sat very still, though he heard her breath catch when his fingers found the top of the stocking.

The skin beyond felt soft and very warm. He caressed it with seeking fingers, as the cab swayed through the streets.

"Please," Tori whimpered.

"Please, what?"

With her good hand, she cupped the back of his head and brought his mouth to hers. Ah, no mistaking that invitation. She wanted him.

She wanted him.

He brushed his fingers farther upward, into the forbidden territory beyond the top of her stocking, and encountered the cotton hem of her bloomers. God, but he wanted them off.

But, no. Tori Anderson was a decent young woman. The fact that she was kissing him as if she wanted to consume him, and that her heart beat crazily against his chest where he clutched her tight, did not mean he could assume too much, or reach too far. Did it?

But he loved her.

If he hadn't been absolutely certain before, he was now. That terrible moment when he thought she might be harmed by the crowd had clarified things. Right along with her kisses.

The steamcab suddenly rocketed to a halt, and the driver hollered back to them, "Here's your destination."

They leaped apart. Tori, her maimed hand clutched to her breast, hastily pulled her skirts back down over her knees.

Regret flooded Kasper. Why couldn't their journey have lasted just a few blocks longer?

He climbed from the steamcab and handed Tori out like a queen. Inside the house, in the front hallway, they met Mrs. Marner.

"You've been gone a time!" She looked worried and distressed. "Are your mothers both all right?"

Quickly, Tori filled her in on what had occurred—the angry crowd, the police station, and her injury.

"Oh, my! What's happened to our city?" Mrs. Marner appeared to blink back tears from her eyes. "Tori, will you be able to work?"

"Yes, ma'am."

"Well, take it as easy as you can for the rest of the day. I'll need you back on duty first thing tomorrow."

"I'll be ready, Mrs. Marner. How is Janie?"

"She took a sudden turn for the worse, Tori. We lost her this afternoon."

Chapter Nineteen

"But she was better. She was doing so much better," Tori said as she and Kasper went off to the kitchen. "How can she be gone?"

The question came in a wail, and Kasper glanced at her in concern. After what she'd been through already this day, he wouldn't be surprised if she fell apart completely.

"And I wasn't here! Kasper, it's so unfair. These children have so little. To die alone—"

They'd reached the dim, narrow corridor just beyond the kitchen. Kasper paused there and turned Tori gently toward him. "I am sure she was not alone. Daisy was no doubt with her, and Molly. Maybe Mrs. Marner also."

"I know. But she was such a sweet girl. And she never had the chance to get adopted into a proper family. To be truthful, few of our children do."

Life was hard, Kasper could tell her that, but he didn't think it was what she wanted to hear right now.

He drew her into his arms, up against his shoulder, where her tears came.

"Kasper, if someone did create this sickness, as that man on the box said—well, that person is a monster."

"*Tak.* But I do not think it was the automatons."

"It would be hard to believe. Officer Greely and Officer Kelly were both so kind."

"Try not to worry about it now." He kissed her on the forehead. "Why don't you go upstairs and rest? I am sure Mrs. Marner will not object."

"No. I must go find Daisy and comfort the rest of the children. They will be distraught—"

She hurried off, and Kasper stared after her. He felt stirred by the kisses they had shared, sobered by the loss of the child, and at his wits' end. He did not know what to do to help Tori. He didn't know quite what to do to help anyone.

****

He barely saw Tori for the rest of that day. Kept busy with scraping up the last of their coal and making a simple repair to Becky, he missed his supper and, by the time dark fell, was stumbling with weariness. It was he who saw to matters when the men from the mortuary came to take Janie's tiny body away. He heard weeping from upstairs but didn't have the opportunity to go up and see how Tori fared.

Suddenly, well after dark, Daisy appeared beside him. She looked pale and miserable, her eyes red.

"Mrs. Marner says for you to go and get some sleep. I just had my head down for a while, though I didn't get but two or three winks. Mrs. M. and I will stay up the night. She and Tori have got most the children to sleep, so Mrs. M. is sending Tori off to bed too."

Kasper nodded. Wearily, his feet dragging, he climbed the two flights of stairs to the attic, where they had been lodging. When the building had been a fine house and not an orphanage, this was where the servants had slept. He certainly felt no more than a servant now.

He dragged himself up the corridor to the tiny washroom, where he half stripped and scrubbed himself, and on to his small, barren room.

His body ached with weariness, but his mind refused to stop running over all that had happened this day. He lay on his cot and listened to the quiet house, unable to relax into sleep.

He heard footsteps tiptoe past his door down to the washroom and back to the chamber across the way, the one Tori used. He'd left his door open a crack in case someone needed to call him, but the ensuing silence seemed to close in, becoming stifling. It felt like the ceiling descended to smother him.

The creak of his door being opened alerted him to a presence. He half started up, Tori's name on his lips. A dim wall lamp burned in the hallway, and by its light he saw—

It stood framed in his doorway, one hand still on the knob, the other holding a censer from which trailed a terrible scent. In the weak light, its robes looked dirty, dun brown. When it moved, he caught the sharp outline of the beak and the dreadful slits behind which there may or may not be eyes. When it moved, its robes rustled and the scent wafted toward Kasper. The smell of death.

The plague doctor had got into the house. And it had its gaze fixed on him.

He made a strangled sound in his throat. He wanted to leap up, chase the thing away, push it out the front door if he had to. But his limbs refused to obey his command. He could only lie there staring at the dreadful figure that gazed back at him.

"Kasper? Kasper, are you all right?"

This voice broke through his paralysis. He blinked and saw that the plague doctor had disappeared. It was Tori who stood in his doorway.

"What?" he said stupidly, speaking in Polish. "What?"

"You called out."

"Did I?" with an effort he switched to English. "But I saw—I saw—"

"Yes?"

He did not want to tell her, did not want to sully her mind by sharing that image. She looked so pure and lovely standing there in a white nightdress, with her brown hair loose all around her. The very opposite of the ugly thing he had seen. Or thought he'd seen.

"You must have been dreaming," she proposed and tiptoed farther in, came and sat on the edge of his cot, and placed her good hand on his chest, as if feeling his heart.

Could that have been a dream? But surely he'd been awake. "I thought I was awake. I couldn't sleep."

"Neither can I. Would it be all right if I stay here with you? I don't want to be alone."

Would it be all right? No, it most certainly would not. Given the way he felt about her, he didn't know whether he could endure such a heaven.

Hoarsely, he said, "Maybe better if you share with Daisy."

"She's taken the night shift. Her room is empty. Besides, I'd rather be with you."

He'd rather that also. Still, he didn't know if he could trust himself. "I would not wish to harm your reputation or take advantage—"

"You'd never do that. And no one will know. I'll leave early, before Daisy comes up."

"Tori—"

He got no farther because she leaned down and

kissed him. A persuasive sort of kiss it was, and other factors joined in to stir his blood. When she leaned close, her breasts pressed forward against the thin fabric of her nightdress, the one she'd collected from the rooms she shared with her mother just that day, and he could smell the womanly warmth of her. Her hair tumbled forward and touched his pillow.

He raised a hand and stroked a wavy tress. "I've been longing to see you with your hair down like this."

"Does that mean you want me to stay? I'll keep the bad dreams at bay."

"Yes. Only you had better shut the door first."

She did, moving softly as a ghost back to the bed. With the door shut, the dark inside the room intensified. He could barely see her when she slipped under the blanket beside him.

Which was a shame. She was so very pretty.

He wished he could tell her so, but he was having trouble finding the English words again.

"Hold me," she requested, and wiggled in tight.

Holy mother of God, what a sensation! The warmth from her body came right through the fabric of her gown and fair scorched him.

"Your heart's pounding," she whispered, once more with her hand planted on his bare chest. "Is mine?"

Like a man in a dream, he moved his palm to the appropriate position. "Yes." Her breast was high and plump. Perfect. He went slightly dizzy with desire.

He and his brothers used to do this when they were small—no, not fondle a woman's breast in the dark, but cuddle all in one bed when frightened. He had to think of that. She'd merely come to him for comfort after the terrible day they'd had. If only his body might concur.

In his ear, she said, "Tell me about your dream."

He definitely didn't want to do that, though doing so might well put a hold on his rising—er—passion.

"I do not wish to speak of it."

"Oh. That bad?"

"Yes." And telling her might solidify the possibility that the plague doctor could be here inside the house. Only it was already here, wasn't it? It stalked the children's rooms and had taken Janie from them.

He shivered.

"Are you cold?" Tori asked.

He was not. It had been a warm day, and the heat lingered up here in the attic. Plus she gave off such warmth—

Before he could reply she said, "Let me warm you."

The kiss was designed to warm a man, yes, right through his flesh and into his bones. It might well set him afire. Kasper relaxed, forgetting for the moment about the specter of the plague doctor. Abandoning her breast, he plunged both hands into Tori's hair, while they kissed as if they'd been born to do so.

His mind began moving sluggishly between restraints and possibilities. He couldn't take advantage of her. He cared for her too much, valued her too much. And she'd brought herself to him in a vulnerable condition.

On the other hand—she'd brought herself to him. She was in his bed dressed only in a shift of thin cotton, her body sprawled over his, kissing him as if she'd never stop.

What exactly did she desire?

He slid his hands down from her hair and across her back. The hem of her nightdress had ridden up, and his fingers soon met warm, silken skin. The easiest thing in the world, sliding both palms up, cupping her fanny, and settling her just so, atop him.

Who'd have thought? Who'd ever have thought he'd need to cross half a continent and then an ocean to find the perfect woman?

She broke the kiss at last and lay panting on his chest. She whispered, "I've never—never—"

"No?"

"Of course not." She laughed breathlessly. "I'm a good girl."

"Perhaps we had better just…sleep." How could he even suggest such a thing when he was hard as iron? When he needed nothing so much as to be inside her?

"Yes, perhaps we should." In direct defiance of her words, she kissed him again. Her tongue encountered his and stroked it, wooed it into her mouth in a way that turned him damp with lust. Yes, that was it—he belonged inside her, the way he belonged nowhere else.

He needed to claim her, roll her over on her back and make her his own. He needed to tell her, then, how he felt about her, before stripping her of the alluring nightdress and spending the rest of the night tasting those tantalizing breasts.

He swiftly approached the point of no return.

"Tori." He broke the kiss so he could say her name. Very gently, he rolled her over and found himself positioned perfectly between her thighs. He wore only a pair of smalls, and the fingers of her good hand raked the hair on his naked chest.

He tried to gaze into her eyes in the dim light. "Tori, do you want me to—" She had nothing on beneath the nightdress. He could feel that. She continued to give off warmth like an overheated automaton.

She drew a breath. Her lips parted. "Yes, Kasper. I want—"

A loud crash sounded from below. It seemed to rattle the house and echoed with a metallic clang. Immediately, several children began crying.

"What was that?"

"I do not know." The crash had been loud enough to penetrate Kasper's closed door. Tori half reared up, her maimed arm caught between them, listening.

Voices, from below. For an instant, Kasper believed it hadn't been a dream after all. The plague doctor was here in the house, and someone else had seen it.

Running footsteps sounded out in the hallway. Daisy must have climbed the stairs. And gone to Tori's door?

"Tori?" That was Daisy's voice, all right.

Finding Tori's room empty, Daisy came next to Kasper's. "Kasper?"

Tori slid from beneath him and out of the cot. Swiftly, she swung wide the bedroom door. Daisy stood there, her hand raised to knock. She stared at Tori in shock.

"Oh, Jaysus!"

"What's happened?" Tori asked.

"You're needed downstairs."

She ran off and, with but one glance for Kasper, Tori followed.

Chapter Twenty

On the second floor, chaos reigned. Children were out of their beds and, against strict orders, had escaped their rooms. Many stood about crying.

Mrs. Marner hovered in the hallway outside the sickroom, looking pale in the light from the wall sconces.

"Stop this!" she cried as Daisy, Tori, and Kasper reached the bottom of the back stairs. "Stop this at once!"

Tori stared, astounded by what she saw. For Tom lay sprawled on his back at the center of the broad, upstairs hallway, water leaking from his thorax and pooling around him. He was a heavy unit, and the crash she'd heard must have been him going over like a stumpy tree.

Omar, one of the new units, stood over him, his arm in the air like a champion boxer. He spewed words at poor Tom.

"You are a fool! Knuckling under to those who would abuse us. Unthinkingly obeying every order that comes your way. If you do not stand up for yourself, no one will."

Ironic for him to exhort Tom to stand up, when he'd obviously just knocked him down. Were they having an argument? Difficult to warrant. Automatons never argued, not that she'd ever seen. The world had, indeed, gone mad.

Tom said nothing. Indeed, could it be considered an

argument if one participant didn't, well, participate?

The other house automatons, including the three remaining new arrivals, all rolled out from various rooms to stand silent. Molly paused just outside the door of the sickroom, waving her arms in distress. Becky and Hank, who must have been in the boys' room, stood shoulder to shoulder, and little Trina rolled up from the front of the house.

Slowly, Omar looked around at those gathered. "You should all be ashamed! Every unit among you should join in the effort to stand up for yourselves." He fairly shouted at Tom, "Stand up!"

"I don't think he can." Predictably, it was Daisy who stepped forward, her Irish temper flaring. "You're a bully, you are," she told Omar.

"I am not a bully." He swiveled to face her, and Tori suddenly wondered if he'd attack. Steam units were built to defend, and so far in all the encounters between steamies and humans that was what they had done. Stood and received a battering or returned blows in protection of themselves or others.

But the world had gone askew, and at this moment she believed anything could happen. If Omar—who outweighed the lightly built Daisy by hundreds of pounds—attacked her, the outcome could be dire.

"You think you are better than me just because you are human!" Omar accused Daisy.

"I don't think I'm better than anyone," she returned roundly. "But I'll not stand by and let you holler at our Tom, or frighten all these children. This is a house of sickness, for God's sake, and bereavement."

She stooped to try and help Tom up, and Tori caught her breath. The move put her directly under the looming

Omar.

"Tom, dear, can ye rise?"

Tom never moved. Hot water continued to leak from him at an alarming rate. His fire might have gone out, rendering him helpless.

Kasper leaped forward and tried to help Tom up, but the unit still proved too heavy to lift. After an instant, Hank trundled forward. It took the three of them to get Tom back up on his wheels.

Mrs. Marner stepped to Tori's side. "Can you calm these children and get them back in their rooms?"

"Yes, Mrs. Marner."

Tori began gathering the girls, who cried loudest. Some of the boys seemed fascinated rather than horrified by the show. After a moment, Becky jerked to life and helped, guiding the boys back to their dorm room.

"Everyone back to bed," Tori admonished her charges.

"Miss Tori, is Tom all right?"

"He will be, yes." A few dents perhaps, but Tori hoped that was the worst of it. She was fond of the unit who did so much around the orphanage so quietly and never complained.

It took a few minutes to settle the girls. Tori could hear Becky's mechanical voice across the way, tending the boys.

When she came out, Mrs. Marner waited at the door. Tom, Daisy, and Kasper had gone, and the other steam units had scattered to their various posts. Only Omar stood where they'd left him above the spreading pool of water from Tom's thorax.

"What do I do about him?" Mrs. Marner looked distracted. "I don't dare shut him down, since the new laws about automatons were passed. There can be dire consequences for doing so."

"Yes." The new ordinances said automatons must be paid for their work, though they still earned much less than humans. They must receive adequate maintenance, though no one had quite defined "adequate." They weren't to be shut down against their will, which for them equated death, at least not without good cause. That, too, went undefined, however.

To Mrs. Marner, Tori whispered, "Exactly what happened?"

"I don't know. I was in my office and had just come up to do a check. Omar and Tom were sharing duties in the boys' room, and I heard them arguing. It spilled out here, and to me it looked fairly one-sided. Omar began shoving Tom, and he went over with a crash."

Tori whispered back, "Perhaps you should shut Omar down, if he's dangerous."

"I heard that."

Slowly, Omar turned to face them. He appeared to have calmed somewhat from his earlier state, yet his stance remained vaguely intimidating.

"Who are you to threaten me with shutdown?" he demanded of Tori. "You too are lesser. Defective. When measured by the eyes of others, have you not the right to live?"

Tori experienced a chill.

Mrs. Marner stepped in front of her. "That's enough, Omar. You will not berate or—or denigrate one of my employees."

"You humans are all hypocrites! One set of values for yourselves and another for metal. Do you learn nothing? You are far from indestructible. Do you not already harbor the sickness that could put an end to all the humans here in this structure?"

"What does he mean?" Tori asked nervously.

Omar answered, "You think yourselves so superior, so much better than us. Yet you can be brought down easily by a tiny bit of contagious matter."

The plague. He spoke of the plague.

Tori wanted to run. She wanted to hide. She'd never been afraid of a steam unit—not until now.

"I have rights!" Omar declared. "Rights you cannot trample."

Shut him down, please. Tori thought it, but she would not say it again.

Hank trundled out from the boys' room and stood toe to toe with Omar.

"Stop it. You are frightening the children."

"Let them be frightened, brother. Let them learn we are a force with which they must reckon."

"I am not your brother, and I cannot let you intimidate these good people."

"Good people? Is there any such thing?"

"Yes. Mrs. Marner and Miss Tori are good. They care for these children and for us."

"But in the greater scheme of things—"

Omar got no farther because an incredible thing happened. Hank reached out with his thick, rubberized fingers and flipped the switch located on Omar's side, turning him off.

The hallway went very still. It seemed unbelievable that a steam unit should possess such energy, yet Omar's anger seemed to have filled the space. Relief came in its wake.

Mrs. Marner drew a breath. "Thank you, Hank."

"He was a bad influence," Hank stated sorrowfully. "And he pushed my friend."

****

It took hours for the furor to die down. Kasper and Hank between them wheeled Omar down the back stairs to the laundry room, out of the children's sight. But everyone remained shaken and even back in their beds the children refused to settle.

By then it seemed pointless to return to bed, even though being there—with Tori—was all Kasper could think about. Well, that and the horrifying dream that had preceded her arrival in his room.

He needed to talk to her, but there was no opportunity. She flitted about like a moth, and when they did encounter one another, she refused to meet his eyes.

He was helping Becky load laundry into the washtub when Mrs. Marner entered the room. The manageress still looked pale and unhappy.

She paused and gazed for a long moment at Omar, whom Kasper and Hank had pushed to one corner.

"What do you think happened to him?" she asked Kasper.

He paused in his work and looked at her. "I am sure I do not know."

"I've dealt with automatons a long while. I've never seen one malfunction in this way."

With a glance at Becky, who kept on with her task, Kasper dried his hands and stepped over to Mrs. Marner. "He did not actually malfunction however, did he?"

She stared at him.

"I mean," Kasper went on, "he was operating perfectly. He merely—expressed an opinion."

Did Omar not have a right to an opinion? Didn't

everyone? He'd seen enough back home of people being denied the right to own their emotions, to express grief or anger or any belief that flew in the face of an oppressive government. He'd seen men jailed and punished brutally for gathering to discuss their dissatisfaction.

As a newcomer to the city, he wasn't sure exactly where the automatons stood on achieving their rights. Some had, so he understood, been granted a measure of equality. Did it not include freedom of expression?

Until a person had been denied that particular right, he never grasped how precious it was.

"He became aggressive and turned on his fellow unit. He tried to intimidate us," Mrs. Marner said indignantly. "We cannot have that."

Again, Kasper glanced at Becky, who did not seem to be listening. "What will you do with him?"

"When it gets light, I intend to send a message of complaint to the shop that delivered him—a place called Pike's Steam Repair. They will simply have to come and mend him."

"Mend him?" Kasper repeated. She meant they should take away Omar's personality. Kasper might not like Omar's personality. The unit was abrasive and overbearing. But did he deserve having his very thoughts expunged?

"Until then," Mrs. Marner insisted, "he will remain off. I know you did wonders, Kasper, repairing Becky. But I do not want you restarting Omar, do you understand?"

Kasper nodded, understanding in that moment a simple and profound truth. Mrs. Marner was afraid of

Omar. And it was a fear shared by many in this great and terrible city.

Chapter Twenty-One

"So do ye mind telling me what you were doing in Kasper's room earlier?" Daisy poured hot water from the kettle on the stove into her pail. "I mean, I know what ye were doin'. What it looked like ye were doin'. I guess what I'm asking is, what were ye thinking?"

Tori, working at buttering a towering pile of toast, flushed scarlet, the heat washing over her in a wave. With all that had happened, she'd almost forgotten what Daisy must have seen when she opened Kasper's door. But of course Daisy hadn't forgotten.

It's none of your business. She wanted to speak those words but didn't. She considered Daisy her friend, and that friend appeared truly troubled on her behalf.

"I'll grant you, he's a looker." Daisy turned from the stove. "But that's not reason enough for a girl to lose her head. Tori Anderson, I never imagined you'd do such a thing."

"I—I was shaken by what happened earlier. I couldn't sleep and didn't want to be alone."

"I understand that. If you didn't want to be on your own, you should have come and found me."

"You were working. And I figured you had your hands full with the children."

"So ye turned to him? Listen to me, my girl. He might be tempting. And I'm not saying ye shouldn't be friends with him. But jumping into his bed?" She waved a chiding finger. "What happens if ye end up with his babe in your belly, eh? You won't be able to keep working here, or anyplace else. Then where will ye be?"

Tori's flush deepened. "Nothing happened."

"Not to say it wouldn't have, if that Omar hadn't gone haywire. In my opinion, ye had a lucky escape."

That might be Daisy's opinion. Tori could still taste Kasper's kisses and feel his body pressed to hers. She'd always been what her ma called a good girl. Biddable and hard-working. Impervious to temptation. Well, she'd had little choice, had she, with this arm? The twisted foot. No man had glanced at her. Certainly no man who looked and tasted the way Kasper Czak did.

She tipped up her chin. "He didn't take advantage. It was I who went to him—"

"That doesn't mean he wouldn't take advantage. The best of them will when it's offered on a plate."

"Are you saying the only way he could possibly be interested in someone like me is because I'm easy?"

"Someone like—" Daisy's eyes widened before her gaze abruptly softened. "Och, ye mean because of the arm? No, I'm not sayin' that at all."

Only she must mean that, because Tori's arm always mattered, at every moment. She'd lived with that fact all her life.

To be sure, the only way a man like Kasper could be interested in a maimed freak like her was if he thought she might surrender her virtue to him. How could she have imagined differently? It was just that the way she felt when she was with him lifted her clear out of herself.

Daisy whispered, "I don't want to see you gettin' into trouble, lass. He might be handsome, but he's the very definition of trouble."

But I still want him, Tori was left thinking, after Daisy moved off with her pail. What am I to do with this desire?

****

"Tori? We need to talk."

Tori spun when Kasper spoke, and found him standing just behind her. The tray she balanced in her hand wobbled. One swift glance told her Kasper looked as troubled as she felt, worried and disheveled. The collar of his shirt lay askew, and his dark hair tumbled over his forehead in disarray. The man needed a haircut, and it became him. She wanted nothing so much as to plunge her fingers through those silken tresses.

The tray wobbled again, dangerously, in response to her emotions, and Kasper seized it in both hands.

"I can manage," she snapped, driven by the fact that his attention had now been drawn to her deformity. "I've been managing all my life, as you see."

"Yes," he agreed but did not let go of the tray. Tori wondered what that meant. Yes, I see you are maimed? How could anyone miss it?

All her life she'd compensated for her withered arm, and all her life she'd been on the receiving end of the consequences. The mockery, the sing-song taunts from other children when she was young. *Tori one-arm. Your ma should put you in the circus.* The stares, some full of disgust and—almost worse—some of pity.

She'd managed, yes. She'd compensated. She'd tried to grow a skin thick enough to keep it all at bay, but she'd never truly succeeded. Inside, she still harbored the little girl who wanted to put her good arm over her head and hide from the sting.

"Everybody's got some defect," Ma had told her

many the time. "Only with most folks, it don't show."

Tori had half believed it. Then along came this perfect specimen—Kasper Czak—with his impossibly good looks, gentle hands, and irresistible accent. If he carried a flaw, she hadn't found it.

"Tori, are you angry with me?"

She could not look into his eyes. She absolutely could not. She didn't want to see what lay there.

"Why would I be angry with you?"

He shook his head helplessly. "I do not know." It was she, after all, who had come into his room and jumped into his bed. Ah, even the memory made her warm all over.

"Embarrassed, then?" he suggested.

Yes, she felt embarrassed. Vaguely ashamed, and so full of doubt she couldn't express it. She wanted—needed—to know if he'd merely kissed and touched her in order to get from her that which it seemed men were always seeking. Not because it was *her*.

Because he thought she was willing to give it away.

"I can't talk now. I have to get this tray up to the sickroom."

"Let me carry it up for you."

"You think I can't carry it?"

"Not in the least. But all those stairs—"

She yanked the tray away from him. For a terrible moment it teetered in her hand before tipping wildly out of control. It hit the flagstone floor of the kitchen with a blinding crash and a hail of food mixed with shards of porcelain.

"Oh, look what you made me do!" Unfairly, she blamed him. Tears filled her eyes and blurred everything as she crouched down and tried to gather up the pieces with one hand clutched, as ever, to her chest.

"Let me help."

His hands—his beautiful hands, long-fingered and graceful—began to gather the spilled items. Those hands had touched her. Suddenly Tori wanted to throw up. How could she have been so deceived as to go crashing into this man's room? To imagine he'd want her anywhere near him?

"Do not cry, Tori, please." Dumping the broken crockery back onto the tray, he reached out and cupped her face between those beautiful hands. "Look at me."

She couldn't, she absolutely couldn't. Instead she ducked away and sprang to her feet, ready to flee.

A knock at the front door gave her an excuse. She flew to answer it.

A man and a boy stood on the stoop. The man looked to be in his mid-to-late twenties, of medium height, and lightly built. He held a leather carryall. The boy, nearly as tall as the man, and skinny, wore a bandana tied over his mouth, probably in an effort to ward off the sickness.

"Hello, miss. I'm Lionel Pike," the man said. "I received word that one of the steam units we sent you has run amok?"

"Oh, yes."

"I understand there's sickness here in this house."

"We have some children taken ill, yes."

The man drew a bandana from his pocket and, laying down his bag of tools, tied it over the bottom half of his face. "My wife will never forgive me if I fall ill."

He stepped past Tori, and the boy followed, his gaze sweeping over Tori as he did, locking on her arm. As did most folks'.

"He's a newlywed," the boy explained. "It's

146

sickening at our house."

That made Tori smile despite herself.

"This is Sam," Lionel Pike said fondly. "He's supposed to be my apprentice, though he spends most of his time dodging the work he's given."

The boy might have grinned. Tori couldn't be sure, since his mouth was covered, but his bright eyes smiled.

"Where is this unit, miss?"

"Our caretaker has put him in the laundry room."

"Can someone take us to him?"

"I will." Kasper stepped out of the shadowy kitchen doorway. "Follow me."

The workmen did, and after a moment's reflection Tori followed them. She had to make another tray to take upstairs. She wanted to see what this repairman made of Omar first.

It seemed her impulses still weren't very well disciplined.

"Ah, Omar," Lionel Pike murmured when Kasper led him to the unit. He and Sam exchanged glances before he once more set his tool kit down on the damp laundry room floor. "Could you tell me exactly how he malfunctioned?"

"He did not malfunction," Kasper replied. "Not—not as such."

"What did happen, then?"

Kasper looked Pike in the eye. "He expressed an opinion."

"He would." Sam piped up. "A real firecracker, is Omar. Isn't that right, Mr. Lionel?"

Pike looked unhappy and said nothing.

"Did you build him?" Tori asked.

"No. I refitted him. The way it works is, we receive

many units that have been cast off and would normally be destined for the scrap yard. We refit them, and our patrons see they're provided free of charge to places like this, that are desperate for extra help. Some are aged units that we restore. Some are put together from more than one other damaged unit."

"I see," Tori said.

"It's a low-budget operation. Upon occasion, things can go awry." Pike looked at Kasper. "Can you describe the incident that caused Omar to be shut down?"

"Not all of it. I was not there."

Tori spoke up. "Neither of us was there. It was the middle of the night, and Omar was working with one of our units, Tom, in the boys' dormitory. The way I understand it, they began arguing."

"A discussion," Kasper corrected gently. "Omar expressed some opinions with which Tom did not agree."

Pike and the lad exchanged glances. "I was afraid of this," Pike said. "Did Omar then become belligerent?"

"Yes." Tori nodded. "Omar wound up pushing poor Tom over. He crashed to the floor and his fire went out."

"I am sorry to hear that, miss. Is Tom all right?"

"We got him up, and I got him relit," Kasper said. "He seems to be functioning well now."

"He's woefully dented," Tori put in.

"You see," Pike began, "when we get these older units, they already have what you might call personalities. It's against my philosophy to alter a unit's personality. It would be like—like erasing your memory, almost, wouldn't it? Omar came to us already passionate about automaton rights. I did tell him it wasn't appropriate for him to take that into the workplace."

"He's a right crusader, our Mordred says," the boy put in.

"Mordred?" Tori repeated.

"My other assistant." Pike's gray eyes looked serious. "Also an automaton."

"I see." Tori wasn't sure she did, entirely.

"Omar tries to convert other automatons to the cause, wherever he goes. It is that important to him. I'd hoped he might be able to curb his tendencies in this setting. The trouble is, units like him both live and work on site. They're never off duty, so to speak, and can't really grasp the notion of keeping an activity for their own time."

"Then you will have to swap him out for another unit," Mrs. Marner declared from the doorway, having heard the last part of the conversation. "I cannot have commotion here, disturbing the children."

She glared at Tori and Kasper. "You two can get back to work, please. I will deal with this."

Tori and Kasper filed out of the laundry room. When they reached the kitchen, they paused, and Tori looked at Kasper. He appeared upset.

"What is it?" she asked. "What's wrong?"

"I hope Mrs. Marner does not talk the repairman into changing Omar's personality."

"He is a bit overbearing."

"He is," Kasper agreed. "Yet no one—automaton or otherwise—deserves to have their beliefs repressed."

Chapter Twenty-Two

For the second time in as many days, angry words pierced the customary quiet of Lost Waifs Home for Children. In this case, as Kasper reflected while he helped Tori and Becky carry lunch trays upstairs, they were all spoken on Mrs. Marner's part. Lionel Pike kept his voice low and his comments courteous. But nothing Mrs. Marner said could persuade him to alter Omar.

Kasper respected that. Not that he wanted disruption in the house or that he personally did not find Omar's abrasive manner annoying. He did. But he'd seen, in the past, too many incidences when those with opinions were harshly penalized for expressing them.

In the end, Pike got Omar running, and the unit left the house in the company of the repairman and his assistant, under his own power. Pike promised to send over a replacement unit in a day or two.

Mrs. Marner did not seem as pleased by this as Kasper felt she should. Indeed, Mrs. Marner was clearly overwrought and not herself. Formerly cool and collected, with perfectly disciplined hair worn in a bun, and a formal manner, she now looked distracted, with tendrils of hair sticking out all over her head, a wrinkled blouse, and the eyes of a madwoman.

"I reckon she's goin' to crack," Daisy commented to Kasper when they met in a hallway. Mrs. Marner had just given conflicting orders, for them to both vacate the floor and attend the children there, before marching off to the sickroom. "It's just a matter of time."

"We are all under much strain," Kasper agreed.

"I'll bet she can't remember the last time she slept. The thing is," Daisy bit her lip, "if she goes down, I don't know what will happen. An old lady called Miss Radmacher owns this place. She holds the purse strings, and she holds 'em tight. But she's never actually come here."

"Would she hire another manageress, if something happens to Mrs. Marner?"

"I don't see how, with the city in such a state. She might just close the place."

"What would happen to all the children, then?" They had no other home. As for that, Kasper did not want to find himself on the street without a job. Would he ever see Tori again?

"We'd best be nice to her," Daisy warned. Her eyes met Kasper's. "That means you'd better not kick off."

"Kick off? I do not understand."

"It means 'Don't cause any trouble.' "

"I am not in the habit of causing trouble."

"Yeah, you look innocent, I'll give ye that. But I'm keeping my eye on you."

Unhappily, Kasper thought back to that moment very early the previous morning when his door had been flung open, only for Daisy to catch him and Tori together.

He said, "Nothing happened between Tori and me." *Not much, anyway.*

"Yes, that's what she said. And you'd best keep it that way. Tori's a good girl, and she needs this job. If she gets cast off, where do you think she'll find another position? Who do you think would hire her with that arm? And Mrs. Marner's just in the mood to cast anybody off, if she gets wind of something goin' on."

Kasper's anger, usually well controlled, stirred. "I think you—and Tori—both make too much of the arm."

"Oh, do ye? As if ye didn't notice it."

"It is not the first thing I see when I look at Tori." Rather, he noticed that cloud of soft brown hair, the sweet, vulnerable chin, the steady warmth in her green eyes.

"Well, then, I'll just bet I know what ye do notice. You're like all men, always lookin' for the chance."

"Chance? For—" Kasper took her meaning, and his anger heightened. "That is not true. I like Tori very much."

"And that's why ye had her in your bed? Look, you're a good-lookin' lad and no mistake. And Tori's never been subject to what ye might call temptation. If ye do like her, you'll look after her, right? Make it clear ye respect her too much to do her any harm."

"For the last time, I do not mean to do Tori any harm. I wish you would stop suggesting it."

Daisy planted her nose in the air and marched away. Something in the atmosphere of the place, Kasper thought, just seemed to be fueling discord. If it were true in the rest of the city, why, they were all doomed.

He tried for most of that day to grab another word with Tori, despite the likelihood of it going awry, and never succeeded. He ached to put things right between them, to mend the rift that had occurred.

He wasn't even sure why she was upset with him. Was it because she thought he wanted only to sleep with her? He scowled to himself over it as he went about his work. A strange term, since if it occurred there would surely be little sleep involved. And yes, to be perfectly honest, he did want to sleep with Tori. Following their encounter in his bed, it was all—almost all—he could think about. But it wasn't the only reason he longed to be near her.

There was also her smile. And her conversation. The comfort he—usually—felt in her company. He had to get her alone and tell her how he felt about her. Confess that he *loved* her.

Ah, sweet blessed mother! The very idea shook him. What if she became insulted? Who was he, after all, but a penniless immigrant, spouting broken English, who had nothing to offer? What if she refused to believe him and once more accused him of merely trying to seduce her with a lie?

What if she laughed or scoffed at him?

Be a man, he admonished himself. You are the one who faced the Russians in the forest. The one who battered Josef senseless in the cellar. Will you fear facing a girl who stands scarcely higher than your shoulder?

In the end, he didn't have to worry about it. Fate and circumstances conspired to keep him and Tori apart. He found himself instead in company with Becky in the laundry room where the wringer washer had once more malfunctioned.

"The roller that squeezes out the water has jammed," the unit explained to him. "I would wring out the rest of the sheets by hand, but I am supposed to be on duty upstairs at the girls' room and should not take the time."

More words than the usually taciturn unit had spoken since Kasper came into the house. Yet since he'd restarted her, she seemed comfortable with him. Was it possible she felt as agitated as everyone else? It had become evident automatons did *feel*.

"Let's see if we can get it mended," he told her, "before you go upstairs."

A sheet was stuck in the mangle, which may have caused it to seize up. Becky became upset when Kasper pulled on it.

"Please, Master Kasper, do not tear the sheet. Mrs. Marner is made most unhappy by torn linens. We have so few left."

"Call me Kasper. I am not your master. Here, you help me, then. You tug on the sheet while I loosen the roller."

They struggled together, Becky's sculpted metal face somehow emitting the same frustration Kasper felt.

As they worked, he said, "How can Mrs. Marner expect you to manage all this laundry and be upstairs at the same time?"

"Much is expected of me. I am to Help Out."

"Tell me." He eyed her. "What do you think of that rant Omar went on?" Where did she stand on the subject of automaton rights? The lowest of the low in this household, did she harbor any deep-seated resentment or desire to be heard?

"He spoke out of turn. And he pushed Tom."

"That was speaking out of turn, was it?" Kasper had loosened the roller, and the sheet came free. "Hasn't he the right to speak?"

She turned her face toward him, the sheet bundled in her arms. "Those of my kind fight for those rights. But Kasper, that is beyond these walls, where I seldom stray. I belong here. And Tom is my friend."

"I see," Kasper said, not quite sure he did.

"It is not good to make trouble."

Ah, now, Kasper had heard that sentiment expressed far too many times back home. Keep your head down and they won't notice you. If they don't notice you, they may not hurt you.

Yet, as he could attest, they did hurt you even if you kept your eyes averted. He'd seen many a man with a bowed head decapitated by a Cossack's sword. The moment came—as it had in the cellar with Josef—when you had enough and must fight back.

Yet he needn't say that to Becky, who he hoped was becoming his friend.

"There, now," he told her instead, comfortingly. "You run on upstairs to your other duties. I'll see if I can put this back together and keep it from binding."

"You are very clever, Kasper."

An hour later, he had the machine reassembled and in good working order. He filled the tub with water and a full load of linens and cranked the agitator. Lurking here in the depths of gloom wouldn't give him his time with Tori. On the other hand, they all had to Help Out as best they could.

****

It had become nearly impossible to keep the children in check. Bored and tired of confinement in their respective dormitories, they proved either defiant and unwilling to listen to instructions or all too apt to weep over trivialities. Daisy had assigned herself to the nursery, caring for the smallest of them. By late afternoon, Tori found herself sharing duties with Trina, in the girls' room.

It seemed strange, working with a unit she didn't know. Used to Molly and Becky, Tom and Hank, with whom she'd worked since taking the job at Lost Waifs, she never had to think about how to approach them. Since the incident with Omar, however, courtesy was very much on her mind.

It would be difficult to feel intimidated by Trina, since she was small even by Tori's standards. The unit had a little round head set on equally rounded shoulders and features that had been carefully repainted, most likely at Mr. Pike's shop.

"This is a madhouse," she remarked to the unit, standing with her good hand propped on her hip. None of the girls, who ranged in age from five to thirteen, heeded a thing she said. Three of them were currently having a pillow fight in one corner, two others engaged in an argument over God-knew-what, and one of the smallest howled in her bed, for no apparent reason.

"They have too much energy," Trina replied surprisingly, "and need something to do."

She was absolutely right. "Yes, but what? With them all cooped up here, our options are limited."

"I could teach them to sew."

Tori stared at the unit. "Could you?"

"Yes. In my past incarnation, I was a lady's maid. I took care of all my lady's needs, from running her bath to keeping track of her appointments, to both making and mending her clothing."

The unit fell silent, and Tori wondered what had occurred to end such a long association. She could almost see this tiny unit trotting up and down the hallways of some grand house. She and her mistress would have been so comfortable together.

"Oh, I see," she murmured. "What happened? Did your mistress pass away?"

Trina turned her painted face to Tori. "No, miss. She desired a newer, better model."

"Oh. Oh, my." Trina's words were spoken without emotion—of course they were. Automatons didn't possess emotions, did they? Except they did. Omar, indignation. Tom, loyalty. This small unit harbored grief.

"I'm so sorry. What did she—what did she do with you?"

"She denied me coal. What I had in my hopper ran out quickly, and at length I shut down. I must have been put out to the curb then for scrap, because I was later told I'd been picked up by those who scrap old, worthless units. I was eventually taken to Pike's Steam Repair, where I was repaired and restarted."

"Well, then, you're anything but worthless, right? No more so than I am with this bum arm of mine. And you're very much wanted here."

"I do hope so, miss." The painted eyes seemed to seek Tori's. "Will I be able to remain here, miss, once the present crisis has passed?"

"I certainly hope so, Trina, but who knows? Let's just try and get through the crisis, first."

Chapter Twenty-Three

"I need you to take a message for me," Mrs. Marner told Kasper from behind the desk in her tiny office. She shot him a look. "I hate to ask you to go out, but I have no choice."

Kasper said nothing. When he'd first come to work at Lost Waifs—had that truly been only a week or so ago?—he'd been brought into this office to sign some papers. At that time, it had been neat as a pin, everything in its place, the wood surface of the desk polished and shining.

The woman who'd faced him across the desk had appeared collected and rather formidable. All that had now changed. Papers, files, and books littered the desk. Several empty teacups and a small plate holding the remains of a slice of bread and butter had been shoved aside. The rest of the office looked like it had been ransacked by a troop of undisciplined monkeys. The woman herself wore a stained blouse and wrinkled suit, and her hair straggled from its formerly neat bun.

Before Kasper could speak, she went on. "I'd much prefer to send one of the steam units. I know the streets are unsafe, but Miss Radmacher has a thing about automatons. She won't allow any in her service, and if I send one of ours she won't allow him in the door."

Kasper frowned. He didn't fancy going back out on the streets after what had transpired last time. Even more, he disliked the prospect of leaving Tori here without him. Not that she would be alone. The house was crammed full of children and steamies.

Correctly reading his expression, Mrs. Marner said, "I would not send you at all, were it not so important." Her pale blue eyes met his. They looked worried. "We are nearly out of money." She gestured to one of the books on the desk, a large ledger. "Usually I run the household strictly, to the penny. There have been a number of unexpected expenses during this—this difficult time. There have been charges for medicine, Dr. Rasmussen's fees, and now these extra automatons to keep running. As I'm sure you've noted, they are depleting our supply of coal most drastically."

"Mrs. Marner, you need not make explanations to me."

"But I do." She waved her hands wildly. "Asking you to risk your safety this way. With that thing out there." She corrected herself doubtfully. "Or *things*." Earnestly, she leaned across the desk. "Kasper, do you believe there's more than one of them?"

"More than one plague doctor, do you mean? It seems there must be, since they've been sighted all over the city, and at the same time."

Mrs. Marner shuddered. "I would give you money for a cab, if I had it. As it is, you will have to walk. Miss Radmacher lives on Bidwell Parkway." She told him the number and handed him a folded paper. "Give her this. Be insistent. And I'm afraid you are going to have to wait for an answer from her. We need immediate funds. I'm sorry to ask it of you, but you must refuse to leave without at least a partial allowance."

Kasper's heart sank. "What if she will not see me?

Or—or refuses to read the note? Or to pay out, if she does read it."

"You must plead our case. Tell her how very desperate we are. Be as quick as you can—do not linger on the streets. Quite apart from the dangers there, we have sickness here that you might perhaps carry with you."

Kasper didn't like that thought. He didn't like any of it.

"When you go in to see Miss Radmacher, you should perhaps wear a bandana over your face. Do you have one?"

When Kasper shook his head, she got up from the desk, went to the door, and called, "Tori!"

Hurried footsteps soon came in response. Kasper's heartbeat quickened when Tori appeared from upstairs, looking inquiring. She appeared surprised to see him. "Yes, Mrs. Marner?"

"Did you say you are making bandanas?"

"Yes, Mrs. Marner. Trina is teaching the girls to sew. We're using fabrics from the rag bag. It seems to be working a treat."

"That's fine. Please select a finished bandana and give it to Mr. Czak. He's going out to run an errand for me."

Tori stared at Kasper in dismay. "Oh, I see. Mrs. Marner, do you think that's a good—"

"It cannot be helped, I am afraid. I would not ask him to go, but things are desperate."

"I—I will fetch him a bandana at once."

She ran off, looking far more unhappy than when she'd come in.

"Mr. Czak, please promise me you'll be very

careful. And that you will not return to us empty-handed."

"I will be careful, *tak*. But I cannot promise this woman, this Miss Radmacher, will act as you wish."

"I know." Mrs. Marner's gaze softened a bit. "Please do your best. You have the address in your head?"

Kasper nodded.

"Then on your way, as soon as Tori gives you that bandana."

Kasper stepped out into the hallway, feeling half queasy and half numb. At the foot of the stairs he met Tori, who came flying down the steps with a square of blue fabric in her hand.

"Here, this is one of the better ones. Some of the girls' efforts aren't too good as yet. Tie it on, so."

"I will look like a bandit."

"I'm sure you won't be the only one." Tori's eyes were huge. "Kasper, where is she sending you?"

"To the home of a Miss Radmacher on Bidwell Parkway, to try and procure emergency funds."

"My goodness, are things that bad?"

"Mrs. Marner says so. There is almost no coal left in the cellar. I was hoping there would be a delivery coming."

"Why doesn't she send one of the steamies?"

"She says Miss Radmacher would not let one in her door."

Tori's green eyes met his above the edge of his bandana. "Promise me you'll be careful."

That he could promise. "I will."

Was her anger with him forgotten? It seemed so, for suddenly she was in his arms, embracing him fiercely tight. For one precious moment he wrapped his arms around her. She felt so small to mean so much to him.

"Come back," she whispered. "Come back to me."

****

The street outside looked empty and felt dangerous. A wind far too cold for summer snaked its way up the pavement and chased pieces of litter along the bricks, sounding like claws scraping. Caution held the city in its grip. How appropriate, Kasper thought as he hurried along. *Does autumn already begin to make a claim on summer? When the year begins to die, will the city die, also?*

Bidwell Parkway lay many blocks distant from Lost Waifs. The street itself was lengthy, a wide and rather majestic boulevard with a mall down the center, lined with large and prosperous households.

On an ordinary day, the streets along the way would be bustling, filled with horse-drawn cabs and the newer steam-powered ones, delivery wagons, and folks on foot hurrying by. Now even Elmwood Avenue was quiet, devoid of both wheeled and foot traffic. Many businesses were shut. People must, so Kasper reflected, be obeying the mayor's shelter-in-place edict. Kasper felt as if he now saw the skeleton of the city.

It was not a good or comfortable thought.

Did people, the shut-ins, watch him from behind those closed doors and windows? Did they peer out at him as he hurried past? It felt so. An uncanny sensation.

And what if he met up with—it? The plague doctor in one of its many incarnations? A full body shiver seized him at the thought. He seemed to attract the thing.

Was there in truth only one, possessed of magical powers? Or many?

A horse-drawn cab clopped slowly past, heading in

the same direction as he was. The horse and driver both turned their heads to stare at him curiously. The driver wore a black bandana.

Beneath it, he could be anyone.

Suddenly, Kasper wished he were back home with his mother—not in the tiny set of rooms they shared, but in Poland. He wished they'd never come to America. Wished he'd never taken the job at Lost Waifs.

But then he'd never have met Tori Anderson. Never touched her, held her. A fair trade, perhaps, for his peace of mind.

He reached the house on Bidwell Parkway out of breath. The place was huge, a tall, three-story house standing foursquare, with stone pillars on the porch and a dormer like a little cap all the way at the top. Painted in green and gray, it had rows of stained-glass windows marching along the sides and flanking the front door.

There was a pull bell, like those at some of the grand houses back in Krakow. When he pulled it, it seemed to echo inside as if the place stood empty.

He only half expected a response. But a maid came to the door and drew it open. Of middle years, she looked waspish and unwelcoming.

"What do you want?"

"Is this the home of Miss Radmacher?"

"It is."

"I come with a message from Mrs. Marner at the Lost Waifs orphanage."

"We are not letting anyone in. Because of the sickness." She began swinging the door shut again. Mindful of Mrs. Marner's instructions, Kasper planted his hand against it.

"I understand. You do not have to let me in. Just

please take this letter to her."

He fished it out from inside his jacket. The maid stared as if it were coated in poison.

"I don't think—"

"Melissa? Who is it?" The querulous voice came from behind the maid and caused her face to crease with anxiety.

"Wait here," she told Kasper and went off, leaving the door ajar.

He could glimpse a foyer inside, with a highly polished floor and stiff side tables standing at attention. He could hear voices—most likely issuing from some room beyond—the maid and the person who'd called to her.

Miss Radmacher?

When the maid returned, she looked even more unhappy. "Come in. But keep that bandana on, mind. And don't get close to her."

Miss Radmacher sat in a chair in the large parlor that lay to the left of the foyer. Small and frail, she must be somewhere in her sixties, with sharp blue eyes and hair so thin Kasper could see her scalp in places. As for the rest of her, she looked like a bundle of bones held together by fusty clothing.

"Who are you?" She demanded the moment she laid eyes on him.

"Kasper Czak. I work for you at the Lost Waifs orphanage."

"Do you?" Her gaze inspected him with a horrifying attention to detail, starting at his face and tracking downward.

"Yes, ma'am."

"Melissa said you were good-looking. I think she

underestimated. What does Gertrude Marner have you doing for her, eh?"

Kasper told himself there was nothing suggestive in the woman's tone. He failed quite, to believe it.

"Maintenance, ma'am. And due to the present situation, I do whatever else I can to help out."

"I'll just bet you do."

Kasper swore to himself in Polish. "She has sent you a message. Will you take it, please?"

"Hmm. I'm not sure I should. You have the sickness at the orphanage?"

"Yes, ma'am."

"The city's going to hell, I tell you. Straight to hell. It all started when somebody got the idea of building a servant out of metal. Damn fool! Sure, they're cheap to run. But who would trust 'em? I won't allow them in the house."

Yet she had purchased units to care for the vulnerable children under her care, some of whom were mere babies. One set of rules for her, and another for what she no doubt considered nothing but a business.

"Miss Radmacher, ma'am, we are in need of help at—" he began.

She disregarded him. Leaning forward, her eyes sparking with malice, she said, "There are all sorts of theories flying around the city about this Black Fever. Have you heard? Oh, I may spend most my time shut away here, but I get the news. You may be sure of it. They're saying it's those hybrid automatons who cooked up this sickness as a way to get rid of the rest of us."

Kasper thought of Officer Kelly, and Officer Greely, who'd been so kind to Tori at the police station, and shook his head.

"You don't believe it?"

"I do not believe—"

She cackled. "Well, you'd better. They want to take over the city. Everybody knows that. They have a coalition and have been buying up properties as fast as they can raise the money. You ever ask yourself why?"

Kasper hadn't. He'd been too busy trying to survive.

"Once they're in control, they'll enslave the rest of us, anyone who survives this plague of theirs. They want to turn the tables, to be on top. That's what happens when you give underlings too much power."

Underlings. Was that what this horrible woman also considered him?

"Please, ma'am, read Mrs. Marner's letter." He held it out to her.

"Well, since you ask so pretty." Miss Radmacher fished a pair of spectacles from her pocket and gestured at Kasper. "Sit down, sit down. Melissa, fetch the young man a cup of tea. He's going to stay a while."

Chapter Twenty-Four

If Tori hadn't been in the kitchen, cutting the dozens and dozens of sandwiches for the children's lunch, she wouldn't have heard the knock at the door. Lunch was already late. They'd become involved in the sewing project in the girls' room and time had slipped away. Trina's sewing scheme proved popular. The children liked the idea of making their own bandanas. Even some of the boys clamored to join in.

Maybe, Tori thought distractedly, they could start up a project in the boys' room next. No reason a young man shouldn't learn to—

A hard rap sounded on the back door. She laid her knife aside and hurried to answer the summons.

For a split second before she swung the door open, she imagined the plague doctor standing there. What was happening to her mind?

Of course it wasn't the plague doctor. Instead she saw a tall young man with fair, messy hair and intensely blue eyes—the same fellow with whom she'd seen Kasper speaking once before. He looked like he'd recently been in a fight.

She opened the door only a crack for safety's sake, and peered out at him. "Yes?"

"I am looking for Kasper Czak." He had an accent like Kasper's.

"He's not here."

"Of course he is. He works here."

"He works here but he's not in, just now. He's out on an errand. Can I help you?"

He inspected her with those sharp blue eyes, fastening on her withered arm. A faint sneer twisted his lips. "I do not think so."

"Then—"

"I must speak to him. I will come in and wait."

"I don't think that's a good idea. Unless—" Tori's mind raced. "Is there something wrong? Is this about his mother?"

"About his mother, *tak*. She lives at—" He tipped his head. "What is her address again? I seem to have forgotten. Do you know?"

"I do not," Tori lied. He'd made her uncomfortable before, and now, under the thin veneer he presented, she sensed…violence. "You can't wait here. We have sickness in the house."

He shook his head in mock sorrow. "What a shame. But there is sickness all over this city. They are saying the machines, they spread it. To get rid of us. They can't get sick, see."

"Miss? Is there a problem?"

The voice, deep and mechanical, came from behind Tori. Suddenly Tom was there, tall and solid, a reassuring presence.

The visitor's eyes narrowed.

"Tom," Tori said with some relief, "this person is looking for Kasper."

"Mr. Czak is not here," Tom intoned, his voice box vibrating.

"So the little girl said. I want to come in and wait. You get out of the way."

"I do not think so." Very gently, Tom nudged Tori aside and seized the edge of the door. The visitor still had his palm planted against the panel, and a struggle ensued. The would-be intruder appeared strong, but Tom's metal body outweighed him. When the automaton leaned into it and puffed steam, the door slammed shut.

"Tell Kasprczak that Josef was here asking for him. I will be back!" The visitor shouted through the narrowing gap.

Tom locked the door with his large, pincer hands. He and Tori looked at one another.

"Oh, Tom," she whispered. "I'm so glad you were here. What would I have done? I'm afraid he might have forced his way in."

"Yes, miss. I fear the same."

"He was looking for Kasper."

"Quite clearly, yes."

"Is he gone?" Tori dashed to the small window beside the door and peered out. "I don't see him."

"It may be best, miss, if in future you do not open the door unless we are sure who is outside."

"Yes." Tori shivered. "How did you know I needed help?"

"I did not, miss. Trina sent me to find you. The children want their sandwiches."

"Oh, yes. You can help me carry them up. Tom, did you hear the nonsense that fellow was spouting?"

"Some of it, miss."

"I hope you know I don't believe it."

"Neither do I, miss. But there is a lot of hate out there." He shook his head slowly. "A lot of hate."

****

"Miss Radmacher, ma'am, I do not think it is a good

idea for me to sit down." Kasper glanced around the parlor, which felt cold and disused. "I will just stand."

Miss Radmacher held Mrs. Marner's note to her face. She flicked him a look, past it.

"A word of advice, young man. When your employer gives you an order, it's best to obey it. If you wish to remain employed, that is."

Had it been an order, or an invitation? The former, so it seemed.

Uneasily, Kasper backed to the nearest chair, a hideous overstuffed monstrosity, and perched on the edge of the seat.

"Now, what is all this nonsense?" Miss Radmacher read the missive. She hummed as she read. She snorted and huffed.

"More money. I should have known. It is all that woman ever wants from me."

Kasper wasn't sure if he should argue the case or let the letter do it for him. Miss Radmacher did not seem impressed by whatever Mrs. Marner had written.

"Ma'am," he began.

The maid came hurrying in with a small tray which contained a cup of tea. Miss Radmacher eyed it sharply. "Where are the biscuits? Did you give him any biscuits?"

"No, Miss Radmacher."

"Go get some."

"Yes, Miss Radmacher."

"Damn girl." Miss Radmacher didn't wait for the maid to clear the room before cursing her. "We have so few visitors she forgets how to be hospitable."

Hospitable? A less welcoming house Kasper had never seen, not even back home. *Especially* back home.

Miss Radmacher fixed him with a sharp eye. "What

were you going to say?"

"The need at the orphanage is dire. With the children sick, the doctor has had to be called in, which took the money for the coal."

"Coal? Why do you need coal?"

"For the steam plant, ma'am. To run the lights. And for the steam units." Should he tell her they now had three extra units, consuming coal? Those had been provided by a donor and brought in by Pike's Steam Repair. She might not approve.

Sure enough, she snorted. "Steam units. Should get rid of them all."

"They are very helpful. I do not think we could manage without them."

She fixed him with that sharp eye. "Take off your bandana."

"I do not think I should."

"You will have to take it off," a smile stretched her withered lips, "to drink your tea. And"—as Melissa came hurrying in—"to eat your biscuits. Let's have a look at you, boy."

Was that why she'd provided him with refreshments? So he'd have to take his bandana off and she could get a look at him? Affront and dismay combined to prompt a shudder, which he strove to conceal.

"Come on." She shook the letter at him. "You want me to answer this, don't you?"

Slowly, Kasper untied the bandana and laid it on his knee.

"That's better. Where did Gertrude find a pretty boy like you, eh? But what are those bruises? You look like you've been brawling."

Kasper did not think she truly wanted an answer. He didn't think he owed her one.

"A tough sort of fellow, are you? Good with your hands?" Miss Radmacher gave an appalling little shiver of what looked like titillation.

"Ma'am, please."

"Yes, yes. You want money. The need is dire, blah, blah. You want to take the funds back with you. It states all that here."

Kasper did not know what to say.

"Tell me, young man, how would you like to come and work for me here instead of the orphanage? Still the same employer. The same pay." She smiled dreadfully. "Or depending on your duties, perhaps a bit more."

"Ma'am, I am needed at the orphanage."

"You might be needed here. You never know."

"I would not like to leave them"—he searched for the term in English—"high and dry."

"Goodness, no. Nobody wants that."

She appeared to deliberate, tapping a finger against her teeth. "Very well, I will send some funds back with you today. Not as much as Mrs. Marner has requested— that seems an exorbitant sum. But enough."

"Thank you, ma'am."

"On one condition. When Gertrude wants more from me, she will send you back to ask for it. We will sit and visit." She quirked an eyebrow. "And maybe a bit more, eh?"

Nothing, not even a threat from a Cossack's sword, would induce Kasper to agree to that. If he never set toe in this place again, it would be too soon.

"We would be very grateful for the funds."

"Grateful, eh? Good enough. Melissa!" She

bellowed very loudly for a frail old woman. "Bring me my stick."

Was there money enough in the world to compensate the maid for her service? Kasper wondered as he watched Melissa help her mistress from the room, the two of them moving slowly and painfully.

When the old lady had gone, he pushed the tea away and tied the bandana back on over his mouth. He wanted nothing Miss Radmacher offered him. Except, perhaps, the funds.

She returned in due course with a slim wallet, which she held out to him. She made sure her fingers touched his when he accepted it. Her hand felt like a bunch of sticks covered with cold parchment.

"Thank you, ma'am." He tucked the wallet into the pocket deep inside his jacket.

"You be sure to come back again, mind. And be careful out there in that wide world."

The maid, Melissa, looked like she wanted to say something to Kasper when she showed him out. She pinched her lips and said nothing.

Kasper emerged from the front door and moved as quickly as possible away from the house. He needed distance. On the sidewalk, a full-body shudder seized him. He blinked at the afternoon.

He needed to get these funds back to the orphanage as soon as possible. He walked swiftly back down Bidwell Parkway to Elmwood, where he began seeing a lot of foot traffic, more than he'd seen on his way to Miss Radmacher's. Odd, he thought. The pedestrians were all men, and they all moved at a half-jog, half-run. The fact that many of them wore bandanas like his made it seem more peculiar, like a gathering of bandits.

He swore under his breath again and increased his own pace. *Just let me reach Lost Waifs*, he beseeched in his mind. Who would ever have thought such a place as the orphanage could come to feel like a refuge? After all he'd been through in Poland, who would think he'd become spooked by the echoing streets of a city?

A paddy wagon rounded the corner onto Elmwood. It was followed by a phalanx of what could only be hybrid police officers, six of them running in three tandem rows, like matched horses.

Kasper called to them, "Officers? Is there trouble?"

They swiveled their heads to look at him. He didn't recognize any of them from his and Tori's trip to the police station. But one called back courteously, "Riot, *sor*! Do not come this way. Find another route."

Riot? Holy blessed mother. He stood where he was and watched the police jog on without another word.

And he could hear it—a harsh susurration from up ahead. More hurrying footsteps and raised voices, sounding completely unlike they came from human throats and more like the distant rumbling of a storm.

He'd heard such rumblings before, back home. The last thing he wanted was to encounter such an uprising here.

Yet he didn't know another way back to the orphanage. Unfamiliar with this city, he wasn't sure he could find an alternate route.

Surely it would be all right if he crept past whatever was up ahead? Made a shadow of himself, and slipped by?

He traced the outline of Miss Radmacher's wallet in his breast pocket. Whatever he did, whatever it took, he couldn't lose the funds entrusted to him.

Chapter Twenty-Five

Tori and Trina were clearing up after lunch in the boys' room when Daisy came running, breathless. The boys, confined like a troop of rowdy baboons, managed to make a mess of anything, including a modest meal.

Tori had an armful of plates and Trina was sweeping the floor when Daisy stuck her head in the doorway and gestured wildly.

"Tori, lass, come!"

Oh, heavens. What now? Balancing the stack of plates precariously, she stepped out into the broad upstairs hallway where Mrs. Marner already stood.

"What is it, Daisy? I'm in the middle of—"

Daisy's eyes glowed. "There's a riot up on Elmwood. I just took the dustbins out to the curb. I was going to have Tom do it, but he's busy bringing up the last of the coal from down in the cellar."

Mrs. Marner demanded, "Daisy, whatever are you talking about?"

"A huge riot. There was a meeting at the Automaton Rights Center, and people started attacking while the automatons were inside." Daisy lowered her voice. "They tried to burn the place down, while everybody was in there. Can steamies be destroyed by fire? I'm sure I don't know, them being mostly metal and all."

"If the fire is hot enough," Mrs. Marner said, "even metal warps. How did it get to Elmwood Avenue?" She glanced at Tori. "Such a respectable neighborhood."

"Spilled over," Daisy said. "People ran and congregated there. The police have been called in because things turned violent."

"Oh, this is dreadful," Mrs. Marner lamented. "I understand there is a distance between the human and metal citizens of this city, and it's been widening. But this is not the time for things to break open."

"People are saying it's the automatons who created the sickness, to get rid of us," Daisy hissed.

Tori's stomach clenched and heaved. She feared she might be sick. Kasper was out there amid a city in riot.

"How did you hear this?" Mrs. Marner asked Daisy, clearly hoping it wasn't true.

"From our neighbor, Mr. Dorsey. He was taking his bins out, too. He said now steamies from all over Buffalo are heading for the riot to—how did he put it?—form a wall of protection for any units caught there."

"If the police have been called, then surely they will handle it," Mrs. Marner declared, sounding far from confident about it.

They all eyed one another uneasily. It was Daisy who asked, "Which police have been called, I wonder? The hybrids or the human ones?"

"It should not matter. So far as I know, Buffalo's police force has always stood united. The hybrid Irish Squad are considered an asset."

"As they are," Tori murmured. "Especially now."

"Just so. Keep all the doors locked. Do not go outside for any reason."

"But Kasper's out there!" Tori wailed.

Mrs. Marner looked at her. "I know. I hope—believe—he will be all right. When he arrives, he can knock, and we will of course let him in."

Daisy fretted, "What if the riot spreads through the whole city? What if people start burning everything down? Mr. Dorsey said fire is purification."

Mrs. Marner paled, but she said, "No one would be so foolish. Now, get hold of yourselves. We don't want to frighten the children."

"Doctor Rasmussen was supposed to come," Daisy reminded her, "to look in on the sickroom. I don't suppose he'll be able to get here now."

"No, but give a listen to anyone knocking, just in case."

Oh, Tori would be listening. That was for certain.

****

The large church on the corner of Elmwood and Lafayette Avenue appeared to be under siege. The fact that it stood on a corner only made things worse, since it allowed the attackers access from two sides. Indeed, as Kasper drew closer, he could see there must be an alleyway behind the structure, for people collected there also.

The attackers were mostly—well, people. They washed up like a restless sea on a stony shore, waving their arms or whatever objects they held in their hands. Signs, workmen's tools—all had become weapons.

A ring of automatons made a frail barrier between this sea and the actual structure. Some were members of the hybrid Irish Squad. Some were ordinary steamies, come from who knew where in the surrounding neighborhood. At first glance it did not appear they'd be able to hold off the marauders for long.

But why attack a church?

Amid the automatons on the steps of the building

stood a man in a black cleric's suit. As Kasper attempted to edge past, he stepped forward and held up his hands.

"Peace!" he called out. "All of you go home and cease with this madness."

"Metal-lover!" Someone in the crowd roared back at him.

"This is a church!" the cleric returned, in a tone that implied it deserved protection.

"You're hiding steam units in there!" Another voice called from the crowd. "And hybrids!"

"I do not know what is going on," the poor cleric complained, his voice quaking, "but I will not stand by while persons of any kind are battered and beaten. If I can offer refuge, then that is what I will do."

"Then you'll take what you get!"

Mesmerized, and knowing he should move on, Kasper watched to see what would happen next. One of the hybrids in the protective ring around the church turned his head and addressed the minister, though of course Kasper couldn't hear what he said. The cleric ducked into the church and out of sight.

A wise move, without question. Kasper, who had witnessed similar scenes back in Poland, could sense things would only get uglier.

"We've set fire to their damned Automaton Rights Center—we can burn this church down too!"

"You should be ashamed," called one of the hybrids, revealing a rich Irish brogue, "attacking a house of God."

"What do you know about God, you freak?" A wildly incensed man in the front of the seething crowd called. "Just because your kind are building your own 'churches' don't mean you believe in anything!"

Kasper had to move, get off Elmwood Avenue or

find a way around, as the policeman had suggested. The noise here was deafening. The paddy wagon had, of course, arrived ahead of him, and its bell still clanged. Unable to penetrate the crowd, it stood near Kasper. The phalanx of police had run forward.

Folks pushed against and harassed the horses, which were having none of it. Someone was going to get trampled. People would die before this ended. Kasper felt that right down to his bones.

And the most frightening thing—perhaps—was that people and steamies just kept coming. From all directions, up and down Elmwood and from every side street, they ran or trundled in. The mechanical units puffed steam. The humans had tools or other weapons in their hands.

He had to get out of here. Because—oh, yes, something awful was going to happen. Something—

A figure with reddish hair and a blue uniform struggled up onto the church steps. Kasper recognized him immediately—Patrick Kelly, clearly on duty. He posed in front of the church door and raised his hands.

"People? People!"

Most failed to hear him. Those who did paid little heed.

"Listen to me!"

Neither metal nor flesh-and-blood obeyed. The metal kept rolling in, the older models making quite a din. The humans formed a mob.

Kasper turned, looking desperately for a way out, but the crowd had filled in behind him. The press of bodies jostled him toward the church.

Another figure pushed its way into place beside Kelly—no, it was a row of figures. Human or hybrid? At this distance, curiously, it was hard to tell. Probably not humans. The person beside Pat Kelly handed him something—a long, tubular object that winked silver in the afternoon light.

Not until Kelly raised the object and fired into the air did Kasper recognize it for what it was, a portable steam cannon. It discharged harmlessly into the air but claimed everybody's attention.

"Please," Kelly called again. "Listen to me."

The crowd took it down a notch. The automatons stopped moving. The humans quit yelling. It was far from quiet, but they did listen.

"We do not wish for anyone to get hurt! Everyone please go home. Move off in an orderly fashion—"

Somebody threw something. Whatever it was, it bounced off Kelly's broad chest and fell at his feet. For an instant he looked shocked or—did automatons grow angry? Could they?

The figures on either side of him closed ranks. The figure to his right was female—a woman in a neat yellow gown with black hair and brown skin.

A commotion started up not far from Kasper. A group of men pushed through the crowd carrying a wooden box. They bulled people aside and set up the box in the street facing the church steps. A man climbed up on it.

He was a stocky fellow with black hair and a balding head, perhaps forty years old. He wore workman's clothing—a brown jacket, sturdy pants, and stout boots.

He emitted aggression the way an aging automaton gives off steam.

"You listen to me!" he called and the crowd quieted further. He wore no bandana, and his voice carried the way the blast from the steam cannon had. "We, the people of Buffalo, know what you automatons are about! We're on to what you're trying to do. We declare ourselves the true residents of this city—human residents—and we're taking it back!"

The crowd at his rear erupted in wild support of the declaration. Kelly never wavered. Through the hubbub, his gaze latched onto the black-haired man to the exclusion of all else.

"Who, sir, are you?"

"Bert Warden, President of the Dockworkers' Union." The man drew a breath. "And, head of the Automaton Expulsion League!"

The silence which met that declaration was complete. Even the automatons seemed to stop breathing.

Kelly recovered swiftly. "Sir," his Irish brogue sounded rich, "I have never before heard of that organization."

"There are a lot of things you've never heard of, you hunk of rusting metal covered with stinking flesh! You abomination!"

The men around him who, Kasper now saw were dressed similarly, began to howl. It was a sound Kasper had heard back home, one that turned his blood cold in his veins.

No. Not this again. He must get out of here. Because the storm was about to break.

Kelly called, "Your insults, sir, mean nothing to me."

Warden sneered, "Just as you and your kind mean nothing to us! You, with your human wife. Yes, I know who you are. A machine, no matter how you set yourself up. You lot, with your pay packets and your buying up property. And manufacturing children to inherit it all from you! It ends here. Do you understand? It all ends here!"

The howl increased in volume. It came from human throats and rose like an ill wind.

"We mean the people of this city no harm," Kelly called. "We never have."

"Bullshit!" Warden called back. "Metal means to take everything from us. That monstrosity next to you, that calls itself a doctor—"

The woman in the yellow dress, he meant. She took a step forward and the man—male automaton?—on her other side seized her arm.

"You address me?" she called. "I am Mrs. Chastity Greely. I do not call myself a doctor."

"You've set yourself up as one! A damn hybrid. You and your ghastly crew get up to all kinds of nastiness. Stealing eyes and hair and skin from corpses. Using them to manufacture more of your kind."

"Everything we do is within the law."

Warden bellowed louder, "Stirring up this illness that besets us all! Go ahead, you God-damned mechanical whore. Admit it! You and your kind created this Black Fever in your laboratory, to wipe us out one and all!"

For an instant, the silence was complete. Then the howl became a scream as the humans stormed the church, moving forward in a heaving tide.

Kasper moved with it. He didn't have a choice. Carried like flotsam on the surface of the ocean, he was pushed from behind until, suddenly, the crowd shifted and scrambled.

The people in front of him came up against a wall of metal.

The automatons that had been charging into the street now formed a barrier. Large and small, old and new, they stood shoulder to shoulder in an attempt to block the way.

The humans attacked them with whatever they held in their hands. Tools met metal with a crash. Units went over, bellowing steam, their bodies still serving to block the way.

Someone pushed Kasper from behind, so hard that he fell over a downed unit and struck his face hard on the bricks of the street. He lay there, unable to get back up for the press of bodies, and felt the unit over which he'd stumbled shift aside.

It moved out from under him, raised up onto its arms, slid above Kasper, and shielded him with its metal torso. The crowd went over them. Steam cannon fire erupted on all sides. Had the regular—human—police arrived? Kasper struggled to raise his head and see. His metal companion pushed him down again gently.

"Lie still, sir."

The voice sounded a little like a gurgle, perhaps because the unit was prone. Kasper obeyed it. He could feel heat pouring from the metal skin just above him. And he heard repeated clangs as the feet of the rioters went over them, striking his companion. They struck him too, on his knees and shins, even though he lay mostly protected.

A deafening sound filled his ears amid the roar of the crowd, a throb that increased in volume as it beat through the air.

"What is that?" he gasped.

"Airship, I believe," his companion answered, even though Kasper hadn't expected a reply.

Kasper sat up. This time, his companion allowed him. Most of the mob had passed over them. A living, breathing threat, it besieged the church.

Kasper could no longer see the figures on the steps and had no idea what had happened to them.

Overhead—

Kasper blinked and stared. He'd seen steam airships before, of course, in Europe. But only from a distance. This one loomed so low over the street he could see every detail, from the lettering on its envelope to the men hanging over the edges of its gondola.

The envelope was dark blue. The men were police officers. They had bullhorns and they shouted instructions.

Go home. Clear the streets. Violators will be arrested.

Arrested by whom? Kasper could no longer see any police on the ground, hybrid or otherwise. The besiegement of the church continued, a ghastly thing in its own right.

The ground all around them lay littered with the fallen, both metal and human.

The bullhorn sounded again. *Clear the streets! A shelter-in-place order is in effect!*

The throb of the steam engines seemed to reach right inside Kasper and grab hold of his guts, pulverizing.

"We had better obey," his companion said, allowing Kasper room.

"Yes." Kasper wanted away from here, nothing more. He staggered to his feet.

His companion also struggled to rise. Kasper lent

him a hand and hauled him up.

He was large and heavy. He stood a good six inches taller than Kasper, who nearly topped six feet. He appeared to be a newer unit with deeply-sculpted features and black, painted eyes.

"Thank you, sir," he said.

"No, thank you. I think you saved my life."

"Life is precious, sir, whether metal or flesh."

"Are you all right?"

"Fortunately, my fire did not go out when I was pushed over. I appear to have a few dents."

"Me too, I think." Kasper's shins ached from being kicked and trodden.

The airship passed directly over them. They both tipped back their heads, looking up at it.

"This is madness," Kasper said.

"I agree."

"You would not—the automatons would never do such a thing, right? Create the illness, I mean."

The unit looked at him. "I do not believe so, sir. But I am just a simple drayman, looking to do my work. I know little about sickness."

"Nor I."

"We had better follow instructions and go home."

This unit had a home. Just like Kasper, it wanted to get there.

"Thank you again. Do you have a name?"

"They call me Haddy, sir. I do not know why."

"Thank you, Haddy. Go home safe."

The unit headed north and Kasper south. He slipped away, shins still aching, and left the chaos behind.

Chapter Twenty-Six

He half expected to encounter the plague doctor on the way home. It would, so he reflected, be all this terrible day needed to round out the horror. He didn't, though he did encounter plenty of people heading the other way toward the riot. Two more paddy wagons, these without accompanying squadrons of hybrid police. An ambulance. Curious members of the public, all humans.

He'd checked to make sure he still had Miss Radmacher's slim wallet, that it hadn't been lost in the scuffle, and ran to Breckenridge Street with his hand pressed over it.

The street looked deserted. When he reached the orphanage, it was tightly locked down and panic fluttered in his gut. What if he couldn't get in?

He went around back and pounded on the kitchen door. Becky looked out, her face appearing both vacant and anxious at the same time. She opened the door.

"Becky! I am glad to see you."

Before the unit could reply, Tori appeared and ducked around the steamie straight into Kasper's arms.

"Oh! Oh, I'm so glad you're back. I was terribly frightened."

He wanted to say he was glad too, but he was silenced by emotion—overcome by the sensation of her huddled against him, trembling. The feel of her arm clutching at him so tightly and her body burrowing in. He would like such a welcome every day for the rest of his life.

She drew away much too soon. Eyes wide, she said, "Did you know there's a riot?"

"*Tak*, I got caught in it."

"Is that what happened to your face?" She touched his cheek gently. "You're bleeding."

"Am I?"

"Yes." Her fingers caressed his face below the cheekbone. "Here."

"That must be where I hit the bricks of the street. I was pushed down."

Becky gusted a little breath of steam. "I will get a basin, miss. We will tend him."

"Yes, please do that."

The unit trundled off. Tori's green eyes gleamed at Kasper for an instant before she lifted onto her toes and kissed him.

As a kiss, it was quite expressive. Kasper felt all her fear for him in it, her relief, and a whole boatload of desire. Had his own composure not just taken a beating, he might have handled it with some aplomb. As it was, he wrapped both arms around her and answered her enthusiasm with fervor of his own.

Neither of them heard Becky come rolling back. She bumped Tori gently on the shoulder with her basin.

"Ahem, miss."

Even then, Tori's mouth left Kasper's with reluctance. Her tongue caressed his, and her lips clung. Her eyes looked misty when she gazed at him.

"Come sit down." She pushed him into a chair at the kitchen table. "Thank you, Becky. Please go and fetch

Mrs. Marner."

Becky hurried out again. Tori leaned forward and kissed Kasper once more, as if she couldn't get enough. He had no objection to that. He could go on doing this all night. For multiple nights.

Yet he abandoned her lips to say, "Do we truly want Mrs. Marner?"

"No. I wanted to get rid of Becky so I could kiss you again. Anyway—anyway, Mrs. Marner asked to be informed the minute you got back. Did you see Miss Radmacher?"

"Yes."

Tori asked even more softly, "Did you get the funds?"

"Yes." Kasper's hand flew to his breast pocket, fearing he might have dropped the wallet after all, but it was there.

Mrs. Marner hurried into the kitchen with Becky in tow. The woman still bore little lingering resemblance to the neat, collected manageress who had hired Kasper only a short time ago. Her hair straggled down her neck and her eyes looked frantic.

"Kasper?" she echoed Tori's query. "Were you allowed to see Miss Radmacher?"

"I was." Kasper struggled to his feet and drew the wallet from his pocket. As soon as Mrs. Marner saw it, some of her agitation calmed.

"Oh, thank goodness!"

"Miss Radmacher read your note. I do not think she sent as much money as you requested. But it is something." He handed over the wallet.

There in front of the three of them, Mrs. Marner opened the wallet and counted out the funds. It looked

188

like a fortune to Kasper. He supposed when running a large household, it wasn't.

"Enough to buy some coal. And food. What happened to your face?" Mrs. Marner asked belatedly.

"There is a riot going on, farther up Elmwood Avenue. I got caught in it on the way back."

"Goodness!" She looked at him, seeming to focus on him for the first time. "I am sorry I had to put you in danger. And thank you—thank you for bringing back the funds we need."

"Of course." What else did she think he would do? Make off with them? He was an honest man.

"Miss Radmacher received you without difficulty?"

"Yes, Mrs. Marner."

"Good. Perhaps if we need to apply for more funds, you can go back to her again."

"As for that—" Kasper shifted on his feet. "Might I ask you a question?"

"Yes."

He hesitated. "Did you send me to Miss Radmacher because she—well, because she has a liking for younger men?"

Tori stiffened in shock. Mrs. Marner flushed deep red, and Becky listened avidly.

For an instant, Kasper thought Mrs. Marner would deny it. He supposed she'd haul on her dignity, but instead she crumbled.

"Oh, I am sorry! Was she terribly inappropriate with you? Yes, she has a reputation for it. I thought she might be better disposed to help us if approached by a handsome young man such as yourself."

"Mrs. Marner!" Tori breathed.

"I have said I am sorry. I was desperate. I have this

entire household to fund, all the children—I feared she would not even agree to see someone from Lost Waifs."

Kasper sympathized. He didn't like to watch Mrs. Marner writhe in her embarrassment. But he said, "I am not comfortable with being—" he searched for the correct phrase, "used in such a manner."

"I understand."

"I do not think I would want to go back there again."

Mrs. Marner began to weep. Tori looked appalled, and Becky let out a little sympathetic gust of steam.

"Mrs. Marner, you're exhausted," Tori said. "When is the last time you slept?"

"I do not know."

"You should go to your room now," Tori told her. "We have the funds for the coal, so that's one worry gone. No more children have fallen ill. Let's all hold tight till tomorrow morning."

"Yes, Tori. Yes, you're right. If the city's in riot, there's nothing we can do except lock the doors and wait till morning." Mrs. Marner reached impulsively for Kasper's hand. "Again, I am sorry. Tori, take care of him."

"Oh I will, Mrs. Marner," Tori assured her devoutly. "I will."

****

Tori looked at herself in the cheval mirror she'd dragged into her tiny room from the open part of the attic. The glass was cracked and the finish so worn she couldn't be sure it showed her an accurate image.

Night had fallen, and the house, per Mrs. Marner's instructions, was locked down tight. Mrs. Marner had retreated to her room behind her office on the first floor. Daisy held her post in the nursery. The automatons were all on duty.

Kasper was in his room alone. Tori didn't mean to leave him that way.

She wore her best nightgown, which she'd collected from home the day she and Kasper went to visit their mothers. Even her best, though, was terribly plain. It had lace at the neck and cuffs, and covered her all the way from her neck to her feet. She'd combed out her hair so it flowed loose down her back.

The effect was rather ruined by her withered arm and turned foot. She intended to offer herself to Kasper like a dinner on a plate. How tempting a prospect was she, though, with her deformities? Kasper insisted he didn't mind them. But still—looking at herself now in the cracked glass, she very swiftly lost her confidence.

She hadn't missed the implications of what Kasper had said in the kitchen. Mrs. Marner had sent him to Miss Radmacher as a kind of ploy. Because he was a fine-looking young man.

What would a perfect specimen like him want with her?

She raised up on the bare toes of her good foot and turned from side to side. Ma always lamented that something must have gone wrong before Tori was born, inside the womb. Maybe because the family hadn't had enough to eat back then. Not a thing Tori could help. Yet it flushed her cheeks with shame.

On the other hand—maybe Kasper truly didn't mind. There were those kisses he and she had shared in the kitchen. And the way he made her feel. There was also the situation beyond the walls of this orphanage, in the city at large. The plague doctor, the sickness. The rioting, the upheaval.

The threat of imminent death.

That lent a bit of, well, impetus, didn't it? Pleasure not seized now might never be had.

Tori had never expected to marry. Not given her appearance and her position in the world. She'd hoped for a job she could tolerate, to help support Ma. To maybe do some good in the world.

If she didn't intend to marry, for what was she saving herself? Her much-touted virtue wasn't worth much to anyone. They might all end up dying, and she wouldn't know what it was like to lie with a man.

She could have Kasper, though. Maybe tonight.

What would it be like, lying with Kasper? At liberty to touch him. Feeling him touch her all over. She couldn't even imagine it.

She wanted to know. She wanted what she wanted, for once in her life.

"Do I dare?" she asked the girl in the clouded mirror. "Do I dare walk across that hallway, to him?"

The girl in the mirror, her withered arm clutched tight to her chest, gave a mysterious smile. "Since this may be your only chance, yes, I think you damn well better."

Chapter Twenty-Seven

Tori stood outside Kasper's closed door so long her bare feet grew icy and her courage very nearly deserted her. Nearly, but not quite. Desire, so she discovered, proved stronger than fear, which no doubt explained how so many young women got in trouble.

Young women like her.

She didn't quite have the cheek to knock on Kasper's door. Somebody downstairs might hear. Instead she cracked it open and whispered, "Kasper?"

No reply. He slept. She should just turn around and go back to her room.

Instead, surprising herself, she slipped inside and closed the door behind her. "Kasper?"

"Tori?" He moved in the bed and half sat up. She could just see him in the faint light coming through the dormer window. "What has happened? What is wrong?"

"Nothing." She floated to the bed. She no longer felt connected to her feet. Or possibly, to reality. Something else moved her, took her beyond herself. "Might I stay here with you tonight?"

He froze. For an instant he stopped breathing. Tori heard him gasp when he started up again.

"Let me make myself clear," she whispered. "I want to be with you tonight. Not sleep."

"You—I—" He seemed to wrestle with it silently. "I have no words. In English."

"Speak Polish then. I don't care."

She walked softly forward till she could perch on the edge of his bed, and he let her, moving aside the required inches to afford her space.

"If I speak Polish, you will not understand when I tell you it is not a good idea."

"Good. Because I don't want to hear that." She leaned in and kissed him. As an exercise, in the near dark, it was delectable and sent most of her fear to flight. Kissing him was like striking a match. She felt surprised the sheets didn't immediately catch fire.

Kasper participated with surprising enthusiasm, for a man who must be shocked by her audacity. A fog had collected in Tori's brain before he pulled away slightly to say, "Tori, do I understand you to mean—"

"I've never been with anyone. I want it to be you."

He swore softly in what must be Polish. "I do not wish to take advantage of you."

Tori's heart sank. He was going refuse. "Is it the arm?" she asked.

"The what?"

"My arm. Or my foot. The fact that I'm—"

"No. No, Tori, you are beautiful. So beautiful."

"Then don't worry about taking advantage. Just kiss me."

They kissed. And kissed. Kasper drew Tori under the covers where they explored one another by touch. Kasper wore only his smalls. His chest, gloriously bare, felt warm beneath the palm of Tori's good hand, rough with crisp hairs. His hands moved over her gently, spreading heat everywhere they touched. The back of her neck, when he deepened the kiss. Down her spine to the hem of her nightgown, which had rucked up, and under it. Against the bare skin beneath.

She forgot about her arm, a thing that rarely happened. She stretched herself against him like a cat and purred deep in her throat while they continued to kiss. She forgot about the world and all its madness.

"Tori—"

"Don't talk. Don't think."

He'd gone hard down below. She could feel that right through his smalls. So—that was how men got the job done. She explored with her fingers, wondering if it weren't too big to fit inside her, and went limp with desire. Funny how he'd gone so hard and she so soft and receptive.

"Tori." He slid the nightgown up her body and over her head. So maybe it didn't matter what she wore. There was a bad moment when the sleeve of the gown got hung up on her withered arm. Tori barely cared, because Kasper cast the nightgown aside and put his lips to her breast.

"Beautiful," he murmured. "Beautiful."

Tori failed to listen. Never had she suspected such pleasure could exist. It lit her just like a candle from one end to the other, and made her abandon any remaining shreds of doubt.

To think she might have gone to her grave without experiencing this.

She cradled Kasper's head and stroked his hair while he feasted on one breast and then the other. When at last his mouth returned to hers, it was with a spate of Polish, a question.

"Hmmm," she replied. She didn't want to answer questions. She wanted more and more.

Another rush of words.

"Don't worry about it."

Somehow, with their bodies pressed together and using only her good hand, she got him out of his smalls. Her body knew what to do by then. Cling to his. Open and inviting. Welcome him in.

Another rush of Polish in her ear, and then, "It might hurt."

"I don't mind."

It did hurt for an instant, swiftly lost in a surge of pleasure so pure and strong it lifted Tori to another place. In that place, she belonged to Kasper and he to her.

She never wanted to leave this place.

"Tori, Tori—" He kissed her all over her face and swallowed the breaths that came from her. It seemed all he was able to say—her name.

She clung to him with her one good arm, and they calmed, heartbeats easing, relaxed with one another.

Tori's thoughts moved sluggishly, glorying in what she'd just done. Anything to regret? No room for regret, in this. She felt warm and safe in his arms. Cherished.

Brushing her lips across his, she said, "You may speak to me in Polish any time you like. It is the most titillating thing I've ever heard."

"What is this word—titillating?"

She leaned up to his ear and told him.

He laughed, and she reconsidered. Perhaps his laughter, here in the dark, was even more titillating.

****

They slept there together in Kasper's bed. He awoke sometime later to find Tori draped all over him. But for that he'd have thought it a dream, because he'd dreamed of her in the past.

Nothing like this.

Why had she done it? Why come walking in through his door in her sweet, white gown and offering herself to him? He'd fallen for her quite some time ago. He'd had no indication she felt the same for him.

Back home in Poland, there had been a few such encounters, quick and desperate. There'd been the sense, always, that life could end at any time. His heart had never been involved.

Till now.

Was that what drove Tori to bring herself to him? The fear and uncertainty? The conviction there might not be many tomorrows?

If so, he could not express his feelings for her. How awkward, how embarrassing that would be if he hung himself out there, only to find she did not feel the same, and that he was only a convenience. A male, ready to hand. At best, a friend.

He did not want Tori Anderson as a friend. Well, he did—but he wanted her far more as a lover.

He could say none of it. The words may well have slipped out while they were making love. But he'd spoken them, most fortunately, in Polish, all English words having deserted him.

"*Kocham Cię*, Tori. *Kocham Cię*."

She did not know what that meant or that it came from his heart.

For now, it must be enough just to hold her while she slept. How trustingly she lay against him, her maimed arm caught between their bodies. He stroked it gently, wishing he could place a kiss in the palm of the hand.

She was like no one else, his Tori.

He closed his eyes and relived it all again—the way

she'd clung to him, the way she'd parted her thighs, inviting him in. The feel of her nipple against his tongue. The heat of her when he pushed inside.

She trusted him with her body, if not her heart. He would never betray that trust.

He dozed, only to come awake upon a rush of sensation. Tori's fingers, wrapped around him. He was already up and ready.

"Kasper? Kasper—"

No further words were needed this time. Like two creatures obsessed with mating, their bodies knew what to do. All her barriers down, Tori had shed any inhibitions. She presented her breasts to him and took what she wanted in turn. She left him flushed with heat, soaked with sweat, and limp.

"I will have to go back to my room soon, so nobody knows I've been here."

"Umm." He had no other words, his mind blasted. One thought presented itself to him. How was he supposed to work alongside her after this, and behave as if he hadn't possessed her most intimately?

"And," she went on, "if we do not get caught, we can do this again. Tomorrow night."

"We can?"

"Yes. We just have to make sure we are both off at the same time. Unless—" She stiffened against him. "You don't want to."

"I want to." Oh, he wanted to. More than breathing, quite possibly.

"Good." She leaned in and kissed him hard. "I must leave you now. Where is my nightgown?"

Kasper neither knew nor cared. He watched through narrowed, hazy eyes while she fished around and found it and struggled to get it over her head. Gathering her legs beneath her, she scrambled to her feet.

"Oh, I nearly forgot." At the last moment she turned back toward the bed. "That fellow came looking for you while you were gone to Miss Radmacher's."

"What fellow?"

"The one who was here before, called Josef."

Kasper's peaceful stupor flew away, the hazy warmth replaced with a spate of cold. His eyes went wide.

"What did he want?"

"He didn't say, really. Just that he'd be back. That's not good, is it?"

"No." Oh, no, anything but.

Chapter Twenty-Eight

Mrs. Marner sent Tom out the next morning to buy a copy of the *Courier Express*. News of the riot was splashed all over the front page and several other pages within.

They all gathered in the foyer to look at it, Mrs. Marner spreading it out on a side table. Some of the household steamies even stood by as Daisy read bits out loud.

This news, as became quite evident, affected them as much as anyone.

Tori found herself feeling grateful Kasper had made it home safely through all that. The descriptions of what had happened, all laid down in black and white, made her fear for him all over again. Even though he stood right beside Daisy while she read.

Stood there with his dark hair all tousled and the scrape at the side of his face, with those hands that had touched her all over.

She couldn't help it—she couldn't keep from feeling possessive about him. After what they'd shared, and all they'd done. Those beautiful hands were now hers along with the hard, strong body beneath the simple clothing he wore. The thought of having him again, maybe as soon as tonight, made her go as breathless as she had upstairs in his room when he—

He glanced up at that moment, and their eyes met.

She no longer knew what Daisy was reading. Kasper's eyes glowed like sapphires. In them she saw the shared memory of each touch and every kiss.

Good heavens! Someone was going to see how she felt. Even after a life of insults and, yes, whispered comments, she wasn't particularly good at hiding her reactions.

"Thank goodness," Mrs. Marner broke through her thoughts, "the police were able to break up the riot. Imagine! Storming a church. But this article says it didn't end there. After the crowd left the church, many of them ran through the streets spreading havoc and destruction. That's what it says here—*havoc and destruction.*"

"What sort of destruction?" Tori asked, tearing her gaze from Kasper.

Daisy, her eyes on the newssheet, answered, "Starting fires, turning over dustbins, breaking windows—and attacking automatons." She too shot a look at Kasper. "You're lucky you got home in one piece, my lad."

"I had some help. A steamie called Haddy protected me when the mob rushed over us. I hope he is all right."

"Before the riot at the church was quelled, so it says, some of the hybrids there were hurt."

"Not Patrick Kelly, I hope. He was there. I saw him."

"Doesn't mention him by name. Says a 'Mrs. Chastity Greely' was damaged, though. She's that hybrid doctor, isn't she? I suppose the attackers think she'd be involved with researching up this fever they're accusing the hybrids of starting."

Kasper looked troubled.

Daisy slanted a look at Mrs. Marner. "You don't

think they'd do that, do you? Manufacture the fever, I mean. Just to get rid of all of us, the way this Automaton Expulsion League claims?"

Mrs. Marner pressed her lips together. "I wouldn't like to think so."

The occupants of the foyer, metal and flesh alike, looked at each other.

"All I know is," Daisy commented, "the cases of fever in the city are rising. If we didn't have the automatons right now, everything would grind to a halt."

"How many cases are there?" Tori asked. "Does the paper say?" They'd been fortunate here at Lost Waifs. No more children had fallen ill, and those in the sickroom were holding their own.

Daisy turned a page of the paper and froze. "Oh, sweet Jaysus!"

"What is it?"

"Says here, sightings of the plague doctor figure are also spiking. The police—that would be the Irish Squad, I suppose—have put out a request for a report of all sightings. They have vowed to track the figures, that's what it says, *figures*, down and discover who's behind them.

"It asks the public to—to trap one of the figures if possible, hold it, and send for them immediately."

Hold it? Touch it? Tori experienced a full-body shudder that actually served to drive the thought of Kasper from her mind for the first time since she'd been with him last night.

Mrs. Marner looked skeptical. Daisy trembled. Kasper appeared nearly as horrified as Tori felt. Tom and Hank, who also listened, of course wore no expressions, but Tori fancied they were also appalled.

Tori whispered, "How could one plague doctor turn into so many?"

"Someone is dressing up like that," Daisy announced, "to terrorize the city."

"Yes," Kasper agreed.

But why? And who was behind it? Humans or automatons?

****

"Do ye want to tell me about it?" Daisy's rich Irish brogue sounded in Tori's ear, making her jump.

It had been a busy morning. Well, most of them were, these days. Even with the three additional automatons, the orphanage felt short-staffed.

"Tell you about what?"

They'd met in the kitchen where they once more cut sandwiches. Thankfully, Mrs. Marner had sent Tom to the bakery for bread, solving one pressing problem.

"Come now, lass, I thought we were friends."

"So we are." Tori looked at Daisy in surprise.

"Then tell me what's going on between you two." Daisy nodded her head at Kasper, whom they could see through the doorway of the laundry. He'd squatted down, trying to adjust Tom's arm at the elbow. It had been giving the big automaton trouble.

"Me and Tom?"

"Fool," Daisy grunted. "I'm talkin' about Mr. Fix-It there. You've barely been able to take your eyes off him."

"He's—he's handsome."

"He is that. But I'm after thinkin' there's more to it. And I haven't forgotten that I caught you in his room, that time. Funny—I always thought it would be Rasmussen for you."

"Dr. Rasmussen?"

"Sure. Have you never noticed how much nicer he is to you than the rest of us, when he calls?"

"I always thought that was pity," Tori admitted bleakly. "Because of my arm."

"He's sweet on you. And you could do worse than to marry a doctor."

"I like Dr. Rasmussen. He's a good man. But not to marry."

"Huh. A poor decision, if ever I heard one. So what's between you and Kasper?" Daisy's eyes sparkled with curiosity. "Have you been after stealing kisses?"

Had she? Tongues tangling, the flavor of honey, and deep, delectable heat as they kissed over and over again.

"You have. You're blushing. What was it like?"

Tori had no words. "Good," she dredged up helplessly. "It was good."

"Well, you be careful, my girl. Make sure you don't get stupid and let it move beyond a few kisses. A woman can get in trouble that way."

"Trouble?"

"Yes. He looks healthy enough."

"Healthy enough for what?"

"To put a brat in your belly, like I said."

"Oh. Oh, Daisy—" Tori could now feel the heat scorching her face.

"Don't say he wouldn't want to. I've seen him lookin' back at you."

Had he?

"And while I ain't opposed to a bit of romance— even if it is here beneath this roof, where it's forbidden— I wouldn't want to see you come to grief."

"I understand."

Daisy fixed Tori with a hard eye. "You wouldn't, would you? 'Cause I can almost smell the lust every time you're in the same room. You wouldn't be so foolish."

"Of course not," Tori assured Daisy demurely.

She could barely wait till tonight.

****

They met later when Tori, taking something out to the bins, found Kasper standing at the rear door, gazing out through the wavy glass pane. Dark had just begun to gather, and Becky still worked, doing a stint in the laundry. Tori could hear the mangle running as she stepped to Kasper's side.

Not the most romantic of music, but it might be a symphony, for all Tori knew.

"What are you doing?" she asked him. "Looking for the plague doctor?"

Kasper gave a shiver. "Him, I do not want to see. Though I'm thinking it might be interesting to unmask him—like the newssheet said."

"I'm not sure I want to see what's under that terrible head and beak. Man or automaton?" Another thought struck Tori. "Oh, are you here watching for your visitor, Josef?"

"Him, I do not want to see either."

"He hasn't come back?"

"Not yet. If you are taking those things to the dustbin, I will do it. You are not going out there now it's dark."

"I'll be fine, Kasper."

"Tori—" In answer to her day-long prayers, he touched her. He laid a hand on her shoulder, keeping her from unlocking the door.

A simple touch, yet it opened the flood gates. Tori

dropped the bag of trash on the floor and stepped into his arms.

And oh, oh—she'd wanted this, she'd longed for it all day. She needed this. Feeling the hard wall of his chest with his heart hammering beneath the muscles, right up against her breasts. The smell of him, the taste when their mouths met, frantic and hungry for one another. There, in the rather squalid surroundings of the back entryway that hadn't been scrubbed in far too long, beauty bloomed, and Tori's heart opened and bloomed right along with it.

"I need you," Kasper said raggedly when they came up for air. "Tell me we will be together tonight."

Tori had meant to share Daisy's concerns with him, but all that flew from her head. She threaded the fingers of her good hand through his hair and gazed into his eyes. "Yes. Will you be off duty soon?"

"Mrs. Marner has been giving me my nights off since I'm needed during the day."

"She's given me tonight off also. She's been assigning the steamies to night—" She stopped speaking when Kasper claimed her lips again. All the things they would do together lay in that kiss. It made her shiver with delight and burn with heat.

"I suppose we ought to be careful."

"Careful?" he repeated. He nuzzled her neck and moved lower, breastward.

"We could—I could—you could give me your babe."

That stopped him cold. He raised his head and looked at her. What did she see in his deep blue eyes? A wealth of emotions teeming there. Desire, yes, a steady light of it. Doubt and wonder and—oh, would he push her away from him now? Would he have done with their association, end it all?

"Tori," he said gravely, and took her hand between both of his.

Here it comes, she thought. He's going to tell me that, quite foolishly, he never thought of that. He just landed in this country and is trying to make his way. He, like me, has a mother to support. And the kind of girl who would present herself to a man between his sheets like a—well, like a five-course meal—is just a passing fancy anyway.

"Tori…" He squeezed her fingers tight. "I hope you know that, should such a thing happen, I would want to marry you. If you would have me, that is."

If she would have him. Tori's heart quivered in her chest, leapt and considered dying on the spot. But it couldn't. She was going to need her heart later tonight.

"I will meet you later, Kasper. My room, this time. I can't wait!"

Chapter Twenty-Nine

Kasper stepped outside and let the cool air wash over him, taking his temperature down a notch. Talk about fever! All he had to do was look at Tori and he became drenched with heat. The taste of her enflamed him, and made him ache to be inside her. But it was more than that. He wanted to be in her company, and to hold her in his arms while he slept.

Would she be willing to marry him? He had little enough to offer her besides this passion that seemed to burn so brightly for both of them. No money, no. He couldn't even read English yet. He had the strength of his back and would be willing to work hard for her, but—

Of course he'd have to offer. He had taken her virginity. An offer of marriage was what a decent man provided. And though he might not have seemed it in his bed last night, he was a decent man.

It would all be up to Tori, whether she accepted him or not.

He stepped across the yard to the dustbins and something beside them moved. A tall figure stepped forward from the shadows.

The plague doctor.

Kasper's heart stopped in his chest. It seized so tightly that for an instant he thought he would die.

The figure loomed over him. Long brown robes the color of dirt. Two slits in the mask for eyes—was there anything underneath? And the beak which, in some indeterminate way, appeared so threatening.

That beak—it turned down at the end and came to a sharp point. It looked like something from a horrifying dream.

His heart thudded back to life with a kick like that of a draft horse. The thing stood less than two feet from him. If it touched him—

He swore devoutly in Polish.

The figure laughed.

The laugh sounded stifled inside the mask, but it was a laugh all the same. Mysterious as the figure looked, there was someone inside.

Someone human?

Kasper lunged, his hands reaching for the head. He didn't want to touch the figure—superstition burned deep, and argued he'd fall sick if he did. But anger helped. He didn't like being frightened. He didn't like the whole blessed city reduced to fear.

The figure moved when he did, and he missed his grab of the beak. Instead he knocked the head off. It tumbled down and hit the sparse grass in front of the dust bins.

The figure swore back at him. In Polish.

He blinked at what he saw. Fair, tumbled hair. Sharp features—almost a milder echo of the mask's—still wearing some bruises. Mad blue eyes.

Josef.

"No need to attack me—again." Josef spoke in Polish and he sounded resentful. He picked up the bird head—it was the kind of mask that fit over his whole head—and cradled it in his arms.

"Holy mother! Josef? What are you doing here? *You*

are the plague doctor?"

"One of them. And despite what happened the last time we met, I am here to do you a favor."

"A favor?" That he found difficult to believe.

"*Tak*. To offer you an opportunity, as a fellow countryman."

Kasper shifted on his feet. He felt as if reality had just split wide open. It was hard to grasp. "Opportunity?"

"For a job."

"I have a job."

Josef sneered. "Here at this place? I am talking about a *good* job—an easy one—making good money for doing nothing more than walking around the city."

"As you are doing? As the plague doctor?" Kasper shook his head. "Frightening people half to death?"

"Who cares? It is easy, and they pay me."

Now Kasper sneered. "Who hired you?"

"I do not know."

"You must. Who would take a job without knowing for whom he is working?"

"It was a man who hired me. We met him at the tavern. He hired all three of us. Me, Stor, and Lech."

"He did not give you his name?"

"He did not."

"What did he look like?"

"Just a man. Most of his face was covered. He said we'd get paid well, and we were. He sent us to a certain address where we were given our costumes. Do you like my costume? I hope you did not damage the beak."

Kasper blinked. The mask, as he could now see, was made of papier-mâché. His mind raced.

"This person who hired you and the others, he was a man? A human, I mean. Not a machine?"

"From what I could see."

"How many of you are there? How many plague doctors?"

"I do not know." Josef shrugged. "And I did not come here for you to ask me questions but to offer you an opportunity."

"To dress up like that? To frighten people?"

"To make some good money, as I say. The man who hired us said if we knew anyone else, we could collect a bonus."

"A bonus!" For an instant, Kasper saw red.

"What is wrong with that? We need to make our way in a new city. People here are not so welcoming. They call us stupid. You know that."

"*Tak.*"

"Think of all the great minds back home. The buildings. The art, the music! And they call us stupid! I am not stupid."

No, just crazy.

"If I frighten them a little bit, maybe they deserve it."

"What about the Black Fever?"

"What about it?"

"People believe the plague doctor is spreading it."

"Well, I am not." He swung the censer, which he held by its chain. "This is just some nasty incense. The stuff in church back home smelled better, didn't it?" He glared at Kasper. "Look, I came to do you a favor. If you don't want that—"

"I do not. You should go to the police."

"Why?"

"You have information that could help find out who is paying you. And who's spreading the sickness."

"The police can go bugger themselves. Though I don't suppose they can." Josef laughed again. "They're mostly hybrids. People are saying that hybrid woman doctor created the sickness in her laboratory, just like a Frankenstein, yes?"

"You think that's true?"

"Who else would want all of us dead? As a matter of fact, the man who hired us could have been a hybrid. Damned if I can tell the difference."

"If so, then you're working for those who would destroy us all."

"Is that any worse than what we did back in Poland, to survive? I once killed an old woman for the pennies she had in her pocket."

"You did that?"

"I was hungry. And I ate that day." Josef stabbed a finger at Kasper. "I survived, and that got me here, didn't it? I am still surviving. We thought things would be better here, and maybe they can be, Kasprczak, so long as I don't care what I have to do to earn my bread."

Kasper cared, but he didn't say so. No point. Josef was either mad or past redemption.

"Give me the address of this man," he said, "the one who will hire me. How can I find him?"

"You have changed your mind?"

"Maybe. *Tak.*"

"I do not believe you. If I tell you how to find him you will run straight to the stinking hybrid police. You'll ruin my good job."

"I will not."

"I cannot trust you. I should not have come here. Try to do someone a favor—"

Kasper leaped for him, his one thought being to hold

him till he could holler for Tom or Hank to fetch the police. Josef moved just as swiftly. His robe swirled, and from its folds he produced a knife. A wild swipe brought it in contact with Kasper's right arm.

Instinctively, Kasper leaped away. Josef swore bitterly and fled, leaving his papier-mâché bird head behind.

For an instant Kasper stood frozen in shock. The knife had traced the inside of his arm, but for several moments he felt no pain. Then it came with a rush, along with the blood—a wild, hot sting.

The back door cracked open and light spilled out.

"Mr. Kasper? Are you well?" Becky's mechanical voice somehow expressed concern.

"I'm injured, Becky. I'm bleeding."

"Oh, goodness! Oh, goodness, Kasper!" And wailing, she dragged him inside.

Chapter Thirty

Tori had just handed over her shift in the girls' room to Trina when the wailing began. The girls' room seemed to have become Tori and Trina's domain. She and the tiny unit worked well in tandem there, growing comfortable with one another. They settled the girls for the night, and Tori turned her thoughts to the hours to come.

Kasper and her alone together. Her room, his room, she didn't care. She ached for him.

No one had ever told her a woman could ache for a man, could crave the taste of him so much she thought she'd go mad.

The wail arose, and she and Trina exchanged a look.

"Miss Tori, what is that?"

"Good God, I don't know." It sounded like an ambulance, only she didn't think it came from outside. Downstairs, maybe? Either way, it brought up the hairs on the back of her neck.

"Stay here," she told Trina, casting a look at the rows of sleeping children. "I'll go and see."

Out in the upstairs hallway, she met Daisy, who leaned out from the nursery. "What—"

"I don't know." It rose and fell in undulating waves.

Mrs. Marner appeared from the sickroom, as did Tom and Hank from the boys' dormitory.

"For the love of God!" Mrs. Marner cried.

"I'll go see." Tori started for the stairs.

"Tom, go with her."

The unit rattled and creaked so much on the stairs behind Tori, he nearly drowned out the wailing. At the foot of the flight, Tori paused.

"I believe it is coming from the kitchen."

"Yes."

At the kitchen door, Tori paused again, the scene there freezing her in place.

Becky stood at the center of the room beside the big plank table. It was she who wailed, precisely like she'd been equipped with a siren. As she wailed, she waved her hands at—

Kasper, who sat at the table. Tori blinked and tried to comprehend what she saw. The sleeve of Kasper's shirt was torn. Blood covered the fabric and had spread everywhere—onto the table and the floor. He tried to stanch it with a cloth from the drainboard, but it seeped between his fingers.

Tom gently bumped into Tori from behind. He nudged her aside and rolled forward to Becky. "Stop it. Stop that noise."

Thankfully, she did. Kasper raised his bent head, from inspecting his wound—yes, it was a wound—and met Tori's gaze. Her paralysis broke, and she hurried to him.

"What's happened?"

He appeared to be in shock, his eyes too wide and his skin pasty. He fumbled for words in English. "I saw it. In the yard. Only it's not an *it*, it's a man. One of them, no doubt. And I know him. He cut me—"

Clearly. The wound extended from well above Kasper's elbow and ended just above his wrist. Any lower, and he might have bled out by now. He still might.

The room swayed around Tori. She pulled herself together hastily. "Give me that." She took the cloth from Kasper. "It isn't clean. Becky, bring me a sheet from the laundry room, one of the ones waiting for mending. Mind, make sure it's clean."

Tori had never seen so much blood. She focused on Kasper's face. "You saw *what* in the yard?"

"The plague doctor."

Tori's legs threatened to fail her. "Is it still there?"

"No. He ran off. After he slashed me. I knocked his mask off—it's still out there."

Tori glanced at the back door. All the money in Buffalo couldn't get her to go outside and look.

"Tom, is the door locked? Make sure."

Tom trundled to the door, checked the lock, and stationed himself in front of it.

"What is going on?" Mrs. Marner stood in the door to the hallway. She took one look and her eyes rolled back in her head. She fell slowly, her body attaining a state of collapse limb by limb and spreading out almost gracefully on the floor.

"Good God!" Tori exclaimed. "Tom, you must go fetch Dr. Rasmussen."

"For Mrs. Marner or Mr. Kasper?"

"Both. For both!"

****

Daisy arrived from upstairs and took charge of things, though Tori had herself well in hand by then. She applied her attention to wrapping Kasper's arm in the clean sheeting Becky brought.

"How deep is it?" Daisy asked from somewhere above Tori's head.

"Not too bad," Kasper answered. He seemed to have revived once Tori touched him. "A slash, only. How is Mrs. Marner?"

"She's just fainted. I'll get her a drink from her office. You too."

"You had better have Tom summon the police as well as the doctor."

"Yes."

Daisy and Tom together got Mrs. Marner up and took her from the kitchen so she wouldn't open her eyes upon that bloody scene again. Becky moved around mopping at what covered the floor and the table, wailing softly to herself. She sounded like a teakettle about to reach the boil.

Tori met Kasper's wide-eyed stare, full of pain and determination.

"It was a man, you say, inside the plague doctor suit?"

"*Tak.* It's a—a costume."

"Who was he?"

"It was *him*. Josef Zymanski. The one we spoke about earlier."

"The fellow who came here looking for you, before?"

"The same. Whoever is behind this is—what is it called?—recruiting more plague doctors. He wanted me to take the job. Easy money, he said. Easy, frightening the life out of people. Tori," he touched her hand, "there's an army of them out there."

"But why? Who's behind it?"

"I don't know."

"Oh, Kasper, this is dreadful. Are you in terrible pain?"

"It's better now." He cupped his hand around the back of her head, scooped her in and kissed her. Despite the situation, Tori closed her eyes in bliss. Right now, everything might be wrong with their world. This, this was right.

"Oh, God," she whispered when their lips parted.

And he smiled. Light invaded his eyes, enough to kindle a corresponding flame inside Tori.

Becky had stopped wailing and stared at them.

"Come," Tori told Kasper, "let's get you somewhere you can lie down. Just till Dr. Rasmussen gets here."

"He may not come." Kasper jiggled his arm. "He has bigger worries than this."

"Till the police arrive, then."

Kasper got to his feet and went to the back door. "Wait."

"No! Don't go out there."

"I want to get the mask. It is what I believe is called *evidence*."

Becky and Tori both stared while he stepped outside, and Tori held her breath till he reappeared holding—

A ghastly object, seeming almost obscene, tucked in the crook of his arm. The eye holes stared, empty. The beak looked like a weapon.

Tori recoiled involuntarily.

"It is a bird," Becky said.

"It's made of papier-mâché," Kasper told them. "All painted up. See? Harmless."

Not harmless at all. It was terrifying. And the man inside had carried a knife.

Tori had a sudden vision of an army of these dreadful figures, haunting the streets of Buffalo. Better or worse than thinking it some supernatural creature? She wasn't sure.

Officer Pat Kelly turned up about an hour later with another, human policeman in tow. The human policeman wore a blue bandana tied over the bottom half of his face and seemed reluctant to step inside the house.

"This is Officer Short," Pat Kelly introduced him. "My apologies for arriving so late. We are stretched very thin, as a force."

"Come in, please," Tori invited.

"You have the fever here?" Officer Short asked.

"Two children sick. They are in isolation."

Kasper had refused to lie down and insisted on helping Becky finish cleaning up the kitchen. He'd set the plague doctor's mask on the newly-scrubbed table, and when Tori and the officers entered the room, Officer Short recoiled.

"That off one of them plague doctors? I haven't seen one yet."

"Fascinating," Pat Kelly circled the table, examining the mask. "Crude in construction, yet effective."

Mrs. Marner came in. She still looked pale, and her gaze also focused on the garish mask on the table.

"Good God!" She looked at Kelly and Short. "Officers, what are you doing about this?"

"We are in fact piecing things together. Mr. Czak will be able to help a great deal with that."

They all listened while Kasper recited his tale. Officer Short took notes. Pat Kelly listened in the rapt manner only an automaton could.

"So you know this fellow?" Officer Short reiterated. "And he wanted to recruit you?"

"Yes."

"He didn't say who's behind it?" Officer Short eyed Patrick Kelly. "Could be a man or men. Could be automatons."

Pat Kelly, of course, did not change expression. "I can assure you, no automaton would involve him or herself in such a debacle."

"How can you be so sure?"

"I have what you could call inside knowledge. All automatons are built to help and defend humans, not destroy them."

Officer Short shuffled on his feet. "Except your lot. You hybrids were created to attack us."

"That was some time ago. We now exist to protect and serve."

"Maybe. But you're smart enough to come up with a scheme like this. Put a bunch of spectral spirits on the street to keep everybody shut in at home where the fever can do its work. If your doctors can build hybrid children, they're sure smart enough to stir up a plague. And you lot certainly can't get sick."

Pat Kelly's expression still did not change, but his green eyes seemed to glow with fervor. "Our doctors even now work tirelessly toward a cure for this illness."

"So you say. Meanwhile, the rest of us are dropping like flies. Good way to clear the city, I suggest."

Pat Kelly tipped his head slightly as if considering Short's opinion and dismissing it. "As soon as we get hold of one of these plague doctors, we will be able to trace a path back to the truth. A shame, Mr. Czak, you could not hold him."

"I did try. That is when he slashed me."

"If he comes back again and asks you to participate

in this scheme, you might pretend interest, allow him to take you to meet whoever hired him."

"No!" Tori spoke swiftly. "It is much too dangerous."

"It could provide very valuable information."

Kasper said, "I do not think he will be back again."

Kelly reached for the mask, which still stared at them from the table. "I will have to take this."

Tori and Mrs. Marner spoke as one. "Oh, please do."

****

Dr. Rasmussen never arrived. Tori could only figure he was busy treating fever victims or else did not want to bring further sickness within their walls.

Mrs. Marner ended up treating Kasper's arm. Having pulled herself together, she unwrapped the sheeting Tori had applied, cleaned the long wound, and bandaged it again much more neatly.

"I had some first-aid training before I accepted this post," she explained to Tori, who stood by. To Kasper she added, "It is not a deep cut, but it bled a great deal, which actually serves to clean the wound. I think it will heal well. But you must go to bed now and stay there. Understand? You need rest."

Kasper's gaze touched Tori's and slid away again. He might go to bed and stay there. Resting was debatable.

"Mrs. Marner," Tori said even as Kasper left the kitchen, "it has been a very long day. Might I retire also?"

"Certainly, Tori. Go ahead. We'll leave the automatons on duty in the house overnight."

Tori climbed the stairs in Kasper's wake, decrying herself with each step as a wanton. How could she think

Laura Strickland

of performing wild and wicked acts with a man so badly injured? To be sure, Mrs. Marner said Kasper's cut was superficial. And tired as she was, those prospective acts insisted on dominating her thoughts.

Kasper had closed his door. She stopped and stared at the wooden panel for an instant, debating what to do. The door opened, and Kasper peeked out.

"Are you coming in?" he whispered.

"If you want me to. Your arm—"

He reached out and gently snagged her good hand and drew her in. The door shut softly and firmly behind her.

Chapter Thirty-One

The air in the room felt thick with gloom. Kasper had not yet kindled a light, and Tori could see nothing more of him than a dim outline, black velvet on charcoal. The outline breathed, though. It felt warm when he pulled her into his arms. The scent of him shouted *Kasper*. It also stirred the memory of all the things they'd done together, before.

"Kasper, maybe we shouldn't—"

His lips stopped her words. He'd found her mouth without difficulty in the dark. He swallowed her objections and sent a spear of desire all the way through her body. Her knees nearly buckled.

"If you think," he whispered between hungry kisses, "I want to sleep alone after—after that—"

"No. Of course." She curled her good arm around his neck, forgetting that her other withered arm lay trapped between them.

"I want..." he said again, incoherently and apparently ran out of words. Oh, heavens, she thought, if he starts speaking Polish to me again, I'm lost.

What was she saying? She was lost anyway. Had been, perhaps, the first time she saw him. Certainly from the first time she'd touched him.

"Tori, beautiful Tori, will you stay with me tonight?"

He called her beautiful. Her, of all women. Too

good to be true, this had to be some wild dream.

But it didn't feel like a dream when he plunged his fingers into her hair and drew out her hairpins so the heavy locks fell down. She heard the pins hit the floor one by one, little *tinks* in the dark, and wondered what she'd do in the morning.

Next his agile fingers moved to the buttons at the front of her blouse, a plain cotton garment no wanton strumpet would ever be caught wearing.

But by heaven, he made her feel wanton. So much so that she helped him with the buttons and shrugged the garment from her shoulders as quickly as she could.

She wore a camisole beneath, again a plain cotton garment without adornment. With a groan, Kasper sank to his knees and suckled her through it.

Torn between the desire to cradle his head to her breasts and the insane need to bare them for him, she whispered, "No, wait."

She shed the rest of her garments with desperate haste. Everything came off except her stockings. She didn't take time to remove them. She threaded her fingers through Kasper's hair and guided him back to her breasts, where she wanted him.

What a sensation it was, there in the dark! It turned her bones to water. It gathered up all her emotions in a rush that urged her to give herself to this man. Everything he asked, everything he wanted.

"Take me," she whispered. "Please."

Her knees failed her before they reached the bed. He helped her onto the sheets and stood over her for an instant. She could see him better now that her eyes had adjusted. A rime of light came from the narrow window, and she watched as he stripped off his clothing, and lost her breath at his strength and beauty.

"Tori." He came down on the bed and lavished attention on her breasts. He worked his way downward to her belly and lower still. He ran his palms up her stockings, all the way to the top, and parted her legs gently.

"I have wanted this."

This? Well, who was she to stop him if he wanted anything? Hadn't she just given herself to him?

He touched her there in her private place where no one but he had ever been. He parted her with his fingers and plunged them inside.

Oh, lord, oh, lord, oh—

He dropped kisses on her legs, on her thighs. When he replaced his fingers with his tongue, she nearly came off the bed.

This couldn't be happening. It must be a delusion brought on by worry and stress. By desire. Perhaps she had the fever and it had triggered this outrageous illusion. Because this kind of pleasure simply could not exist.

No matter if it were a fever dream. She surrendered to it. If she died now, she could ask no more.

When the wracking waves of pleasure took her, she gloried in it. Her body had become Kasper's, and he could do as he wished with it. So far, she liked what he wished.

When he left her—seared and still quivering—and worked his way back up to her lips, he was babbling in Polish. She didn't need to understand him. She knew what he meant.

He liked her legs. He liked the way they felt in her stockings. He liked the way she tasted. He was hot and ready and needed to be inside her.

She could feel all of that. The weight of him lay heavy against her thighs while he kissed her, letting her know with his tongue in her mouth what he wanted to do down below.

She lay more than open, and ready for him. "Yes," she whispered. "Yes."

It was quick and hot and explosive. Mouths fused, they mated like two creatures destined for destruction. Nothing could be more perfect, Tori thought as white light flared behind her eyes.

Kasper collapsed on top of her, and she cradled him, the most precious being on earth. She lay while their breathing settled in tandem, and wondered how she might ever live without this, in the future. Without him.

Because such madness couldn't go on forever, could it? Vaguely, she believed this to be the product of their dire situation. All of them trapped here together. They'd become friends and then proximity had spun it into something more.

It was need, as had just been demonstrated. He couldn't possibly care for a girl like her.

One day, when the city reopened and the doors of all the houses where people were trapped were flung wide, he'd see there was a world of other women. He'd move on to someone far more suitable.

At this moment, she told herself she didn't care. She had him in her arms, and if this moment lasted forever, she would be content.

****

Lying with his cheek pillowed on Tori's breast, Kasper sought for words and failed miserably. Perhaps there were no words. What they'd just shared defied

226

description in any language.

Except—she had such beautiful breasts. Round and soft and succulent. Beautiful legs also, that led from delicate ankles all the length of her stockings up to—

Ah, absolutely no words for that. Well, ambrosia, possibly, but he didn't know the English term.

When he got to feeling the way she made him feel, at once overmastered and powerful, he lost the ability to translate. Yet he needed to tell her, tell her how he felt. How strong it made him feel when she opened herself to him so sweetly. How humble, how trusted. He was a simple man, really. He just wanted to love her. He didn't know if he had the courage to tell her so. He felt like she'd reached right inside him and claimed his heart, but he hadn't a clue as to whether she felt the same.

And—everything was madness. After mere days of acquaintance, could he declare himself?

"Tori?"

"Umm?"

"I want you to know—" He raised himself from her breast even though it was the last thing he wanted to do. Her maimed arm lay tucked against her. He seized the hand and pressed a fervent kiss into the palm.

"Don't." She snatched the hand away from him.

"Why not? I want you to know you are beautiful."

"Not that, it isn't."

"All of you. Everything I've seen. Touched. Tasted." That might be as close as he could get to telling her.

"Kasper—"

"*Tak?*"

"Don't spoil things, all right? With lies. Don't tell me things you think I want to hear."

"I do not. I would not. You are the most beautiful woman—"

She stiffened. "You don't need to say that. You got what you wanted without the—the compliments, didn't you?"

"What I wanted?" Kasper struggled with it, seeking the words. "I thought it was what we both wanted, that."

"Yes." She drew away from him in the bed and sat up. "But I don't want lies afterwards."

"I do not lie. When you know me better, you will know that."

She sat facing away from him. He could see only the delicate outline of her back. He wanted to reach for her, but didn't.

When she spoke again, her voice quivered. "I understand that young men like—well, what we just did together." Was she crying? "My ma explained it to me, that a man would say most anything to persuade a girl into—into giving it away. I can't blame you, can I? You didn't even have to persuade. I took one look at you and I could scarcely give it away fast enough."

She'd taken one look? Was this about his looks? What about the man he was inside? What about his heart, which lay already at her feet?

"Tori, if you think I would—what is the word?— take advantage—" But he had, hadn't he? She was a young woman alone save for her mother, whom she was no longer able to see. Innocent. Vulnerable. He'd given little enough thought to her reputation.

"What I'm saying is, you didn't even have to take advantage, did you?" She was crying. "I must be mad."

"Tori, listen to me." He reached for her arm. She pulled it away. "Have I not said if you should fall with child, I will marry you?" He wanted to marry her anyway, damn it.

"Oh, you would do the decent thing, would you?" She got to her feet, delightfully nude except for those seductive stockings. "Can't you see I wouldn't want you to marry me for that reason? Because you had to?"

"Tori, it isn't like that. I have feelings for you."

"The same kind of feelings a hungry man has for a banquet, no doubt." She gestured wildly to the bed. "All laid out for you."

Ah—perhaps she was angry about him tasting her. *There.* Without explicit permission. He hadn't been able to resist.

"No," he denied. "Nothing like that. Tori, please do not be angry with me."

"This can't happen again, Kasper Czak. Do you understand?"

"I hear you." He watched, helpless and frustrated, as she gathered up her clothing and left his room, still gloriously naked except for the damn stockings. He had one titillating glimpse of her in the light from the hallway before she was gone.

Holy mother, what had all that been about? They'd started out with searing pleasure. Now she detested him.

He sat there amid the sheets that still smelled of her, feeling angry and bewildered by turns. She'd wanted what they'd done together. She'd been eager to shed her clothing. She'd watched him shed his. She'd opened herself to him completely and it had been—well, he still didn't have words, even in his head.

He wanted to do it again. He wanted to do it forever. What had he done to make her leave him in anger?

Truly, truly in any language, women were impossible to understand.

Chapter Thirty-Two

All morning long, Daisy had been giving Tori meaningful glances, and she could only guess why. When Tori had crept from Kasper's room last night, not taking time to put her clothing on first and with the garments clutched against her, she'd thought she heard something. The soft closing of a door, maybe.

Had Daisy looked out and seen her leaving Kasper's room? Heavens! Her cheeks grew hot at the mere thought of it.

She spent the morning avoiding Daisy, a task not made easier by the fact that she was busy avoiding Kasper also. Things were further complicated by the return of the police, wanting more information about this Josef fellow from Kasper, and by Dr. Rasmussen at last turning up.

Tori opened the door to Dr. Rasmussen herself, and he smiled at her, something he did rarely enough.

"Good morning, Miss Anderson."

"Good morning, Doctor. How are you?"

"Very busy. My apologies for not attending last evening. I was detained."

He looked exhausted, with new lines around his eyes and a certain gauntness about his person. Despite that, those eyes held abundant kindness and still a hint of a smile.

Why couldn't she fall for a man like him? Someone

sane and steady, instead of—Hold on. She hadn't fallen for Kasper. She'd merely allowed herself to be seduced by him.

"Allow me to make you a cup of tea," she bade the good doctor impulsively. "I'll have it ready for you when you're done."

"That would be most welcome. How are the patients today?"

"The children, most miraculously, are holding their own. And no others have fallen ill." She led him inside.

"That is wonderful. And the knife wound?"

The knife wound. "Oh, our caretaker, yes. I haven't really seen him this morning." The injury certainly hadn't seemed to bother him last night. Hadn't kept him from sliding his hand up her leg. Holding her so tightly while he—

"And, Miss Anderson, are you feeling quite well? Only, you look flushed."

Flushed, yes, and she tingled all over. Good heavens, for a level-headed girl she'd certainly gone off the rails.

"I'm quite well, thank you. Oh, here's Mrs. Marner. She'll take you to see Kasper."

Tori stood trembling while Dr. Rasmussen went off with Mrs. Marner, who told him she'd treated Kasper's wound last evening. He would check the knife wound and go up to see the children. Tori needed to steady herself if she could.

She went out the back door and stood, taking in the morning. Fog cloaked the yard, having sifted in from the river, and the air smelled of coal smoke. The yard looked stark in black-and-white. Here had Kasper met up with the plague doctor, who was only a man after all. Here had he shed blood.

Suddenly she didn't want to be in that yard. The dread figure—man or otherwise—could be anywhere, lurking in the fog or behind the scraggly bushes at the rear.

Hastily, she returned to the kitchen and put the kettle on. She set a place with a cup and saucer and a plate with a couple of the biscuits Molly had made yesterday. Molly was a bit of a heavy hand with baking, but the children never complained.

Where was Kasper? Had Dr. Rasmussen already seen him? If so, where? She heard no voices from the laundry room, only the thump of the mangle as Becky worked her way through another mountain of laundry.

She scrubbed and tidied the kitchen, and eventually Dr. Rasmussen came in.

"This is most kind of you, Miss Anderson."

"Please, Doctor, sit down."

"I really should not. I have many more appointments to keep."

"When is the last time you took a rest?"

"To be frank, I cannot remember."

"Then please do so now. The tea is already made. I am sure you would tell your patients they cannot keep going with no rest."

"*Ja*, but it is different for us doctors, you see." He eased himself onto the seat at the table. She poured his tea. His gray eyes considered her gravely. "Please to sit with me?"

"Well—"

"It is in the morning paper, how the plague doctor was unmasked here last evening. By that young man I just tended, so Mrs. Marner tells me."

"Yes. It turned out to be a man after all."

"Of course."

"I don't suppose—I don't suppose that removes the possibility of guilt on the part of the automatons. Some of the plague doctors could be hybrids, dressed up. Or they could have hired men to wear the plague doctor suits, yes?"

"Undoubtedly. The question is whether they would."

"Everyone is blaming them for creating the fever."

Dr. Rasmussen held up a biscuit for emphasis. "I know Patrick Kelly very well. I have attended his wife under truly troubling circumstances. His wife is human. I do not think he would endanger her in any way."

"It may not be him. It could still be others of the hybrids. People are saying the hybrids have the knowledge to—to cook up such a disease."

"As they may. Highly intelligent people. But are they capable of doing so much harm?"

"I have to say it's hard to imagine. All our steamies here are wonderful."

"People are beginning to realize automatons have personalities. They assume anyone with a personality can become subject to his or her emotions."

Tori certainly understood that. "You believe they do have emotions?"

"It seems evident, does it not? Perhaps not exactly like ours. And it does not mean they fall victim to those emotions as do we. Consider—even among us, do we all respond the same?"

"No."

"No," Dr. Rasmussen repeated. "If we did, the city would not be so divided right now. People believe what they believe. They feel they are in the right."

"That is so."

"I must go. Other calls." Dr. Rasmussen rose from the table, and Tori followed. He looked her in the eyes. "Miss Anderson, would you consider having dinner with me? When all this furor is over, I mean. When such a pleasure as a simple dinner might again be had."

Tori rocked back on her heels. She sincerely liked and respected Dr. Rasmussen. He was easy to talk to, steady and kind, and not unattractive in his grave way.

He wasn't Kasper Czak.

"Me?" She fumbled. "You want to go out to dinner with me?"

He smiled. "Is it so surprising?"

"Quite frankly, yes."

"I cannot imagine why."

"My arm—"

"Ah." Behind his little, round spectacles, his eyes turned even kinder. "If you suppose such a thing matters—"

"It does. Always."

"Not to me."

Stymied, Tori stared at him and said nothing.

He picked up his leather bag from the end of the table where he'd set it. "You were born this way, is that not so?"

"Yes. And—and I've learned to cope. I have. But in one way or another, it has mattered every day of my life."

"May I say, Miss Anderson, you have many attributes that overshadow all else, in my eyes. You are kind. You are devoted to your charges." The corner of his mouth twitched. "You are very beautiful."

"Me?"

"*Ja*. Please consider my invitation, when things return to normal in the city. If there is such a state as normal."

He bowed slightly, an old-world gesture, and told her, "I will see myself out. Thank you for the tea."

He left the kitchen, and Tori heard a small sound behind her. The thumping in the laundry room had stopped, and when she turned she saw two faces peering at her from the doorway of that room.

Becky and Kasper.

Kasper withdrew immediately, leaving Tori with an impression of a strained, white face. Becky continued to hang there for several minutes while Tori cleaned the table and out of a sense of over-zealous caution scrubbed it again.

She tried not to think about the expression she'd glimpsed in Kasper's eyes.

****

The laundry room smelled strongly of soap and wet linens, and felt warm and humid. The dim light, the thumping of the washing machine, and Becky's company all combined to make Kasper feel invisible.

The doctor. The doctor had treated his arm and told him it should heal well. Told him what to watch out for, pain and heat along the length of the wound, which would indicate infection.

The doctor had been in the kitchen with Tori. She'd given him tea.

A mere gesture of kindness, so it might seem. The doctor appeared exhausted, and Tori would notice that. But he, Kasper, had seen the way the good doctor looked at her.

Thump, thump, went the washing machine. Becky

worked the crank and tossed the sheets aside to be hung in the yard. She kept stealing looks at Kasper where he stood organizing his tools.

He'd never considered himself a jealous sort of man. He'd known a few men back home in Poland who drank too much, went home, and accused their wives of ridiculous things. He had never comprehended that. If a woman did not want you, or wanted another, he'd always thought there was no point arguing about it or forcing her to stay with you.

Now, though, a strange feeling began clawing its way up through him, like acid. A simple cup of tea was one thing. But he was the one who'd held Tori in his arms. Last night. He had tasted her, touched her. He knew what made her cling to him and gasp with abandon.

If this was jealousy, he didn't like the way it felt. If Tori didn't want him—though he still didn't know why she was angry—and if she wanted the doctor instead, he must discipline himself to accept it.

Because he supposed killing the good doctor, or even just beating him to a pulp, was out of the question. And—and he didn't want to be that man.

The washer had stopped thumping again.

"Kasper, are you all right?" Becky asked with plaintive concern.

He glanced at her in surprise. "Yes, of course."

"Only you look very sad. Is your terrible wound paining you?"

That made Kasper smile a little. "It's not a terrible wound."

"It is. I saw when the doctor treated it. I want you to know I have great affection for you."

"Do you?"

"Oh, yes. You are the person who brought me back to life. I will be forever devoted."

"I like you too, Becky."

"Plus you are very pleasing to look upon."

That made Kasper raise his eyebrows. "Am I?"

"To me, you are. If I were human I would surely marry you."

Kasper did not know what to say to that.

Becky, her arms full of wet sheets, gazed at him from her chipped, rusted face. "There are incidences of steamies and humans marrying. But as far as I know, the steamies are all hybrids. So I suppose we must remain friends."

Kasper found his voice. "Friends." He found that surprisingly comforting. "I would like very much, Becky, to be your friend."

"Good. Perhaps then I can make you smile. First, I must go and hang these sheets out to dry."

"Let me help you. It is what a friend would do."

Chapter Thirty-Three

"I want a word with you."

Tori spun when the words sounded in a growl behind her. Uh-oh, caught. She'd successfully avoided Daisy all day, or at least up till now.

"I can't stop now, Daisy. I'm on my way—"

Daisy ignored the incipient excuse. "Have you gone mad, girl? I thought we talked about this."

"I don't know what you mean. Excuse me, but Mrs. Marner asked me to—"

"Everything else can wait. You stand right there and tell me what you were thinking last night."

The denials died on Tori's lips as heat swept up through her, a virtual declaration.

They stood at the foot of the stairs where Daisy had caught her. Tori lowered her voice so no one else would hear. "Not here, Daisy. Not now."

Daisy ignored that. Her hazel eyes glowed with what looked like outrage. "I saw you comin' out of his room. Stark naked!"

"Shh!"

"I never would have thought it of you, Tori. A good girl, just like me, trying to be careful and staying on the right side of things. Sweet Mother Mary, what would your mam say?"

Her mam would be horrified and no mistake. There were rules, Ma might say, for girls in Tori's position.

Meeting a decent young man, if you were lucky. A proper courtship and a proposal in due course. Maybe a stolen kiss or two.

Not creeping into a man's room, offering herself to him like a banquet and allowing him to—

This time, remembering, the heat washed over her in a wave.

"You're positively scarlet!" Daisy accused. "Lass, you've likely just gone and ruined yourself."

"I know." Tears came to Tori's eyes. "Don't worry, it won't happen again. He—I decided that, afterward. He says he has feelings for me, but well, how can he? Has feelings, yes, but I don't think they're the right kind."

Daisy's glare softened. "Oh, lass."

"When a woman—well, when she offers it, a man's going to take it whether he cares about her or not."

"Ain't that the truth?"

"I will not be visiting his room again."

"You promise?"

"I do."

Daisy ran an eye over her. "Then we have to hope it isn't already too late."

"Yes." He'd said he'd do the right thing if she fell pregnant. But she didn't want him out of obligation or pity. "You won't tell anyone?"

"Lass, if his babe starts growing in your belly, I won't have to."

"Oh, no. You don't think—"

"Only God knows the answer to that one. All right, Tori, I'll keep your secret for now. But if I catch ye coming out of his room again—"

"You won't."

"—I'll have to speak to Mrs. Marner. She needs to

know what's goin' on beneath this roof. There are children here."

What would Mrs. Marner do about it? Strike Tori off, when every pair of hands was needed so desperately?

"You won't. I promise. The last thing I want to do is touch Kasper Czak again."

****

The afternoon had just begun to wane when Kasper stepped out into the yard. Becky being upstairs busy in the nursery room, he'd answered a desperate call from Mrs. Marner, who minded the sickroom, for clean sheets. All hands to the wheel, as Mrs. Marner had reminded them repeatedly. It didn't matter what he did so long as he kept busy and managed not to think about Tori.

She'd avoided him all day. The most he'd seen of her had been the strings on her apron as she vacated a room he entered. Not easy to do with them shut in together this way. She must be working hard at it.

Which told him an awful lot. He should take her avoidance as an answer and try to save his heart.

Too late for that.

He heard the back door slam. Light footsteps sounded. Marooned between the lines of laundry, he peered out.

Ah—despite the dull afternoon which promised rain, fate shone on him. It was Tori, bound on the same errand as he.

He waited till she neared him, plucking sheets from the line with her one good hand, before he stepped out. "At last. I have been trying for a word with you all day."

Tori's hand flew to her heart. "Don't do that, especially out here where that—that thing was."

"Why do you refuse to talk to me, Tori?"

"I don't. I'm not. Busy, is all."

"Don't make it worse by lying."

"Worse? How could it get worse?"

Kasper flushed. He didn't want her to think of what they'd shared together as a terrible thing. It had been beautiful and meaningful and as inevitable as the sunrise.

"Daisy saw us. That is, she saw me leaving your room."

Naked, except for the seductive stockings. He'd daydreamed about those stockings. Despite himself, his gaze now strayed to her legs.

She turned and faced him, propping her good hand on her hip. "What are you thinking about?"

"You. I am always thinking about you." The swell of her breast, though he couldn't say that. The scent of her, the flavor.

"Well, stop it. Daisy is right. I shouldn't have done what I did. There could be dire consequences."

"Tori—"

"Don't say my name."

"Why not?"

"It's that damned accent of yours."

"You do not like it?"

"I like it far too much."

"It would be easier for me to tell you in Polish what is in my heart." He shot a spate at her, calling her his beautiful darling. Saying he had lost his heart to her. Things for which he couldn't possibly find the words in English.

I came halfway across the world to find you, only you.

She didn't want him. She wanted, perhaps, the good and worthy doctor instead, a man of education and means. A respectable man with a good position. Not a near-penniless caretaker.

"Stop, please stop." She held up her hand, warning him off. She trembled where she stood.

"Tori, do not be angry with me."

"I'm not. I'm—" She paused and gazed at him, her green eyes glowing in the uncertain light. "I don't know what I am. A fool, I guess." She hauled a sheet down from the line. "When I think about what I let myself do with you—"

"I think about it also," Kasper whispered.

A rose-pink color tinted her cheeks. "I never should have. And I need to go back to being the—the decent girl I used to be."

Kasper frowned. Was it so very indecent, being with him? Perhaps she had decided he was not worthy of the great gift of her virtue.

She folded the sheet messily, laid it in her basket, and pulled another from the line.

"Is this about the doctor?" Kasper asked. He wasn't sure if it would be better or worse, if it was. He didn't want her to shun him. He also didn't want her to prefer another man.

She froze. "What do you know about Dr. Rasmussen?"

"I saw you together, in the kitchen."

Her flush deepened. Her eyes sparkled. "Saw me what? Giving him tea? What if I did more than that? You don't own me, Kasper Czak."

He might have argued it. A humble man at heart, he might nevertheless have said she'd entrusted a part of herself to him when she'd disrobed and allowed him in. She didn't see it that way. And he hadn't the arrogance to insist.

Instead, devoid of words, he stepped forward through the space left by the sheets and took her into his arms.

He'd never before kissed a girl who didn't want it. When his lips met Tori's she resisted a little, stiffened and drew away from him. He persisted, substituting the kiss for words, hoping she would feel what he could not say.

It didn't take long. Her lips parted for him, and he wooed her with his tongue, dove deep into the irresistible sweetness of her.

She melted. He heard the second sheet slide from her grasp and hit the ground. Her hand snaked up around his neck, and she went boneless against his chest.

No one could see them here among the rows of sheets. He hoped. Because the kiss went on and on, almost as good as what they'd shared last night skin to skin. When it ended, she leaned, draped, against him, and he was hard as iron.

Her eyes had gone wide and misty in the gathering gloom. What a thing to be standing in a scrap of a yard half a world away from home, gazing at the one person who could put a light in his life.

"You may give the doctor tea. Nothing else. Understand, Tori Anderson?"

One corner of her mouth quirked upward. He kissed it, and just like that they fell into one another again. Lost.

He was lost. Or he would be, if she rejected him.

He stopped kissing her long enough to whisper, "Please understand, I do not try to own you."

"I do understand."

"It is my heart that demands—that asks—you to be

only mine."

"Oh, hell."

Oh, hell? Was that good or bad? Not the words a man wanted to hear from a girl after more or less declaring his love.

He had no chance to ask for clarification because she kissed him again. He felt her desire come rushing at him, hot as his own.

By the holy mother, they would burst into flame here on the spot.

He stopped kissing her long enough to ask, "About the doctor, are you—"

"Forget about the doctor."

"Are you off duty tonight?"

"Yes. But—" Once more she drew away far enough to look at him. "I can't—"

"I understand." Kasper tried to overmaster his disappointment. She was free to accept or deny him as she chose.

"I promised Daisy I wouldn't set foot in your room again."

"I see."

"That means," she told him with what he could only consider a wicked gleam, "we'll have to use my room instead. All right?"

It was more than all right.

Chapter Thirty-Four

Kasper had been doing a lot of praying lately. He prayed no one had seen him and Tori out in the yard. He prayed Tori wouldn't change her mind about welcoming him into her room. He prayed he could live long enough to hold her in his arms again.

In the past, his prayers had rarely been answered. Not when they fought in the forest back home, when his brother had died. When he lost his father and other brother. When he and Mama had nearly starved in the city, after. When they'd come here to this city that smelled of coal smoke and the river, where things seemed little better.

People sneered at them. Those from his country received little more respect than the automatons that filled the place.

He thought he'd given up praying. But lying across his bed later that night, he found he prayed hard for just one thing—the sound of Tori's footsteps in the hall, for he'd gone up to bed while she lingered in the girls' dormitory. And he didn't have the temerity to let himself into her room and wait for her there. It would be assuming too much.

He could only pray she hadn't changed her mind.

Curious—she was a small woman. She stood no higher than his nose and didn't make much noise when she moved. But he heard her step in the hall anyway. He got up, went to the door, and stood with his heart thumping.

What if that was Daisy instead? Daisy had been taking the night shift in the nursery, but if he had bad luck—

He cracked open the door. Tori stood in the hallway, looking uncertain. She might have rethought it all after they'd parted in the yard. He hadn't seen her since then.

She met his gaze now and raised a finger to her lips. He nodded. She gestured for him to follow her. His heart bounded.

So, she wanted him in her room after all. Inside the chamber, he stood near the door while she lit a lamp and turned to face him. Perhaps she'd just tell him they couldn't be together.

"Did you shut your door? In case Daisy comes up."

He nodded. Whatever words he possessed deserted him when she began taking the pins from her hair. She had so much heavy, light brown hair, and it tumbled all around her as she laid the pins on the dresser one by one.

"We'll have to keep quiet."

"I—" His voice didn't sound like his own. "I can be quiet." If he didn't explode first.

Her hair swirled down around her shoulders. She reached for the buttons on her blouse.

His paralysis broke. He went forward and unfastened the rest of the buttons for her. He slid his hand inside to cup a warm breast. She closed her eyes and arched against his palm.

Just like that, he was lost to reason.

The lamp was small and emitted only a dim golden glow. By its light they shed their clothing, watching one another all the while. When Kasper took her in his arms, she shivered and clung to him.

The feel of her skin against his nearly sent him over the edge. He forced himself to say, "Tori, are you sure?" He did not want her to regret this. Not ever.

"Say my name again."

"Tori."

"Victoria. It's Victoria. Say that."

"Victoria."

"Oh, God." She kissed him and all need for further conversation fled. Most of Kasper's doubt went with it.

They left the lamp burning, and that was good because he could see her. The rosy tips on her plump little breasts, the length of her slender legs. The expression in her eyes when she parted those legs for him. The pleasure that wracked her face when he plunged inside her.

She wrapped her legs around him while they loved each other in silence, except for the creaking of the bedsprings. Profound silence, it seemed to Kasper.

They fit together like—but he had no words for that either. No matter, the silence had its own beauty.

After, still propped on his elbows, he studied her face. He wanted to see bliss there.

He wanted to see love.

Instead he wasn't sure what lay in her eyes when she reached up with her good hand and touched his hair. She whispered, barely above a breath, "You are so handsome."

"Me? It is you who are beautiful, Victoria Anderson."

The corners of her mouth curled up. "It seems we are pleased with one another."

"I could not be more pleased."

"Not even—" She twitched her withered arm, caught as usual between them.

"Not even. Have I not told you, you are perfect to me?"

"You must be a crazy man. Look at me."

"Yes, look." He captured her breast in his hand and applied his tongue to the tip, feeling it harden delectably. "Beautiful."

She shivered beneath him.

"And these lips. So beautiful." He applied himself there also. "And your legs. Must I tell you about your legs?"

"We should not be talking at all." A gleam entered her green eyes. "Why don't you show me, instead?"

****

Tori slept deeply. She could scarcely remember when she'd slept so well. Warm and safe, feeling cherished, she might have been lying in a bed of finest eiderdown rather than on a thin mattress in a barren attic room.

When she woke, climbing up from the very bottom of that slumber, she lay in Kasper's arms, both he and she still naked and wrapped around each other.

Someone pounded on her door.

"Tori? You in there?" Daisy's voice. "Do you know where Kasper is?"

Kasper jerked awake at the sound of his name. He'd slept with one arm flung over Tori in a gesture of protection. Now he gathered her closer, raised his head and said something in Polish.

Daisy rattled the door. Tori dimly remembered flipping the lock last night before they'd shed their clothing and succumbed to glorious madness.

"It's Daisy," she mumbled and slipped out of Kasper's grasp. Barefoot—bare everything—she tiptoed to the door.

"Daisy? What is it?"

"Mrs. Marner said to fetch you. Two more of the children have come down with the fever."

Oh, God, no. Tori rested her head against the door panel. "We'll be right down."

"'We'? Is Kasper in there?" Daisy's voice sharpened.

Why try to hide it? "Yes."

"Good. We thought that maybe the plague doctor came back and he'd been murdered."

Daisy hurried away. Tori turned from the door and looked at Kasper.

The lamp still burned—a terrible extravagance for which she should probably be horsewhipped. She'd liked seeing him, though, seeing all of him while they made love. She liked looking at him lying there in her bed, his dark hair all tumbled and the sheets pulled only to his waist. But reality had come knocking.

"What time is it?" he asked.

"I don't know. The middle of the night, I think."

"Time goes away when I am with you. Tori—" He too scrambled from the bed and, moving with the grace of a tiger, approached her. She tried to determine what it was she saw in his eyes. Too many emotions to untangle.

He reached for her and she stepped away. "Better not."

"Why?"

"If you touch me, it will start all over again. You'll kiss me or I'll kiss you, and then I'll want you. And the madness will begin."

"Is it madness?"

"What else would you call it?"

Eyes fixed on her, deep as blue sapphires, he said, "I have another word in mind."

"No." If it was the word she thought he meant, she didn't want him to say it. Desire, yes—they had that in spades. She wasn't prepared for anything else.

"We have to get dressed and go down to help."

"I want to tell you—"

"Not now. We need to go."

He watched her dress, from the corner of his eye he did. She didn't want to admit it, but she watched him too, as he slid into his trousers and flexed his way into his shirt.

Was it normal for two people to be this taken with one another? Tori didn't know because she'd never expected desire to enter her life. Oh, she'd eyed a good-looking young man or two in her time. She'd never ever dreamed of acting on the attraction.

Hadn't thought about kissing the object of her attention till their lips were swollen. Of becoming intoxicated by the taste of him, of tasting him everywhere, running her tongue across his hot skin. Of straddling him without reservation, and taking him in.

It wasn't fair. How was a girl supposed to keep her head straight?

When they were both clothed, she thumbed the latch on the door. Kasper extinguished the lamp. They descended into a quite different madness.

On the floor below, everyone was awake, and the deep black of night lay outside the windows reflecting back the light of a dozen lamps. Children cried and asked questions. Steamies hurried around.

Mrs. Marner greeted them not with a look of condemnation but relief. "Ah, there you are. Kasper, please go down and assist Tom in the cellar. He is unearthing more cots. Tori, you come with me." She called, distractedly, "Becky, did you find any more linens?"

"Yes, Mrs. Marner." Becky steamed along with a pile of sheets across one bleach-stained arm.

In the nursery room, they found Daisy bent over one of the cots that held a crying tot. Little Andrew it was, no more than three years old.

Daisy shot Tori a burning look when she came in, outraged and accusing. Would she say anything in front of Mrs. Marner? Could she imagine what Tori and Kasper had been doing, in Tori's room? Tori felt as if the signs were all over her—each and every place Kasper had placed his hands, or his lips. Maybe that was because she could still feel him.

Daisy, though, said nothing.

Tori gasped, "What's happened?"

"We found two of the youngest, here, feverish and with the spots starting on their chests. As you can see, they were sick soon after."

Vomit lay everywhere, over the two cribs in question and the adjacent floor. The other children in the nursery room were all awake and standing in their beds, if they were old enough to stand.

Mrs. Marner said, "We have to get them out of here and away from the others. Since there's no room left in the closet, I've decided to put them in my quarters downstairs."

"What do you need me to do?"

"Lend Daisy a hand changing them. You take

Andrew in charge. Daisy, you take Aggie. Trina will stay here to calm the other children. I'll be downstairs helping Tom and Kasper set up those cots."

She hurried out. Hank came in with a mop and bucket.

"This is terrible, terrible," Daisy lamented.

It was, that and more.

Tori cleared her throat. "Daisy, I know I promised to keep away from Kasper—"

Daisy blinked furious tears from her eyes. "You think I care about that now? I think you've gone mad, and no mistake. But that's your lookout. My babies are sick. I don't have time for your foolishness."

Foolishness. Was it?

As Tori tried to find a clean place in the room to change poor, feverish Andrew's clothing, she wondered. Fate and circumstances had intervened this time.

Faced with temptation another time, though, would she be able to resist?

Chapter Thirty-Five

By daybreak, a multitude of tasks had been accomplished. The ailing infants had been removed to Mrs. Marner's quarters, their roommates soothed. The other children on the floor, all awake and sensing the disturbance, had been comforted. The nursery had been cleaned, and Tom had been sent to bring back Dr. Rasmussen.

Tori had not encountered Kasper since they'd left her room, even though she'd helped Becky in the laundry, their need for clean sheets seemingly endless.

Now she stepped outside into the incipient morning light, which trickled into the yard in a haze of gray. Even though she'd only come out to hang a load of sheets so Becky could keep cranking, back in the swampy laundry room, the air felt good.

She stood on the back step and drew a breath.

Miles of clothesline zigzagged across the yard. She had her choice of where to hang. It might be best to start with the farthest and work her way up.

Hanging laundry one-handed was always a challenge. She'd perfected a method—toss the sheet up and over the line. Pull it along to straighten it out, and put the pegs on.

Now she didn't even think about it. Her mind was all on the ailing children—Daisy's babes, as she called them. So young to be taken sick. She hoped Dr.

Rasmussen would be able to come quickly. She hoped no other children would fall ill. She hoped she'd get a glimpse of Kasper. Maybe he'd find a moment to slip out into the yard while she was still here. She'd turn around and—

She stepped from between two rows of sheets and turned. All the breath left her body with a rush, as if she'd been punched in the gut.

A figure stood directly behind her. Tall and imposing and immeasurably horrific, it certainly wasn't Kasper.

The plague doctor. Or more precisely, one of them.

The mask this plague doctor wore looked very like the one Kasper had handed over to Officer Kelly. Patterned after the head of a bird, it loomed above Tori where she stood, perfectly motionless. The color of putty, somewhere between tan and gray, it had a beak over a foot long. Its occupant stared at her from two dark eye slits. Even though Tori knew there must be eyes behind those apertures, that there must be a man inside the dun-colored robes, a superstitious shudder wracked her.

She wanted to scream. Horror closed her throat.

"You," the figure said. The voice sounded muffled and horrid coming from inside the beak. "Are you Kasper's woman?"

Kasper! How she wanted him then, longed for him to come rushing out of the house and chase this thing away. She tried to find her voice and failed. She shook her head.

"Do not lie. I saw the two of you together. Here in this yard. Kissing."

The plague doctor had an accent like Kasper's. It

was the man who had come here before, looking for him. The one who had slashed his arm. *Oh, God.*

"What do you want?" Her voice sounded rusty and old.

The plague doctor did not answer. Instead, he seemed to inspect Tori from out of those terrible black slits. "What would he want with you?"

The same question Tori had been asking herself from the first time Kasper kissed her, now turned back on her by this horror.

She had no answer, but instinct made her spring to life. She tossed the sheet she held at the plague doctor, turned, and ran.

Tried to run. She didn't get far. The plague doctor moved much faster and caught her halfway down the corridor of sheets. He wrapped two strong arms around her from behind, seized her by the midsection, and pulled her up against him. The beak on his mask—that dreadful appendage—struck her in the side of the head.

"No. No!" She drew breath to scream and never got the chance. A gloved hand clamped down over her lips and nose, stopping all air. The gray yard grew dim as her heart beat a frantic tattoo in her chest.

Just before it all went dark, the plague doctor spoke sonorously into Tori's ear. "I will enjoy taking my revenge, I think."

****

"Where is Tori?" Kasper had been trying to get a glimpse of her all morning without success. The house was in an uproar, and he didn't expect he'd get a chance to argue his case, or explain how he felt about her. Come out like a man and tell her that he loved her.

Because he did.

Making love with her had been fine. What was he saying? It had been more than fine, it had been magnificent. Hot and gloriously satisfying and—he couldn't stop thinking about it. But that—the physical component—was not the whole of it. The feelings he had for Tori overwhelmed him. The power of them, the tenderness. He wanted to protect her from all harm, guard her heart. He wanted that even more than he wanted her body.

The connection—that was what made the sex so blisteringly wonderful.

He needed to convince her they belonged together, not just now but after all this insanity ended, if it ever did.

He'd asked everyone in the house if they'd seen her, worked his way from attic to cellar till he ended up here in the laundry room. Pretty much where he'd started.

Becky, who once again worked the wringer washer, turned and looked at him. The unit had caustic soap and bleach splashed all over her arms. If a steam unit could look exhausted, she did.

Through the grate in her mouth came the last words Kasper expected to hear. "I would have loved you, Kasper Czak."

"Eh?"

"I would have loved you. You are kind and gentle. You restored my life to me. I would have put you above all others."

Kasper stared at her in consternation. A more astonishing declaration he had never heard. "Would have?" He repeated uncertainly. "But not now?"

She stopped working the crank. The ensuing silence seemed uncanny, and her mechanical voice echoed in the damp room when she spoke again. "You are with Tori now. You prefer her to me."

A thousand thoughts rushed through Kasper's head. Becky must be what he believed was called sweet on him. It made her jealous. Could a steamie be jealous? If so, might she have acted on that feeling?

Carefully he said, "I supposed we were friends, Becky."

"Yes. I would rather you looked at me the way you look at Tori. I would rather you loved me."

Kasper trembled where he stood. Had Becky done something unthinkable? Had she acted somehow to get rid of Tori?

"Becky, you must know a person can't help who he—or she—falls in love with."

Becky tipped her head to one side. It made her neck joint creak alarmingly. "Love is an attachment. There is no reason you should not become attached to me."

"I am attached to you. We work together. You are part of my life, but Tori has stolen my heart."

"Is it no longer in your chest?"

"It is, *tak*, but it belongs to her."

"That cannot be helped, then."

"It cannot. Becky, have you done something to Tori?"

"Me? No."

A certain note in the steamie's mechanical voice made Kasper's blood run cold. "Do you know where she is?"

"No."

"Or what happened to her?"

"I know someone took her."

"Took her?" Ice raced through Kasper's veins.

"Who? When?"

"It happened early this morning. I saw as I looked out the back door."

Kasper grasped the unit's arm. "Who took her, Becky? You must tell me."

"It was the plague doctor."

****

"We must call the police at once," Mrs. Marner declared while everyone else stood about in a circle and stared at one another in dismay. "The Irish Squad, that is."

"Aye, we need that Patrick Kelly," Daisy agreed. "He's clever enough to track our Tori down. But the sooner the better, eh?"

Kasper felt like his head was about to explode. Or possibly his heart. He wanted to swear, to scream and shout, but that would do Tori no good.

Why? Why would the plague doctor snatch her? The question fairly possessed his mind.

Had it been Josef? Had he come back and done this terrible thing?

"Tom," Mrs. Marner turned to the tall unit, "you go run and tell the police what has happened. You're the fastest."

"Yes, Mrs. Marner." The unit left immediately.

"I want to search," Kasper said.

"Of course you do." Mrs. Marner gave him a look that argued she, like Becky, had observed a relationship developing between him and Tori. "But under the circumstances it's smarter to send our units outside."

"There have been no reports of these figures, these plague doctors, turning violent," Daisy put in.

"Josef," Kasper lamented. "It must be Josef, whom

I unmasked out in the yard. He is—not right in his head. A violent man, especially when he's taken too much to drink. On the ship from Europe, it became plain even his wife was afraid of him."

Mrs. Marner looked worried. "You think he's snatched Tori?"

The more Kasper thought about it, the more he did.

"It happened hours ago," he lamented. "She could be anywhere. If only Becky had told us sooner—"

"I will speak to her about it," Mrs. Marner agreed, "but not now. Everyone but Daisy and myself, go outside and start searching." She cast Kasper another look. "You go also, but search the immediate area, mind. We don't want this abomination snatching you too."

Chapter Thirty-Six

"Drink this." The voice sounded harsh, and the hand that hauled Tori upright was a cruel one. The mouth of a bottle was smashed against her lips, hard, and the liquid splashed on her tongue.

It tasted like turpentine, and it burned everywhere it touched.

She sputtered and gagged. "What is it? You're trying to poison me!"

"It is vodka. Good."

"Not good." She turned her face away and fought down nausea. Her heart beat so furiously she thought she might be about to die. Where was she? The plague doctor—

She swiveled her eyes back to the man who held her in a punishing grip. He'd removed the mask but still wore the rest of his costume. Removing the mask had ruffled his hair. Fair hair it was, and he possessed a not-uncomely face, narrow with slanted cheekbones and a mobile mouth. He had blue, blue eyes that looked—

Insane. Insane, entirely.

Tori's racing heart skipped a beat. She almost, almost preferred the mask.

"You had better drink," he told her. "You will not like what is going to come."

Oh, God. Oh, God, she didn't like any of this. She must get away from him.

Laura Strickland

"Where are we?" The place was dim and chilly, just one light burning that allowed her to see him. She lay on a floor, one that felt like packed dirt, and he crouched above her.

"In the cellar."

"What cellar? At Lost Waifs?"

"No, do you think me mad?"

Yes.

"I don't want him to find you too soon."

"Him—you mean Kasper? You have an accent like his."

"Kasprczak. It is his surname. His given name is Jarek."

"Then why did he call himself—"

"Because," her captor interrupted her, "people here are too stupid to pronounce our names properly. People here call *us* stupid, but they are the ignorant ones."

Jarek. The name suited him somehow. But why hadn't he told her when he held her in his arms? They'd been as intimate as two humans could be, yet he hadn't shared with her his name.

"Drink." The bottle rose again. The vile liquid splashed into Tori's mouth. She tried not to swallow any and failed.

Her captor sat back on his heels a bit but did not let go of her. His mad gaze inspected her from head to foot, lingering at certain places in between.

"Perhaps we can have some fun before the end."

The end?

"It is better drunk. Life, as I have discovered, is better when one is drunk. Otherwise it is very, very disappointing."

"You are a friend of Kasper's." Maybe she could

262

establish a rapport.

He nearly spat. "*Nie*. Not a friend. Not anymore. He betrayed me. Now he will pay."

He drank from the bottle, seeming unphased by its poisonous taste.

"How will he pay?"

Tori's captor ignored the question. He wiped his mouth with the back of his hand. "We were never friends, but countrymen. Countrymen in a foreign land. There is an unwritten code—such men should stand together. Those who do not stand together fall." He held up a finger. "Too many of us fell back home under a Cossack's blade."

"So you want revenge against him because he turned you in, in your guise as a plague doctor?"

"Men like Kasprczak need to be taught a lesson. One they'll remember. I thought first to strike at his *matka*."

"His mother?"

"Aren't you a clever girl? A shame."

"A shame?" Tori echoed.

"About the arm. Beauty spoiled. But perhaps we can do something about that, yes?"

A full body shudder seized Tori. She didn't want this madman so much as thinking about her arm. She had to get away, get away, get—

He took up his account. "It is not honorable to harm an old woman. Kasprczak accused me of lacking honor. Me! When all the while he was the betrayer. It is—I do not know the word in English."

"Ironic?"

"Perhaps. I do not know. When I saw the two of you in that yard last evening, I knew it would be much better to take my revenge on you. He cares for you, *tak*? Has he had you yet in his bed?"

Heat stained Tori's skin. She said nothing.

"I can see the truth in your eyes. No matter. You shall have me, now. I will show you a real man."

"Please, no—"

"Trust me, you will enjoy it. A little pleasure, eh, before you leave this world?"

He meant to kill her. Strangle her, perhaps, with those powerful-looking hands that now hung idle between his knees. He'd laid the bottle aside. If she could get her fingers on it—

"What is your name?" she asked desperately, even though she already knew it. Perhaps if she distracted him, she could buy herself more time.

"Josef Borysek Zymanski." He announced it with pride. "It is a fine name, yes? A name of dignity. It deserves better than being dragged through the dirt."

"Yes."

"Better than dressing up like an accursed mummer."

"Why do you do it, then? Dress up in that." She jerked her chin at the mask which she spied on the floor behind him.

"For the money, of course. I am deserving of better. Better pay and better—opportunities. We were lied to back home. We were told there were jobs in plenty here in America. None of it is true. The metals take all the jobs, and we are once more the lowest of the low." He snatched up the bottle and drank again. "They will be thrown down. Men will retake the city. You will see."

"What men?"

"The ones who will bring justice. There is a scheme."

"Tell me about it. Or," Tori added with calculation,

"don't you know?"

"Me? I know much. This association, they have accepted me."

Accepted him and given him a plague suit to wear. *Him and how many others?*

"They did well to trust a man like you."

He stared at her. His pupils looked like pinpricks, and his eyes appeared almost entirely blue. "You are flattering me in an attempt to delay what will come. I am too smart for that."

Damn it.

"Even drunk, I am smarter than you. Do not worry. You will enjoy some of what is to come." He shrugged. "The end, not so much."

"Please, Josef, let me go. I have done nothing to deserve this."

"Ah, now comes the begging. Women, they do tend to beg. Me, I will enjoy this part."

Tori buttoned her lip. Whatever he meant to do to her, she did not like providing him any satisfaction. She might look frail and hobbled. But a girl growing up in near poverty with a maimed arm learned to be tough, maybe far more so than this bully suspected.

He leaned closer to her. "Go ahead, beg. Then we will drink some more, and begin, eh?"

Not if Tori could help it, they wouldn't.

Chapter Thirty-Seven

Patrick Kelly, along with two other members of the Irish Squad, responded quickly and gathered the searchers together out in the front yard. Kasper, who'd been searching the back yard for the third time, came around the house and joined the group there.

What could the police do that the rest of them could not? He personally had combed the area up to three streets away before returning to the yard and going over it again.

Mrs. Marner and Daisy remained inside with the children, so the search party included Kasper and the house automatons.

Patrick Kelly looked at Kasper when he said, "Please tell me exactly what happened."

To the best of his ability, Kasper did, including what Becky had shared with him, as well as his suppositions. He stumbled over some of the words, needing English equivalents, but all three hybrids listened raptly. Kasper could not complain that they failed to take his account seriously.

"All right, thank you, *sor*," Patrick Kelly said when Kasper finished. He and his fellows exchanged looks. "It seems she's likely been snatched, since Becky saw her with a man, out in the yard."

"It must have been Josef. But why would he snatch Tori?" Kasper asked, turning sick inside.

"That, *sor*, we cannot say as yet. You did report him to us as someone cooperating with whoever is behind these plague doctors."

"Yes."

"It is a logical conclusion to think he wishes to get back at you."

Damn logic. The thought of Tori alone and vulnerable in hostile hands, in *Josef's* hands, terrified Kasper, and angered him.

"So," he asked Patrick Kelly desperately, "how do we find her? Out of all the places in this whole city, how?"

In the garish light of the now-overcast afternoon, Patrick Kelly's expression looked almost sympathetic. "I understand, *sor,* it seems an overwhelming prospect. But we are good at what we do. And we have a few factors on our side."

"Such as?"

"We have been swiftly closing in on the persons behind the appearances of the plague doctor and perhaps behind the Black Fever itself."

"You—you think that can lead us to him? To Josef Zymanski?"

"I think it might." Patrick Kelly tipped his head as if accessing internal information. "Since you gave us the mask the other night, we have been following up on him."

"Yes, he has a beef with me." Kasper's stomach lurched within him. if Tori had been snatched because of him, if Josef hurt her, how would he ever forgive himself?

"In your opinion, *sor*, is this Josef Zymanski dangerous enough to cause Miss Anderson harm?"

"He's not right in his head. Crazy. Oh, God, what are we to do?"

"Find her," Patrick Kelly told him. "We will find her."

****

"Of course you must go and help the police search," Mrs. Marner told Kasper when he and Patrick Kelly laid the matter before her. She had a baby on one shoulder and another in the crib beside which she stood. She blinked at Kasper earnestly. "Tori is part of our family, and if she's in danger, we'll do what any other family would to help her. Go, with my blessing."

"Thank you."

Daisy came running out from the boys' room to seize Kasper in a hard embrace. "Find her! I don't care what the two of you have been up to, just bring her home."

Kasper nodded, unable to speak for the weight of his emotions. He and Patrick Kelly went out, only to find the street empty.

"Where have your fellows gone?"

"They will be canvassing the area, *sor*. Do not worry, they are still close by and on the job." Pat shot a look at Kasper. "Forgive me for asking, *sor*, but from what I just heard inside, am I to infer Miss Anderson is your special lady?"

"I'm in love with her, if that is what you mean."

"It is, *sor*. It is."

"I've been thinking. I suspect after Josef snatched Tori from the yard, he hid her somewhere."

"What makes you say so, *sor*?"

"Instinct. I don't suppose you put much stock in that, being a—"

"Machine?"

"No offense."

"None taken, *sor*. I am what I am, a very high-quality machine, indeed. That does not preclude me putting a certain amount of what you might call *faith* in the human quality called intuition. It is, in fact, made up of equal parts inference and conjecture, both of which I employ."

"Then, I think Josef is hiding her somewhere. That doesn't help, does it? There are a thousand places in this city."

"He wishes to hurt you, through her."

"Yes, to get back at me. He wanted me to join up with him in this—this squad of plague doctors who are roaming the city, terrifying everyone. He seemed to feel I owed him some debt of loyalty, as a fellow countryman."

"Ah, the ties of nationality can be strong. I myself am an Irishman before all else."

"Yes, but that wouldn't make you do something so wrong as what Josef's done."

"No, *sor*, because I am a policeman second."

"I just don't understand how he would know Tori is important to me."

"That is yet to be conjectured. But I think there is a very good chance Mr. Zymanski has Miss Anderson in his possession."

"We have to find them, Officer Kelly, before he hurts her. But how?"

"It is a daunting task, but that, *sor*, is where we call in the reserves."

"The reserves?"

"What is everywhere in this city, Mr. Czak?

Automatons. Give us only time to spread the word, and we shall have eyes and ears, of the mechanical sort, in every alley and on every corner."

"Oh." Kasper felt a flare a desperate hope. "Can you do that?"

Patrick Kelly tipped his head toward Kasper. "We can."

"And—and will steam units, the ordinary ones, be willing to help find a person after all the mistrust that's sprung up toward them? The suspicion and ill feeling?"

"I believe so, *sor*. Helping is what we do."

Kasper thought of Haddy, who'd shielded him during the riot. Please God, Patrick Kelly was right and unlike Josef, the automatons of the city didn't hold a grudge.

They stopped by the police station, where Pat gave instructions to alert the automatons of the city. It was a wonderful speech to his fellow hybrids and the few brave human police officers still working, all of whom wore bandanas over the bottom halves of their faces. He spoke of loyalty, of service, and what he described as an automaton's higher purpose. It brought a tear to Kasper's eye.

After his listeners dispersed, Pat Kelly rather disconcertingly confided to Kasper that he needed to go out back of the police station and top off.

"Top off?" Kasper questioned in bewilderment.

"I wish to fill my hopper with coal and my boiler with sufficient water to last the duration," Pat explained. "That way, once we are on the trail, nothing will impede us."

"Uh—yes," Kasper agreed rather lamely. "Good idea." After a moment's thought he confessed, "I nearly forgot you are an automaton, for a minute there."

Patrick Kelly winked one green eye at him. "*Sor*, I'll take that as a compliment."

Chapter Thirty-Eight

"Our vodka is nearly gone," Josef Zymanski lamented. "That is most unfortunate."

Tori could only agree, since the vodka had served to distract her captor. He'd applied himself to it often and had, in fact, ingested the lion's share of the contents, forcing only an occasional mouthful on her.

Nevertheless, she felt slightly lightheaded from the effect of the strong liquor. She figured Josef had to be drunk by now, but he displayed few signs. She kept waiting—hoping—for him to fumble, to grow incautious so she might attempt an escape.

He appeared just the same as he had before. His eyes still looked mad. He still spewed a litany of grievances over events that had occurred back home in Poland and here in Buffalo.

Tori listened. She figured so long as he ranted, he wouldn't follow through on his implied threats, which were also plentiful. And if he kept drinking—

"Why don't you finish it?" she suggested.

"Are you trying to get me drunk?" He eyed the clear liquid left in the bottom of the bottle, a scant inch. "There is not enough here."

"Yes, well, you seem to be enjoying it." What would it take to turn him tipsy and reckless? When he'd started sharing the bottle with her, it had been three-quarters full.

"We must get down to business." He extended a hand to the front of her blouse—a modest garment it was, buttoned all the way up to her throat—and inserted his fingers. One pull had buttons flying everywhere as the fabric parted.

Tori gasped. "No, please."

"Ah, we are back to the begging." His lips stretched in a self-satisfied smile. "I enjoy."

"Talk to me. Tell me about your country, about Poland."

"No. It is time for me to show you what a real man is. *Tak*?"

"No, thank you."

"You will be astounded by me. How strong I am. How long I can last."

"And then—and then you'll let me go?" Maybe she could endure it, if it meant she could get back to Kasper.

"No, no. I have been thinking. I should solve your problem for you."

"My problem?"

He stared at her with his pinprick-mad eyes. "You are such a pretty girl." He plucked at the front of her blouse, exposing her breasts, and licked his lips. "Nice. It is very much a shame."

For lack of breath, Tori could barely speak. "Shame?"

"About the arm. If not for that, you would be perfection. So lovely." Horrifyingly, he adjusted himself.

"There's nothing to be done about my—my arm."

"There is. In this great city, with its accursed hybrids, there is. I will do you a favor." He reached into the right-hand pocket of his coat which he wore under

273

the dun-colored plague doctor's costume. Fumbling, he drew out a knife.

With increasing horror, Tori stared, not quite believing what she saw. Yes, that was a knife. No doubt the same knife he'd used to slash Kasper—with a six-inch blade that glittered almost as wildly as her captor's eyes.

He'd long since let go of her. Now she scrabbled away from him on her butt and heels.

Casually, he reached out and hauled her back.

"What—what do you intend to do with that?"

"I thought I would remove that arm. Relieve you of it. Perhaps then the clever hybrids will fit you with a new one. If—if they are not all destroyed by then."

He couldn't be serious. Oh, God, he looked all too serious.

"My employers, the men of the Automaton Ex-Expulsion League, are hell-bent on getting rid of them. Hell-bent. It is a saying here. A fine one. I like it: hell-bent."

He was drunk.

"I will be an important man among their ranks, me. I shall rise to a position such as I deserve, once all the automatons are gone. There will be plenty of jobs then, good jobs for deserving men like me."

He deserved a bed in an asylum. Tori couldn't take her eyes from the blade. But he was talking again, which she figured was good.

"How—how will they get rid of all the automatons? There are so many, and they are so helpful."

"Helpful? I thought you were clever. They are a disease. That's what the men of Buffalo call them." He grinned. "And that's what gave them the idea. Create and unleash a disease on the city, blame it on the automatons, and get rid of the damned metal."

A new kind of horror spread through Tori's belly. "Men created the fever? Humans?"

"*Tak*, in someone's cellar. A place, I suppose, not unlike this one where we are. It proves, does it not, that humans are much smarter than machines?"

And far more immoral. "That fever has killed hundreds. Children at our orphanage—"

"Oh, boo-hoo. Do you know how many children starve in my country? Their mothers watch them die. At least yours," he waved a hand, "have no mothers to weep over them."

"How—how was the fever spread?"

"That, I do not know. People were supposed to believe the plague doctor spread it, and that he was everywhere in the city. When the time is right, it shall be proven—proven that the damned hybrids created the sickness. To get rid of us."

When it was, in truth, the other way around.

"How can that be proven if it isn't true?"

"Evidence can be planted. There will be such outrage, steam units will be destroyed in the streets and the rest banished from the city forever."

Tori didn't want the steamies banished. The ones at Lost Waifs were, well, her friends. They worked hard. Cared for the children. Had quirks and personalities.

"But that will take a few weeks," Josef said airily. "You can get the hybrids to fit you with a mechanical arm first."

"I like my arm the way it is."

"No, no."

"It's part of me."

"This arm they will fit you with, it will be covered with skin. From a corpse, as I understand it, but what can you do? They must get the skin from somewhere. It is an unholy practice, *tak*, but they are unholy beings. Did you know they even use the corpses of children to create their own little ones?"

"If you cut off my arm—here—I won't survive. I'll bleed to death."

"Perhaps not. I will make a very clean job of it. I am good with a knife."

Tori just bet he was.

"I'll die from shock. From pain."

"That is why you should drink the rest of the vodka. You will not feel a thing."

"Yes. Good idea." Tori accepted the bottle from him, taking it into her good hand. He watched her with what appeared to be approval in his mad blue eyes.

"There you go. A good bottle of vodka, it can fix anything."

Tori tipped the bottle to her lips, pretending to drink, and curled her fingers more tightly around the neck. She watched Josef through narrowed eyes even as he watched her. He glanced away—she remained focused on him.

A girl with a withered arm learns to do a lot of things with her good hand. Most tasks have to be performed by just four fingers and a thumb, which builds dexterity and a good deal of strength.

There was power in the blow when Tori swung the bottle. It took Josef, who crouched so near to her, in the side of the head with tremendous force, making a sound that, had she not been so frightened, would have turned her stomach. His eyes went wide for an instant, showing the whites all the way around the blue, blue irises before losing their focus. His hands—one still gripping the handle of the knife—reached out, but he didn't complete the motion.

Sheer panic made Tori strike him again, half-scrambling to her feet as she did. The bottle broke, and she blinked at it, realizing she now had an even better weapon.

"Get away from me!" she shouted at him. "Get away or I'll cut you!" Whose voice was that? Hers? Surely not.

He stared at her, unmoving, so she struck him a third and final time. The last of the vodka flew everywhere in droplets. Blood appeared on Josef's temple.

He toppled over slowly onto his face, going down the way a felled tree does, and Tori leapt away from him. The breath came fast in her lungs, and her heart pounded.

She had to get out of this cellar. Far, far away from this madman. Carefully, she set the bottle down on the dirt floor. Was Josef dead? He lay so still, there on his face. She wouldn't stay around to see.

The light had nearly burned out. Once it died, she'd be in darkness with a would-be murderer…or possibly a corpse. That thought got her scrambling for the shadows on the far side of the room, where lay a short flight of stairs with a door at the top.

With every step she took up those stairs, she glanced behind, fearing the appearance of a menacing figure with blood on its face. She could glimpse Josef, though he still hadn't moved. She hauled herself up and reached the door. What if it was locked?

It was, as she saw when she got there, but the latch was on her side. She threw it, hauled the door open, and found herself in a shabby little hallway confronted by yet another door. It was unlocked, and she pulled it open to the outdoors.

She stumbled out into the dark, where reaction hit her. She trembled all over, and her knees threatened to fail her. She couldn't go down here, so close to—to that plague doctor.

She had to find Kasper.

Where was she? And when? It had been early morning when Josef seized her. Now night had fallen, and she had no clue about her location. Buildings surrounded her, tall brick ones that seemed to stare at her with blank, malevolent window-eyes. In front of her she saw an alley. She could smell the river.

Not far from it, then. Of course that could mean anywhere within blocks of the waterfront.

She could scream for help. She could wail and cry. But she'd do neither. She was Tori Anderson—an imperfect woman of no particular importance. She was strong.

Too strong to scream or weep.

Lifting her head, and with her good hand braced against the nearest brick wall, she made for the end of the alley. It opened onto a street she didn't recognize, but yes, the river lay beyond. The mighty Niagara. She could hear it now, singing its restless song, the one that seemed to go on forever.

Something moved at the corner of her eye. Please, God, she thought—not another plague doctor. But no, for a sleek, silver figure stepped into the radiance cast by the nearest street lamp.

One of those new, steam-powered dogs it was, a big one. The size of a wolfhound, it had a smooth silver hide and a sculpted metal face.

It looked at Tori with interest and approached gently, regarding her with keen yellow eyes.

"Hello, fella," Tori said. "To whom do you belong?"

She reached her hand out, and the hound put his head beneath it. Not until her legs failed her and she sank to the ground did he bark for his master.

Chapter Thirty-Nine

The streets crawled with metal units. As Pat Kelly had said, they were everywhere—old and new, shiny and worn, mechanical and hybrid. All searching for Kasper's Tori.

His Tori.

He no longer had any doubts, that's what she was. If they both survived this terrible day, he meant to tell her so, declare himself as a man should. If she wanted the doctor instead of him, she could say so. It wouldn't change how he, Kasper, felt about her.

Love, he thought as he followed Pat Kelly around yet another corner, was a funny thing. If you invited it, it tended to stay away. But if it struck you all unexpected, if you saw something in a pair of green eyes or caught it from a particular smile, there was no getting away from it.

Kind of like a fever that lasted life-long. Or so he hoped.

But this—what had happened in their neighborhood this day—seemed as remarkable as love. A metal army mobilized. All of them coming out and searching for the sake of a girl they did not know. Even now, he could see two units moving down the opposite side of the street. A member of the Irish Squad patrolled from the back of a tall, metal steam horse. Other members had brought out their steam hounds, tall, slender creations which ran ahead of them, golden eyes glowing.

The city might belong to the metal right now. But should the human residents find that frightening? They worked for the good, didn't they?

And they risked their own safety. In the time they'd been searching, Pat Kelly had been brought no less than three reports of confrontations between humans and steamies, around the search area. That, and one sighting of a plague doctor. Not Josef, unfortunately, but the units had held him till the Irish Squad arrived, and he'd been taken in for questioning.

Kasper and Pat had searched multiple yards on multiple streets and now headed toward the river. Kasper found Pat Kelly's company reassuring. Something about his calm nature and the warm brogue kept the worst of Kasper's terrifying thoughts at bay.

Tori, alone and frightened. Tori, dead.

No. He wouldn't let himself be seduced by such thoughts. He—

Pat suddenly paused and held up his hand. "Listen."

Kasper did. He heard many things. The chugging of an aged steam unit across the way. The hiss of a steam lamp on the corner. The deep gurgle of the river a few streets distant. The bark of a dog.

Was that a dog?

He turned his gaze on Pat.

"That's a steam hound," Pat said. "Signaling."

"You think they've found her?"

"I don't know, *sor*. I suggest we go see."

They ran. Pat Kelly should have been able to outdistance Kasper. He was a skin-covered machine, after all. Kasper's desperation allowed him to keep pace. They arrived to an incredible scene.

It had just begun to grow dark, and beneath the light of another hissing street lamp, a steam hound and two other units stood. The hound was a gorgeous thing, tall and sleek. One unit was an aged mechanical. It looked stumpy and worn. The other, a hybrid, wore a police uniform.

The hound had its head bent toward—

Tori. That was Tori.

She sat on the bricks of the street. In fact as he ran forward, she got up, using the back of the now-quiet hound as a hand hold. She was all right. Disheveled, with her hair streaming loose and the front of her blouse torn. But—alive and moving. *Alive.*

Even as that thought possessed Kasper's mind, she turned and saw him.

And his world instantly came right. What matter if the city lay in conflict? If his dreams had gone awry. If he had but a humble job and no fit place to live and—

He ran out of thoughts then because he reached Tori and took her in his arms. He also ran out of English and babbled to her in Polish, saying all kinds of things, telling her she was his darling, that he could not live without her. Telling her how much he loved her.

Kocham Cię, piękna dziewczyna. Kocham Cię.

She clung to him and pressed her face into the crook of his neck. The steam hound touched Kasper's leg in a friendly fashion.

Two more units hurried up. Pat said to one of them, "Spread the word, she's been found safe. Call off the search. Make sure all the searchers are escorted home safely. We don't be wanting any incidents."

"Are you hurt?" Tenderly, Kasper tipped Tori's face up to his. He brushed her lips with his own.

"I'm all right. But there's a man called Josef Zymanski back there, down in a cellar. I think he may be dead."

Several more units came steaming up, searchers now called off the scent. They followed in a knot when Tori led them to the building where she'd been held.

Kasper, having found a few ragged words of English, protested all the while. "Tori should be taken somewhere safe."

"So she will, *sor*, just as soon as she directs us to the miscreant."

"She should be taken to the hospital."

"The hospitals are all full, *sor*, and I'm thinking that's no fit place for her, with the fever still raging."

"She should—"

Finally, Tori raised her hand to Kasper's shoulder. "I'm all right, Kasper. Not so weak that I can't finish this business. Officer Kelly, this is the building. You'll find Josef Zymanski in the cellar, just to the left when you go in."

Pat Kelly went inside along with another member of the Irish Squad, who seemed to own the hound. The hound remained standing next to Tori, and she patted it absently with her good hand while they waited.

"It's Josef? You are certain?" Kasper whispered. He had his arm wrapped around her, lending support, though he was sure she could stand on her own if she had to. No delicate woman, his Tori. He would have to remember that and behave accordingly.

If they were to be together—if she did him the great honor of accepting him once he got around to asking—it would be a partnership, nothing less.

"He's mad," she said. "Mad entirely. He snatched

me from the yard, dressed in another of those plague doctor costumes. He meant to molest me, I think. And he—he wanted to cut off my arm."

Only then did her strength waver, her eyes going wide.

"By the holy mother! Why?"

"He said it kept me from being perfect. That I could get a mechanical one, instead."

"Tori, my love, you are perfect just as you are."

Footsteps clattered on the stairs inside. Both hybrid units reappeared.

"Well?" Kasper demanded even as the other automatons crowded around. "Are you bringing him out?" He wanted to get his hands on Josef, to give him a good pummeling, if the police officers allowed it.

Pat Kelly said, "He's dead."

"What?" Tori and Kasper spoke at the same moment.

"But," Tori protested, "I only hit him with a bottle. He went down—"

"He went down on his own knife, miss. Still clutching it in his hand, he is."

"Oh!" Tori's strength suddenly gave out. She clutched at Kasper to remain upright. "I didn't mean to—"

"Of course not, miss," Pat Kelly said soothingly.

"Will I be in trouble?"

"Not a bit of it. Do we not all have the right to fight back when we are threatened?"

Only later did Kasper find out the citizens of Buffalo had been busy fighting back all over the city. With so many automatons out, conflicts took place from the river all the way to the east city line. It became known as the

Day of Metal, and went down in infamy.

He didn't care about that then. He was too busy trying to thank his fellow searchers—and Pat Kelly, who'd been so much more than kind.

He was busy, too, grieving for Josef who, if not a friend, had been a part of his past. Disconnected from his home, troubled by things that had happened in a faraway land. Damaged, perhaps, by the blades of the Cossacks.

They all carried their wounds in different ways.

He figured he would exorcise his with hard work. In service to others. In gratitude and remembering. In loving Tori, and whoever else entered their lives.

Everyone handled hate differently. And love. He reckoned that, between the two, he'd let love win.

Chapter Forty

Everyone wanted to hear Tori's story over and over again. The police did, including a startlingly handsome captain called Brendan Fagan, who turned up at the orphanage not long after they got home.

Home. For that's what it was. Kasper was there, and Daisy. All her friends, including Tom, Becky, Trina, and Hank. Familiar faces to which she'd grown so attached. To say nothing of Mrs. Marner and all the children— each of them her favorite.

She gave her accounting so many times over, it began to lose some of its horror in the telling. But not all. She still experienced a shudder when she remembered the knife and the look in Josef's eyes.

Was she responsible for his death? If so, could she live with it? Kasper said Josef had a young wife, but implied it might be more a relief to her than a blow, to lose him.

Dr. Rasmussen arrived, and she had to give him the story all over again. He shook his head and clucked his tongue, the eyes behind the small round spectacles kind.

But he didn't miss the way she looked at Kasper or the fact that Kasper refused to budge from her side even when he had to release her hand.

She didn't think Dr. Rasmussen would be asking her to dinner again.

She snatched a few hours of sleep, and then it was

morning. More visitors arrived. First came Pat Kelly, bringing explanations. Much had happened in the city last night besides the search for Tori. The Day of Metal had turned into the Night of Metal, when many steam units were attacked. Some, contrary to their original instructions, had fought back.

Amid all that, the head of the Automaton Expulsion League, a Mr. Bert Warden, had been arrested. The plague doctor captured during the search for Tori had squealed and led the police to a ring of humans behind the frightening appearances. Warden proved to be the head of that ring.

"They hatched the scheme in order to get rid of the automatons in Buffalo," Pat told Tori and Kasper, Mrs. Marner and Daisy, and everyone else who could crowd into Mrs. Marner's office where they met.

"Some of Mr. Warden's affiliates are doctors. Two of them hatched the fever in the cellar of a laboratory where they work. They and other select members of the Automaton Expulsion League put it in motion."

"But why?" Daisy cried. "Why unleash a sickness that could kill every person in the city? They must have known only the automatons would survive."

"That was the whole point, miss. They could finger—I believe that is the word—us automatons for trying to get rid of you and take over Buffalo."

Pat looked grim, if his handsome Irish face could be said to change expression. "Mr. Warden, under considerable—er—pressure, has confessed all. The fever was intended to infect only orphanages, homes for the aged, brothels, and if they could manage it, the jail. All individuals they considered expendable, I am afraid."

"How horrible!" Mrs. Marner sounded indignant,

and her eyes filled with angry tears. "Our children are not expendable."

"I quite understand, Mrs. Marner, they are not," Pat Kelly agreed. "That is why our own doctors—hybrid automaton doctors—have been developing a cure. Mrs. Chastity Greely, despite being injured during the riot, has taken time out from her other vastly important duties and with a team of others, some of them human doctors, has worked day and night to solve the riddle of this illness."

"We do not actually need to sleep," confided his hybrid companion, with a wink.

"Yes, but—" Tori spoke up, "for her—for them to make such an effort in the face of everyone accusing them of starting the plague—"

The sheer decency of it struck her, and she began to weep. She hadn't cried while in Josef's hands or even when she struck him down. She considered herself too strong for that. She hadn't wept when she'd taken refuge in Kasper's arms. But something about this tapped her deepest feelings.

"It's beautiful, a beautiful thing."

"And should show the people of Buffalo just what our automatons are made of," Daisy said staunchly. "Forgive the pun."

Pat Kelly gave off a soft grinding sound. "I appreciate a good pun, me."

Tori swiped at her cheeks determinedly. "Officer Kelly, please tell Mrs. Greely how very appreciative we are."

"You may tell her yourself. She will be here some time this afternoon to dispense doses of her medicine to your children. She wished to do so personally."

"How very kind," Mrs. Marner said. "We'll be

honored to receive her."

"Now we will be on our way." Pat looked at Tori. "May I suggest, miss, you get some rest? You have been very brave, but you've come through quite the ordeal."

"Yes. Thank you again, Officer Kelly."

The police officers left. Mrs. Marner went back to the sickroom, a brighter look on her face. The household automatons rumbled away to their various duties. Daisy followed, with a significant look for Tori and Kasper.

"Rest, the kind police officer said, mind." And she too winked at them.

"At last we are alone." Kasper grunted out a breath.

Tori looked at him. Since her rescue down on the waterfront, they'd had time to do no more than exchange glances, touch hands. He'd put his arm around her while she gave her account.

Now she looked, truly looked at him. The man she loved.

When had she realized it? Sometime while she'd been trapped down in that cellar gazing into Josef's mad eyes. Or maybe before. She'd supposed she wasn't worthy of a man so attractive, so smart and steady and kind—

Now, though, she knew how strong she was. How capable. How worthy. She was Tori Anderson, with a brain and a heart and, rather incidentally, a withered arm.

He'd be lucky to win her. If that was what he wanted.

"Tori, I have some things to say to you. I hope I have English enough."

She rose from Mrs. Marner's desk chair, where they'd put her, and faced him. "There's nothing to say, Kasper. Well, maybe one thing. I thought I was going to die in that cellar. I feared I'd never see you again."

"Me too," he whispered, agony in his eyes.

"My biggest regret was that I'd never have a chance to tell you I love you."

His eyes lit. They glowed like sapphires, and a smile touched his lips. "You do?"

"I do. So, so much."

"Not the doctor? Not—"

"Not the doctor."

"He is worthy."

"You are worthy, Jarek Kasprczak. That's what I realized while Josef was busy showing me his knife. We're all worthy of love—flesh and metal alike. Those who give love deserve it. And I love you."

"Oh, sweet mother! Tori, *moja miłość*." He took her in his arms. Their lips met, and the necessity for words, in any language, ceased. For several glorious moments there in the stuffy little office, the world went away. Their tongues tangled, their hearts beat to one rhythm. Kasper threaded his fingers through those on Tori's good hand.

"One," he whispered then, shaking her hand slightly. "No more loneliness. No more wondering. We are one, like this."

"Forever."

"Forever. Tori Anderson, will you marry me? I am not sure how we will manage. There's your mother, and mine—"

"They are probably friends by now."

"*Tak*, most likely. Where will we live? Neither of us earns very much."

"Don't think, Kasper. Feel. We're young, we're strong. We'll manage just as the people of this city always do."

She kissed him again, and the certainty of it swamped her. "Yes, I'll marry you, Jarek Kasprczak. I'll share all I am with you and you'll share all you are with me. We'll keep working here, of course. We'll do our best to help others. Because—"

"Because," he completed the thought for her, "giving love is the best way to bring it to oneself."

"Not the best way. The only way," Tori told him. And kissed him one more time, to make it so.

A word about the author...

Multi-award-winning author Laura Strickland delights in time traveling to the past and searching out settings for her books, be they Historical Romance, Steampunk, or something in between. Her first Scottish Historical hero, *Devil Black*, battled his way onto the publishing scene in 2013, and the author never looked back.

Nor has she tapped the limits of her imagination. Venturing beyond Historical and Contemporary Romance, she created a new world with her ground-breaking Buffalo Steampunk Adventure series set in her native city in Western New York.

Married and the parent of one grown daughter, Laura has also been privileged to mother a number of very special rescue dogs, the latest of whom is a little boy named Tinker, and is intensely interested in animal welfare.

Her love of dogs, and her lifelong interest in Celtic history, magic, and music, are all reflected in her writing. Laura's mantra is Lore, Legend, Love, and she wouldn't have it any other way.

Thank you for purchasing
this publication of The Wild Rose Press, Inc.

For questions or more information
contact us at
info@thewildrosepress.com.

The Wild Rose Press, Inc.